MURDER BY THE BOOK

MURDER BY THE BOOK

MYSTERIES FOR BIBLIOPHILES

Edited and Introduced by
Martin Edwards

Contents

Introduction

What could be more appropriate than a British Library Crime Classics anthology of short stories concerned with the world of books? This collection gathers together an assortment of mysteries linked by a literary theme of one kind or another.

Both readers and authors of crime fiction are likely to be drawn towards "bibliomysteries," a word which is unlikely to be found in a dictionary, despite supplying the title for a fascinating monograph by the legendary American editor, publisher, bookseller, and bibliophile Otto Penzler. Penzler readily accepted that the term is apt to be defined in a subjective way, and said: "If much of the action is set in a bookshop or a library, it is a bibliomystery, just as it is if a major character is a bookseller or a librarian. A collector of rare books…may be included. Publishers? Yes, if their jobs are integral to the plot. Authors? Tricky… If the nature of their work brings them into a mystery, or their books are a vital clue in the solution, they probably make the cut."

The uncertainties of definition make it difficult to identify the "first" bibliomystery. One candidate, favoured by Penzler, is the little-known *Scrope, or, The Lost Library*, which was published as long ago as 1874 by Frederic Beecher Perkins, in his day a prominent editor and librarian from a well-known American family, but which is long forgotten by crime aficionados. Much of the action of the story takes place in a secondhand bookshop and at book auctions.

Another early example of this type of story was "The First Customer and the Florentine Dante," by Fergus Hume, which was included in *Hagar of the Pawn-Shop* (1898), a collection of puzzles investigated by a female detective, Hagar Stanley. Hagar is confronted by a riddle concerning a second edition of Dante's *La Divina Commedia*.

During the twentieth century, the bibliomystery became increasingly popular, particularly (but by no means exclusively) in the United States. Just after the end of the First World War, Christopher Morley published *The Haunted Bookshop*, a popular light thriller crammed with book lore. As the critics Jacques Barzun and Wendell Hertig Taylor pointed out in their monumental reference book *A Catalogue of Crime*, at the end of the story "the hero characteristically remarks: 'Thanks to that set of Trollope, I think I'm all right.'"

On the other side of the Atlantic, Helen Simpson and Clemence Dane collaborated on *Printer's Devil* (1930), in which a publisher called Horrie Pedler is found dead at the foot of the twisted staircase leading to her London flat. (It has to be said that, over the years, many crime writers have succumbed to the temptation to kill off publishers in their fiction; I leave it to readers to deduce why that may be.) In the story, a manuscript goes missing, and there are rumours that it contained many secrets known only to Horrie and the author. This is an unorthodox novel, which features the authors' actor-detective Sir John Saumarez, but is as much a comedy as a mystery.

In E. C. R. Lorac's *These Names Make Clues* (1937; to be reissued by Poisoned Pen Press in November 2022 as a British Library Crime Classic), Chief Inspector Macdonald is invited to a treasure hunt party by a publisher called Graham Coombe; the fun is cut short when the body of thriller novelist Andrew Gardien is discovered. The same year saw the publication of Clifford Witting's debut novel *Murder in Blue*, a whodunit about the killing of a policeman, set in a thinly veiled version of Sussex and narrated by a likeable bookseller, John Rutherford.

The publishing business in Britain has supplied the background to a good many crime novels, several of them written by authors who, like Simpson, Dane, Lorac, and Witting, were members of the Detection Club. Examples include Nicholas Blake's *End of Chapter* (1957), a case for Blake's regular detective Nigel Strangeways, and P. D. James's *Original Sin* (1994), in which Adam Dalgliesh investigates the murder of Gerard Etienne, head of the Peverell Press.

Bookshops make a delightful background for detective puzzles. The little-known *Death of Mr. Dodsley* (1937) by the Scottish author John Ferguson concerns the murder of a bookseller in his shop on Charing Cross Road, a case investigated by the private detective Francis MacNab as well as Scotland Yard. The poet Ruthven Todd produced a series of detective novels under the name R. T. Campbell in the 1940s, including *Bodies in a Bookshop* (1946), in which two corpses are discovered in the back room of a bookstore in central London; the amateur criminologist Professor John Stubbs helps Chief Inspector Bishop of the Yard to unravel the mystery. Bernard J. Farmer, a former policeman, published *Death of a Bookseller* in 1956. The crime is solved by the dogged bibliophile Sergeant Jack Wigan, and the text is crammed with book-collecting lore.

One of the most intriguing premises for a murder mystery puzzle concerns a crime story where the fictional events are somehow mirrored in real life. An early example of this type of story was *Murder Rehearsal* (1933) by Roger East, an accomplished author whose forays into the genre were regrettably infrequent. A likeable young crime writer, Colin Knowles, has an admiring secretary, Louie, who notices a series of links between a book Colin has been working on and three apparently unconnected recent deaths. What follows is rather far-fetched, but the final twist offers a pleasing and unexpected revelation. A later and more sophisticated variant on the same theme is to be found in John Franklin Bardin's *The Last of Philip Banter* (1947). The eponymous Banter is an advertising man with marriage trouble and a drink problem. He finds a typed manuscript on his office desk, apparently typed by himself, which confuses past and future. It describes what is going to happen as though it had happened already. Then the "predictions" start to come true...

Bardin's focus was on psychological suspense, and the same is true of Renee Knight's recent bestseller *Disclaimer* (2015). The terrifying flavour of the opening is captured by the tagline on the cover: "Imagine if the next thriller you opened was all about you." Catherine Ravenscroft, a middle-aged woman who has pursued a highly successful career in TV, finds a novel called *The Perfect Stranger* on her bedside table; she doesn't know where it has come from, but starts reading, and finds to her horror that it tells a story about the most horrific experience of her own life, one she had believed was safely buried in the past. We soon discover that the author of the mysterious book is a man called Stephen, a retired teacher whose wife has died recently, and who is pursuing an agenda as a result. Stephen's obsessiveness and mental disintegration is revealed gradually, while Catherine's own seemingly perfect life begins to fall apart.

A number of authors have developed a specialism in various forms of bibliomystery. Examples among American crime writers include Elizabeth Daly, whose series detective was the bibliophile Henry Gamadge; the academic Amanda Cross, a pen-name for Carolyn G. Heilbrun; and John Dunning, while their British counterparts include the Oxford don J. I. M. Stewart, who wrote detective fiction as Michael Innes; Bruce Graeme, who wrote a series featuring bookseller-detective Theodore Terhune; and Robert Barnard, who takes aim at authors of romance in *Death in Purple Prose* aka *The Cherry Blossom Corpse* (1987). George Sims, two of whose novels have appeared in the British Library's Classic Thrillers series, was a professional bookman whose expertise in the field is evident throughout his work in the field of crime fiction.

Murder by the Book brings together examples of the book-related mystery from a variety of notable practitioners, including E. C. Bentley, famous as the author of the legendary country house puzzle *Trent's Last Case*; A. A. Milne, who in addition to creating Winnie-the-Pooh was a founder member of the Detection Club; that highly accomplished plotsmith Christianna Brand; Michael Innes; Julian Symons, several of whose postwar crime novels have been published as British Library Crime Classics; and the highly prolific John Creasey, who founded the Crime Writers' Association in 1953.

Anyone who enjoys books in general and crime fiction in particular will find rich variety and entertainment in this sub-branch of the genre. As a lifelong fan of bibliomysteries, I've derived a good deal of pleasure from researching this anthology and I hope the range of stories and information supplied here will encourage readers to make further discoveries of their own.

—Martin Edwards
www.martinedwardsbooks.com

A Note from the Publisher

The original novels and short stories reprinted in the British Library Crime Classics series were written and published in a period ranging, for the most part, from the 1890s to the 1960s. There are many elements of these stories which continue to entertain modern readers, however in some cases there are also uses of language, instances of stereotyping, and some attitudes expressed by narrators or characters which may not be endorsed by the publishing standards of today. We acknowledge therefore that some elements in the stories selected for reprinting may continue to make uncomfortable reading for some of our audience. With this series British Library Publishing and Poisoned Pen Press aim to offer a new readership a chance to read some of the rare books of the British Library's collections in an affordable paperback format, to enjoy their merits, and to look back into the world of the twentieth century as portrayed by its writers. It is not possible to separate these stories from the history of their writing and as such the following stories are presented as they were originally published with minor edits only, made for consistency of style and sense. We welcome feedback from our readers, which can be sent to the following address:

Poisoned Pen Press, an imprint of Sourcebooks, 1935 Brookdale Road, Ste. 139, Naperville, IL 60563

A Lesson in Crime

G. D. H. and M. Cole

George Douglas Howard Cole (1889–1959) and his wife Margaret (1893–1980) were prominent socialists who wrote detective fiction as a money-making sideline. They married in 1918 and worked together for the Fabian Society for several years thereafter. Douglas Cole's nonfiction included such racy titles as *Trade Unionism and Munitions* and *The Intelligent Man's Guide through World Chaos*. After his death, Margaret wrote his biography, as well as her own memoirs.

In 1923, Douglas published a detective novel, *The Brooklyn Murders*, which introduced a diligent cop called Henry Wilson. Thereafter, Douglas and Margaret collaborated on more than two dozen novels, many of them featuring Wilson. Their books include a pleasing "inverted mystery," *End of an Ancient Mariner* (1933), as well as a number of neat plots. Increasingly, however, the authors' weariness with writing fiction became evident; perhaps they felt it got in the way of worthier endeavours, but in any event, their collaboration as novelists fizzled out in the 1940s. "A Lesson in Crime," an example of the Coles in their sharpest form, was the title story in a collection published in 1933.

———

Joseph Newton settled himself comfortably in his corner of a first-class compartment on the Cornish Riviera express. So far, he had the compartment to himself; and if, by strewing rugs, bags, books, and papers about he could make himself look numerous enough to drive fellow-travellers away, there was hope he might remain undisturbed—for the long train was far from full. Let us take a look at him, and learn a little about him before his adventures begin—and end.

Age? Forty-five would not be a bad guess, though, in fact, he is rather less. As for his physical condition, "well-nourished" is a polite description; and we, who desire to have no illusions, can safely call him paunchy, and, without positive grossness, flabby with good living. His face is puffy, and whitish under the eyes; his mouth is loose, and inclined to leer.

His fair hair, which is rapidly growing thin, is immaculately brushed, and his clothes are admirably cut and well-tended, though he has not the art of wearing them well. Altogether he looks a prosperous, thoroughly self-satisfied, and somewhat self-indulgent member of the British middle class; and that is precisely what he is.

His walk in life? You would put him down as a businessman, possibly a merchant or a middle-sized employer, not a professional man. There you would be both right and wrong. He is a professional man, in a sense; and he is certainly in business.

In fact, he is Joseph Newton, the bestseller, whose crime stories and shockers were plastered all over the bookstall he has just left with his burden of newspapers under his arm. He has sold—heaven knows how many million copies of his stories, and his serial rights, first, second, and third, cost fabulous sums to secure.

But why describe him further? All the world knows him. And now he is on his way to Cornwall, where he has a pleasant little seaside cottage with twenty-seven bedrooms.

The train starts, and Newton's carriage still remains empty save for himself. He heaves a fat sigh of relief and picks up a magazine, in which he turns instinctively to a story by himself. For the moment he cannot remember who wrote it. Poor stuff, he thinks. He must find out which "ghost" was responsible, and sack him.

Joseph Newton was interrupted in his reflections at this point by the consciousness that someone was looking at him. He glanced up and saw the figure of a man who was standing in the corridor and staring fixedly at him, with a curious air of abstraction. Newton stared back, trying to look as unwelcoming as possible. It would be really bad luck, he felt, if someone were to invade his compartment now.

The newcomer, after a moment more of staring, pushed back the door and came in, flinging down on top of one of Newton's bags a rug and a pillow done up in a strap. He seemed to have no other luggage. Newton unwillingly got up and cleared a corner of his belongings, and the stranger sat down and began to unbuckle his strap. Then he settled himself comfortably with the pillow behind his head, and closed his eyes. "I hope to goodness he doesn't snore," Newton thought.

While our second traveller is thus peacefully settling himself for a doze, we may as well take a good look at him also; for it may be important to know him later on. He is a scraggy little man, probably of sixty or more, with a completely bald pink head and a straggling grey beard which emerges from an incredibly folded and puckered yellow chin. His height is hardly more than five foot six, and his proportions are puny; but there is a wiriness about his spare person that contrasts strongly with Newton's fleshy bulk.

He is dressed, not so much ill as with a carelessness amounting to eccentricity. His clothes, certainly cut by a good tailor, hang in bags all over him. His pockets bulge. His waistcoat is buttoned up wrong, and sits awry, and his shirt has come apart at the neck, so that a disconsolate shirt-stud is hanging out on one side, while his red tie is leaning towards the other. Moreover, the sole of one of his boots has come loose, and flaps helplessly as his crossed legs swing slowly to the rhythm of the train.

Yet, despite these appearances, the newcomer is certainly a gentleman, and one is inclined to deem him eccentric rather than poor. He might be an exceptionally absent-minded professor; though, as a matter of fact, he is not. But who he is Joseph Newton has no idea.

For some time there was silence in the compartment, as the Cornish Riviera sped westward past the long spreading ribbon of London. Newton's fellow-traveller did not snore. His eyes were closed whenever Newton glanced at him; and yet between whiles the novelist had still a queer feeling of being stared at. He told himself it was nonsense, and tried to bury himself in a Wild West story; but the sensation remained with him. Suddenly, as the train passed Maidenhead Station, his companion spoke, in a quiet positive voice, as of one used to telling idiots what idiots they were. A professorial voice, with a touch of Scots accent.

"Talking of murders," it said, "you have really no right to be so careless."

"Eh?" said Newton, so startled that his magazine dropped from his hand to the floor. "Eh, what's that?"

"I said you had no right to be so careless," repeated the other.

Newton retrieved his magazine, and looked his fellow-traveller contemptuously up and down. "I am not aware," he said, "that we were talking of murders, or of anything else, for that matter."

"There, you see," said the other, "you did hear what I said the first time. What I mean to say is that, if you expect intelligent people to read your stories, you might at least trouble to make them plausible."

Newton suppressed the rejoinder that rose instantly to his lips. It was that he had far too large a circulation among fools to bother about what intelligent people thought. He only said, "I doubt, sir, if you are likely to find my conversation any more satisfactory than my books," and resumed his magazine.

"Probably not," said the stranger. "I expect success has spoiled you. But you had some brains to begin with... Those Indian stories of yours—"

Perhaps no other phrase would have induced Joseph

Newton to embark upon a conversation with the stranger. But nobody nowadays ever read or bothered about his Indian stories, though he was very well aware that they were the best things he had ever done.

"—had glimmerings of quality," the other was saying, "and you might have accomplished something had you not taken to writing for money."

"Are you aware, sir," Newton said, "that you are being excessively rude?"

"Quite," said the other with calm satisfaction. "I always am. It is so good for people. And really, in your last book, you have exceeded the limit."

"Which of my last books are you talking about?" asked Newton, hovering between annoyance and amusement.

"It is called *The Big Noise*," said the other, sighing softly.

"Oh, that," said Newton.

"Now, in that book," the stranger went on, "you call the heroine Elinor and Gertrude on different pages. You cannot make up your mind whether her name was Robbins with two 'b's or with one. You have killed the corpse in one place on Sunday and in another on Monday evening. That corpse was discovered twelve hours after the murder still wallowing in a pool of wet blood. The coroner committed no fewer than seventeen irregularities in conducting the inquest; and, finally, you have introduced three gangs, a mysterious Chinaman, an unknown poison that leaves no trace, and a secret society of international Jews high up in the political world."

The little old man held up his hands in horror as he ended the grisly recital.

"Well," Newton asked, "any more?"

"Alas, yes," said the other. "The volume includes, besides many misprints, fifteen glaring inconsistencies, nine cases of gross ignorance, and enough grammatical mistakes to—to stretch from Paddington to Penzance."

This time Newton laughed outright. "You seem to be a very earnest student of my writings," he said.

The stranger picked up the rug from his knees and folded it neatly beside him. He removed the pillow, and laid that down too. He then moved across to the corner seat opposite Newton and, taking a jewelled cigarette case from his pocket, selected a cigarette, returned the case to his pocket, found a match, lighted up, and began to smoke. Then he again drew out the case and offered it to Newton. "Lavery's," he said. "I know your favourite brand."

As a matter of fact, Newton never smoked Lavery's; but for a handsome sum he allowed his face, and a glowing testimonial to their virtues, to appear on their advertisements. Well, he might as well find out what the things were like. He took the proffered cigarette, and the stranger obligingly gave him a light. Newton puffed. Yes, they were good stuff—better than might be expected, though rather heavy.

"Now, in my view," the stranger was saying, "the essence of a really good murder is simplicity. All your books—all most people's books—have far too much paraphernalia about them. A really competent murderer would need no special appliances, and practically no preparations. Ergo, he would be in far less danger of leaving any clues behind him. Why, oh why, Mr. Newton, do you not write a murder story on those lines?"

Again Newton laughed. He was disposed to humour the

old gentleman. "It wouldn't make much of a story," he said, "if the murderer really left no clues."

"Oh, but there you are wrong," said the other. "What is needed is a perfectly simple murder, followed by a perfectly simple solution—so simple that only a great mind could think of it, by penetrating to the utter simplicity of the mind of the murderer."

"I can't abide those psychological detectives," Newton said. "You'd better go and read Mr. Van Dine." ("Or some of those fellows who would give their ears for a tenth of my sales," his expression added.)

"Dear me, you quite misunderstand me. That wasn't what I meant at all. There would be no psychology in the story I have in mind. It would be more like William Blake's poetry."

"Mad, you mean," said Newton.

"Crystal sane," replied the other. "Perhaps it will help you if I illustrate my point. Shall I outline the sort of murder I have in mind?"

"If you like," said Newton, who found himself growing suddenly very sleepy.

"Very well," said the stranger. "Then I'll just draw down the blinds."

He jumped up and lowered the blinds on the corridor side of the compartment.

"That's better," he said. "Now we shall be undisturbed. Now supposing—only supposing, of course—that there were two men in a railway carriage just like us, and they were perfect strangers, but one of them did not really care for the other's face—Are you listening, Mr. Newton?"

"Yes," said Newton, very sleepily. He was now having real difficulty in keeping his eyes open.

"And, further, supposing neither of them had brought any special paraphernalia with him, except what any innocent traveller might be carrying—say, a rug, a pillow, and a rug-strap—"

As he spoke, the stranger picked up the rug-strap from the seat beside him.

"Hey, what's that about a rug-strap?" said Newton, roused for a moment by a connection of ideas he was too sleepy to sort out.

"Except, of course, just one doped cigarette, containing an opiate—strong, but in no wise fatal," the other went on blandly.

"What the—?" murmured Newton, struggling now vainly against an absolutely stupefying drowsiness.

"There would really be nothing to prevent him from committing a nice, neat murder, would there?" the old man continued, rising as he spoke with startling agility and flinging the loop of the rug-strap over Newton's head. "Now, would there?" he repeated, as he drew it tight around his victim's neck, and neatly fastened it. Newton's mouth came wide open; his tongue protruded, and he began to gurgle horribly; his eyes stuck out from his head.

"And then," said the stranger, "the pillow would come in so handy to finish him off." He dragged Newton down on the seat, placed the pillow firmly on his upturned face, and sat on it, smiling delightedly. The gurgling slowly ceased.

"The rug," the cheerful voice went on, "has proved to be superfluous. Really, Mr. Newton, murder is even easier than

I supposed—though it is not often, I imagine, that a lucky chance enables one to do a service to the literary craft at the same time."

Newton said nothing; for he was dead.

The stranger retained his position a little longer, still smiling gently to himself. Then he rose, removed the pillow from Newton's face, and, after a careful survey of the body, undid the strap. Next, he picked up a half-smoked cigarette and threw it out of the window, folded his rug neatly, did it and the pillow up in the strap, and, opening the door into the corridor, walked quietly away down the train.

"What a pity!" he murmured to himself as he went. "It would make such a good story; and I am afraid the poor fellow will never have the sense to write it."

The body of Joseph Newton was actually discovered by a restaurant-car attendant who was going round to collect orders for the first lunch. Opening the door of a first-class compartment, which had all its blinds drawn down, he found Newton, no pleasant sight and indubitably dead, stretched out upon the seat where his companion had left him.

Without waiting to do more than make sure the man was dead, he scuttled along to fetch the guard. A brief colloquy of train officials then took place in the fatal compartment, and it was decided to stop the train short of Newbury Station, and send for the police before any one had a chance of leaving it. It seemed clear, as there had been no stop since they left Paddington, that the murderer must still be on it, unless he had leaped from an express travelling at full speed.

The police duly arrived, inspected the body, hunted the

compartment in vain for traces of another passenger—for the murderer had taken the precaution of wearing gloves throughout his demonstration—took the name and address of every person on the train, to the number of some hundreds, had the carriage in which the murder had occurred detached, with much shunting and grunting, from the rest of the train, and finally allowed the delayed express to proceed.

Only those travellers who had been actually in the coach of which Newton's compartment had formed a part were kept back for further inquiries. But Newton's companion was not among them. Having given his correct name and address to the police, he proceeded quietly upon his journey in the empty first-class compartment two coaches farther back to which he had moved after his successful experiment in simplicity.

There were 498 passengers on the Cornish Riviera express whose names were taken by the police at Newbury; or, if you count Newton, 499. Add guards and attendants, restaurant-car staff, and the occupants of a travelling Post Office van—total 519.

Of these 126 were women, 153 children, and the rest men. That allowed for quite enough possible suspects for the police to follow up. They were followed up, exhaustively. But it did not appear that any single person among them had any acquaintance with Joseph Newton, or any connection with him save as readers of his books. Nor did a meticulous examination of Newton's past suggest the shadow of a reason why he should have been murdered.

The police tried their hardest, and the public and the Press did their best to assist, for the murder of a bestseller, by a criminal who left no clue, was enough to excite anybody's imagination. Several individuals, in their enthusiasm, went so far as to confess to the crime, and gave Scotland Yard several days' work in disproving their statements. But nothing helpful was forthcoming, and at long last the excitement died down.

It was more than three months later that the young Marquis of Queensferry called upon Henry Wilson, formerly the chief official of Scotland Yard, and now the foremost private detective in England. His modest request was that Wilson should solve for him the mystery of Joseph Newton's murder.

When Wilson asked him why he wanted it solved, the Marquis explained that it was for a bet. It appeared that his old uncle, the Honourable Roderick Dominic Acres-Noel, had bet him fifty thousand pounds to a penny he could not solve the problem, and he, who had the title but not the money, would be very willing to lay his hands on fifty thousand pounds which his uncle, who had the money but not the title, would never miss. Asked the reason for so unusual a bet, he replied that the reason was Uncle Roderick, who was always betting on something, the sillier the better.

"Our family's like that, you know," the Marquis added. "We're all mad. And my uncle was quite excited about the case, because he was on the train when it happened. He even wrote to *The Times* about it."

Wilson rejected the idea that he could solve a case which had utterly baffled Scotland Yard when the trail was fresh, now that it was stone cold, and all clues, presumably, vanished into limbo. Even the most lavish promises of shares in the fifty thousand pounds did not tempt him, and he sent the young Marquis away with a flea in his ear.

But, after the Marquis had gone, he found that he could not get the case out of his head. In common with everybody else, he had puzzled his brains over it at the time; but it was weeks since he had given it a thought. But now—here it was again—bothering his mind.

Hang it all, it wasn't reasonable—it was against nature— that a man should be able to murder another man and get away without leaving any clue at all. So, at any rate, the Marquis's crazy old uncle seemed to think, unless, indeed, he was merely crazy. Most likely he was.

Wilson could not say exactly at what moment he decided to have one more shot at this impossible mystery. Perhaps it was when he recollected that, according to the Marquis, Mr. Acres-Noel had himself travelled on that train to Cornwall. It might be that Mr. Acres-Noel had noticed something that the police had missed; he was just the sort of old gentleman who would enjoy keeping a titbit of information to himself. At any rate, it was one thing one could try.

Wilson rang up his old colleague, Inspector Blaikie, at Scotland Yard, and Blaikie guffawed at him.

"Solve it, by all means," he said. "We'll be delighted. We're sick of the sound of Newton's name... Yes, old Acres-Noel was on the train—I don't know anything more about him... Oh, mad as a hatter. Completely... Yes, he wrote to *The Times*, and they printed it... Three days afterwards, I think. Shall I have it looked up for you?... Right you are. Let us know when you catch the murderer, won't you?"

Wilson sent for his own file of *The Times*, and looked up the letter of Mr. Acres-Noel. *The Times* had not thought it worth the honour of the middle page, but fortunately had not degraded it into the "Points" column.

"SIR," it ran,

> "The methods of the police in dealing with the so-called Newton Mystery appear to show more than the usual official incompetence. As one of the passengers on the train on which Mr. Newton died, I have been subjected to considerable annoyance—and I may add compensated in part by some amusement—at the fruitless and irrelevant inquiries made by the police.
>
> "It is plain the police have no notion of the motives which prompted the murder. Their inquiries show that. If they would devote more attention to thinking what the motive was, and less to the accumulation of useless information, the apparent complexity of the case would disappear. The truth is usually simple—too simple for idiots to see. Why was Newton murdered? Answer that, and it will appear plainly that only one person could have murdered him. Motive is essentially individual.
>
> "I am, yours, etc.,
>
> > "R. D. ACRES-NOEL."

"Upon my word," said Wilson to himself, "that's a very odd letter."

He read it several times over, staring at it as if the name of the murderer was written between the lines.

Suddenly he leaped to his feet, and with an excitement he seldom showed, dashed down Whitehall to Inspector Blaikie's office. Within ten minutes he was making a proposition to that official which left him starkly incredulous.

"I know," Wilson persisted, "it isn't a certainty, it's a thousand to one chance. But it *is* a chance, and I want to try it. I'm not asking the Department to commit itself in any way, only to let me have a couple of men standing by. Don't you see, the whole point about this extraordinary letter is the way it stresses the question of motive? And, more than that, it suggests that the writer knows what the motive was. Now, how could he do that unless—"

"But, if that's so, the man's mad!" Blaikie protested. "Whoever heard of anybody murdering a complete stranger just to *show* him?"

"Well, he certainly is mad, isn't he? You said so yourself, and his family's notoriously crazy."

"He'll have to be pretty well off his rocker," Blaikie remarked, "if he's to be kind enough to come and shove his neck in a noose for you."

"One can but try," Wilson said. "If you won't help me I'm going to try alone. I must have one shot at getting to the bottom of it." And eventually Blaikie agreed.

The upshot was that Wilson, immediately after his interview, arranged for the posting of the following letter, forged with extreme care so as to imitate the handwriting of the supposed author. It was dispatched from the pillarbox nearest to Joseph Newton's Cornish cottage.

"DEAR MR. ACRES-NOEL," it said,

> "*Ever since our chance meeting a few months ago,
> I have been thinking over the very interesting demon-
> stration you were kind enough to give me on that occa-
> sion. May I confess, however, that I am still not quite
> satisfied; and I should be even more deeply obliged if
> I could induce you to repeat it. As it happens, I shall
> be returning to London this weekend, and travelling
> down again to Cornwall on the Riviera express next
> Wednesday. If you too should chance to be travelling
> that way, perhaps we may meet again.*
>
> "*Yours very truly,*
>
> "JOSEPH NEWTON."

Someone remarkably like the late Joseph Newton settled himself comfortably in the corner of a first-class compartment in the Cornish Riviera express. He had the compartment to himself, and, although the train had begun to fill up, no other traveller had entered when the train drew out of the station. Very discreetly, passengers who came near it had been warned away by the station officials.

The train had not yet gathered its full speed when the solitary traveller became conscious that someone was standing outside the compartment, and staring in at him. He raised his eyes from the magazine he was reading, and looked back. Slowly, the newcomer pushed back the sliding door, entered the compartment, and sat down in the far corner.

He was a little old man, with a straggling beard, wearing

very shabby clothes. He flung down on the seat beside him a rug and a pillow tied up in a strap. Undoing his bundle, he settled himself with the pillow behind his head, the rug over his knees, and the strap on the seat beside him. Then he closed his eyes.

Wilson did and said nothing. It was nervous work, waiting for his cue. But by this time he knew he was right. The millionth chance had come off.

The train flashed at length—it seemed hours—through Maidenhead Station. Suddenly the old man spoke.

"Talking of murders," he said, "it is my turn to apologise. I am afraid I bungled it last time."

"Not at all," said Wilson, hoping that his voice would not give him away; "but if you would kindly just show me again how—"

"With pleasure," said the old man.

He moved with alacrity to the corner opposite Wilson, took from his pocket a jewelled cigarette case, and proffered it. Wilson took a cigarette, and did a second's rapid thinking before the match was produced. A cigarette was something he had not allowed for, and it might even turn out to be poisoned. However, no use to hesitate now. He suffered Mr. Acres-Noel to light it, and the heavy sweetish taste confirmed his fears.

Fortunately, however, it was hardly alight before the other rose and went to the window.

"You won't mind my pulling down the blinds, will you?" he said; and Wilson took advantage of his movement to effect a lightning exchange of the suspicious cigarette for one of his own. This was a relief, but clearly he must show some signs of being affected by it. Sleepiness seemed the most likely cue. He yawned.

"You follow me so far, I trust," said the other.

"Perfectly," said Wilson slowly. "Please—go—" Slowly his eyes closed, and his head began to wag.

The old man seized the rug-strap.

"This is the next step," he said, attempting to cast it over Wilson's head. But Wilson sprang to his feet, warded off the strap, and pressed a button beside him which had been fixed to communicate with the adjoining compartment.

Almost as he grappled with his now frenzied antagonist, two stalwart policemen in plain clothes rushed in to his aid. Mr. Acres-Noel, alternately protesting his innocence and shrieking with wild laughter, was soon safely secured. The train slowed down and stopped at the deserted station of Newbury Racecourse, where captors and captive descended almost unnoticed. Then it sped upon its way.

Mr. Acres-Noel, safe in Broadmoor, has only one complaint. The authorities will not supply him with Joseph Newton's new books. He wants to see whether that popular writer has benefited by his lesson in practical criminology.

Trent and the
Ministering Angel

E. C. Bentley

Edmund Clerihew Bentley (1875–1956) is celebrated by detective fiction fans as the author of a novel which, arguably, was the catalyst for the Golden Age of detective fiction. *Trent's Last Case* aka *The Woman in Black* (1913) was a country house mystery intended to debunk the notion of the omniscient detective in the Sherlock Holmes vein, by having the ingenious solution dreamed up by the gentlemanly detective Philip Trent turn out to be wholly mistaken. However, the twisty nature of the plot ensured that the novel was seized upon as something new and inspirational in the field of whodunits. After the First World War, authors such as Agatha Christie and Dorothy L. Sayers, both of whom were fervent admirers of Bentley, proceeded to develop the classic murder mystery novel.

Bentley was a school friend of G. K. Chesterton, whose Father Brown stories include a bibliomystery, "The Blast of the Book," and after Chesterton's death in 1936, Bentley succeeded him as President of the Detection Club. Philip Trent appeared, after a long absence from the scene, in a second novel, and Bentley also wrote short stories about the character. In 1938, twelve of these were collected in *Trent Intervenes*. A thirteenth story appeared in the *Strand Magazine* in the November of that year; this was "Trent and the Ministering Angel."

———

"WHATEVER THE MEANING OF IT MAY BE, IT'S A DEVILISH unpleasant business," Arthur Selby said as he and Philip Trent established themselves on a sofa in the smoking-room of the Lansdowne Club. "We see enough of that sort of business in the law—even firms like ours, that don't have much to do with crime, have plenty of unpleasantness to deal with, and I don't know that some of it isn't worse than the general run of crime. You know what I mean. Crazy spite, that's one thing. You wouldn't believe what some people—people of position and education and all that—you wouldn't believe what they are capable of when they want to do somebody a mischief. Usually it's a blood relation. And then there's constitutional viciousness. We had one client—he died soon after Snow took me into partnership—whose whole life had been one lascivious debauch."

Trent laughed. "That phrase doesn't sound like your own, Arthur. It belongs to an earlier generation."

"Quite true," Selby admitted. "It was Snow told me that about old Sir William Never-mind-who, and it stuck in my memory. But come now—I'm wandering. A good lunch—by the way, I hope it *was* a good lunch."

"One of the very best," Trent said. "You know it was too. Ordering lunches is one of the best things you do, and you're proud of it. That hock was a poem—a villanelle, for choice. What were you going to say about good lunches?"

"Why, I was going to say that a good lunch usually makes me inclined to prattle a bit; because, you see, all I allow myself most days is a couple of apples and a glass of milk in the office. That's the way to appreciate a thing: don't have it too often, and take a hell of a lot of trouble about it when you do. But that isn't what I wanted to talk to you about, Phil. I was saying just now that we get a lot of unpleasantness in our job. We can usually understand it when we get it, but the affair I want to tell you about is a puzzle to me; and of course you are well known to be good at puzzles. If I tell you the story, will you give me a spot of advice if you can?"

"Of course."

"Well, it's about a client of ours who died a fortnight ago, named Gregory Landell. You wouldn't have heard of him, I dare say; he never did anything much outside his private hobbies, having always had money and never any desire to distinguish himself. He could have done, for he had plenty of brains—a brilliant scholar, always reading Greek. He and my partner had been friends from boyhood; at school and Cambridge together; had tastes in common; both rock-garden enthusiasts, for one thing. Landell's was a famous rock-garden. Other amateurs used to come from all parts to visit it, and of course he loved that. Then they were both Lewis Carroll fans—when they got together, bits from the *Alice* books and the *Snark* were always coming into the conversation—both chess players, both keen cricketers when they were young enough, and never tired of watching first-class games. Snow used often to stay for weekends at Landell's place at Cholsey Wood, in Berkshire.

"When Landell was over fifty, he married for the first time. The lady was a Miss Mary Archer, daughter of a naval officer, and about twenty years younger than Landell, at a guess. He was infatuated with her, and she seemed to make a great fuss of him, though she didn't strike me as being the warm-hearted type. She was a good-looking wench with plenty of style, and gave you the idea of being fond of her own way. We made his will for him, leaving everything to her if there were no children. Snow and I were both appointed executors. In his previous will he had left all his property to a nephew; and we were sorry the nephew wasn't mentioned in this later will, for he is a very useful citizen—some kind of medical research worker—and he has barely enough to live on."

"Why did he make both of you executors?" Trent wondered.

"Oh, in case anything happened to one of us. And it was just as well, because early this year poor old Snow managed to fracture his thigh, and he's been laid up ever since. But that's getting ahead of the story. After the marriage, Snow still went down to Landell's place from time to time, as before; but after a year or so he began to notice a great change in the couple. Landell seemed to get more and more under his wife's thumb. Couldn't call his soul his own."

Trent nodded. "After what you told me about the impression she made on you, that isn't surprising."

"No. Snow and I had been expecting it to happen. But the worst of it was, Landell didn't take it easily, as some husbands in that position do. He was obviously very unhappy, though he never said anything about it to Snow. She had quite given up pretending to be affectionate, or to consider him in any way, and Snow got the idea that Landell hated his wife like poison, though never daring to stand up to her. Yet he used to have plenty of character, too."

"I have seen the sort of thing," Trent said. "Unless a man is a bit of a brute himself, he can't bear to see the woman making an exhibition of herself. He'll stand anything rather than have her make a scene."

"Just so. Well, after a time Snow got no more invitations to go there; and as you may suppose, he didn't mind that. It had got to be too uncomfortable, and though he was devilish sorry for Landell, he didn't see that he could do anything for him. For one thing, she wouldn't ever leave them alone together if she could possibly help it. If they were pottering about with the rock-plants, or playing chess, or going for a walk, they always had her company."

Trent made a grimace. "Jolly for the visitor! And now, what was it you didn't understand?"

"I'll tell you. About a month ago a letter for Snow came to the office. I opened it—I was dealing with all his business correspondence. It was from Mrs. Landell, saying that her husband was ill and confined to bed; that he wished to settle some business affairs, and would be most grateful if Snow could find time to come down on the following day.

"Well, Snow couldn't, of course. I got the idea from this letter, naturally, that the matter was more or less urgent. It read as if Landell was right at the end of his tether. So I rang up Mrs. Landell, explained the situation, and said I would come myself that afternoon if it suited her. She said she would be delighted if I would; she was very anxious about her husband, whose heart was in a serious state. I mentioned the train I would come by, and she said their car would meet it.

"When I got there, she took me up to Landell's bedroom at once. He was looking very bad, and seemed to have hardly strength enough to speak. There was a nurse in the room: Mrs. Landell sent her out and stayed with us all the time I was there—which I had expected, after what I had heard from Snow. Then Landell began to talk, or whisper, about what he wanted done.

"It was a scheme for the rearrangement of his investments, and a shrewd one, too—he had a wonderful flair for that sort of thing, made a study of it. In fact—" Selby leant forward and tapped his friend's knee—"there was absolutely nothing for him to discuss with me. He knew exactly what he wanted done, and he needed no advice; he knew more about such matters than I did, or Snow either. Still, he made quite a show of asking my opinion of this detail and that, and all I could do was to look wise, and hum and haw, and then say that nothing could be better. Then he said that the exertion of writing a business letter was forbidden by his doctor, and would I oblige him by doing it for him? So I took down a letter of instructions to his brokers, which he signed; and his wife had the securities he was going to sell all ready in a long envelope; and that was that. The car took me to the station, and I got back in time for dinner, after an absolutely wasted half-day."

Trent had listened to all this with eager attention. "It was wasted, you say," he observed. "Do you mean he could have dictated such a letter to his wife, without troubling you at all?"

"To his wife, or to anybody who could write. And of course he knew that well enough. I tell you, all that business of consulting me was just camouflage. I knew it, and I could feel that he knew I knew it. But what the devil it was intended to hide is beyond me. I don't think his wife suspected anything queer; Snow always said she was a fool about business matters. She listened intently to everything that was said, and seemed quite satisfied. His instructions were acted upon, and he signed the transfers; I know that, because when I came to making an inventory of the estate, after his death, I found it had all been done. Now then, Phil: what do you make of all that?"

Trent caressed his chin for a few moments. "You're quite sure that there *was* something unreal about the business? His wife, you say, saw nothing suspicious."

"Of course I'm sure. His wife evidently didn't know that he was cleverer about investments than either Snow or me, and that anyhow it wasn't our job. If he *had* wanted advice, he could have had his broker down."

Trent stretched his legs before him and carefully considered the end of his cigar. "No doubt you are right," he said at length. "And it does sound as if there was something unpleasant below the surface. For that matter, the surface itself was not particularly agreeable, as you describe it. Mrs. Landell, the ministering angel!" He rose to his feet. "I'll turn the thing over in my mind, Arthur, and let you know if anything strikes me."

Trent found the house in Cholsey Wood without much difficulty next morning. The place actually was a tract of woodland of large extent, cleared here and there for a few isolated modern houses and grounds, a row of cottages, an inn called the Magpie and Gate, and a Tudor manor-house standing in a well-tended park. The Grove, the house of which he was in search, lay half a mile beyond the inn on the road that bisected the neighbourhood. A short drive led up to it through the high hedge that bounded the property on this side, and Trent, turning his car into the opening, got out and walked to the house, admiring as he went the flower-bordered lawn on one side, the trim orchard on the other. The two-storyed house, too, was a well-kept, well-built place, its porch overgrown by wistaria in full flower.

His ring was answered by a chubby maidservant, to whom he offered his card. He had been told, he said, that Mr. Landell allowed visitors who were interested in gardening to see his rock-garden, of which Trent had heard so much. Would the maid take his card to Mr. Landell, and ask if it would be convenient—here he paused, as a lady stepped from an open door at the end of the hall. Trent described her to himself as a handsome, brassy blonde with a hard blue eye.

"I am Mrs. Landell," she said, as she took the card from the girl and glanced at it. "I heard what you were saying. I see, Mr. Trent, you have not heard of my bereavement. My dear husband passed away a fortnight ago." Trent began to murmur words of vague condolence and apology. "Oh no," she went on with a sad smile. "You must not think you are disturbing me. You must certainly see the rock-garden now you are here. You have come a long way for the purpose, I dare say, and my husband would not have wished you to go away disappointed."

"It is a famous garden," Trent observed. "I heard of it from someone I think you know—Arthur Selby, the lawyer."

"Yes, he and his partner were my husband's solicitors," the lady said. "I will show you where the garden is, if you will come this way." She turned and went before him through the house, until they came out through a glass-panelled door into a much larger extent of grounds. "I cannot show it off to you myself," she went on, "I know absolutely nothing about that sort of gardening. My husband was very proud of it, and he was adding to the collection of plants up to the time he was taken ill last month. You see that grove of elms? The house is called after it. If you go along it you will come to a lily-pond, and the rock-garden is to the left of that. I fear I cannot entertain anyone just now, so I will leave you to yourself, and the parlour-maid will wait to let you out when you have seen enough." She bowed her head in answer to his thanks, and retired into the house.

Trent passed down the avenue and found the object of his journey, a tall pile of roughly terraced grey rocks covered with a bewildering variety of plants rooted in the shallow soil provided for them. The lady of the house, he reflected, could hardly know less about rock-gardens than himself, and it was just as well that there was to be no dangerous comparing of ignorances. He did not even know what he was looking for. He believed that the garden had something to tell, and that was all. Pacing slowly up and down, with searching eye, before the stony rampart with its dress of delicate colours, he set himself to divine its secret.

Soon he noted a detail which, as he considered it, became more curious. Here and there among the multitude of plants there was one distinguished by a flat slip of white wood stuck in the soil among the stems, or just beside the growth. They were not many: searching about, he could find no more than seven. Written on each slip in a fair, round hand was a botanical name. Such names meant nothing to Trent; he could but wonder vaguely why they were there. Why were these plants thus distinguished? Possibly they were the latest acquisitions. Possibly Landell had so marked them to draw the attention of his old friend and fellow-enthusiast Snow. Landell had been expecting Snow to come and see him, Trent remembered. Snow had been unable to come, and Arthur Selby had come instead. Another point: the business Landell had wanted done was trifling; anyone could have attended to it. Why had it been so important to Landell that Snow should come?

Had Landell been expecting to have a private talk with Snow about some business matter? No: because on previous occasions, as on this occasion, Mrs. Landell had been present throughout the interview; it was evident, according to Selby, that she did not intend to leave her husband alone with his legal adviser at any time, and Landell must have realised that. Was this the main point: that the unfortunate Landell had been planning to communicate something to Snow by some means unknown to his wife?

Trent liked the look of this idea. It fitted into the picture, at least. More than that: it gave strong confirmation to the quite indefinite notion he had formed on hearing Selby's story; the notion that had brought him to Cholsey Wood that day. Snow was a keen amateur of rock-gardening. If

Snow had come to visit Landell, one thing virtually certain was that Snow would not have gone away without having a look at his friend's collection of rock-plants, if only to see what additions might have been recently made. And such additions—so Mrs. Landell had just been saying— had been made. Mrs. Landell knew nothing about rock-gardening; even if she had wasted a glance on this garden, she would have noticed nothing. Snow would have noticed instantly anything out of the way. And what was there out of the way?

Trent began to whistle faintly.

The wooden slips had now a very interesting look. With notebook and pencil he began to write down the names traced upon them. *Armeria Hallerii*. And *Arcana Nieuwillia*. And *Saponaria Galspitosa*—good! And these delicate little blossoms, it appeared, rejoiced in the formidable name of *Acantholimon Glumaceum*. Then here was *Cartavacua Bellmannii*. Trent's mind began to run on the nonsense botany of Edward Lear: *Nasticreechia Crawluppia* and the rest. This next one was *Veronica Incana*. And here was the last of the slips: *Ludovica Caroli*, quite a pretty name for a shapeless mass of grey-green vegetation that surely was commonly called, in the vulgar tongue—

At this point Trent flung his notebook violently to the ground, and followed it with his hat. What a fool he had been! What a triple ass, not to have jumped to the thing at once! He picked up the book and hurriedly scanned the list of names… Yes: it was all there.

Three minutes later he was in his car on the way back to town.

In his room at the offices of Messrs. Snow and Selby the junior partner welcomed Trent on the morning after his expedition to Cholsey Wood.

Selby pushed his cigarette box across the table. "Can you tell it me in half an hour, do you think? I'd have been glad to come to lunch with you and hear it then, but this is a very full day, and I shan't get outside the office until seven, if then. What have you been doing?"

"Paying a visit to your late client's rock-garden," Trent informed him. "It made a deep impression on me. Mrs. Landell was very kind about it."

Selby stared at him. "You always had the devil's own cheek," he observed. "How on earth did you manage that? And why?"

"I won't waste time over the how," Trent said. "As to the why, it was because it seemed to me, when I thought it over, that that garden might have a serious meaning underlying all its gaiety. And I thought so all the more when I found that Mary, Mary, quite contrary, hadn't a notion how her garden grew. You see, it was your partner whom Landell had wanted to consult about those investments of his; and it was hardly likely that your rock-gardening partner, once on the spot, would have missed the chance of feasting his eyes on his friend's collection of curiosities. So I went and feasted mine; and I found what I expected."

"The deuce you did!" Selby exclaimed. "And what was it?"

"Seven plants—only seven out of all the lot—marked with their botanical names, clearly written on slips of wood, *à la* Kew Gardens. I won't trouble you with four of the names—they were put there just to make it look more natural, I suppose; they were genuine names; I've looked them up. But you will find the other three interesting—choice Latin, picked phrase, if not exactly Tully's every word."

Trent, as he said this, produced a card and handed it to his friend, who studied the words written upon it with a look of complete incomprehension.

"*Arcana Nieuwillia*," he read aloud. "I can't say that thrills me to the core, anyhow. What's an *Arcana*? Of course, I know no more about botany than a cow. It looks as if it was named after some Dutchman."

"Well, try the next," Trent advised him.

"*Cartavacua Bellmannii*. No, that too fails to move me. Then what about the rest of the nosegay? *Ludovica Caroli*. No, it's no good, Phil. What *is* it all about?"

Trent pointed to the last name. "That one was what gave it away to me. The slip with *Ludovica Caroli* on it was stuck into a clump of saxifrage. I know saxifrage when I see it; and I seemed to remember that the right scientific name for it was practically the same—*Saxifraga*. And then I suddenly remembered another thing: that Ludovicus is the Latin form of the name Louis, which some people choose to spell L-E-W-I-S."

"What!" Selby jumped to his feet. "Lewis—and Caroli! Lewis Carroll! Oh Lord! The man whose books Snow and Landell both knew by heart. Then it *is* a cryptogram." He referred eagerly to the card. "Well, then—*Cartavacua Bellmannii*. Hm! Would that be the Bellman in *The Hunting of the Snark*? And *Cartavacua*?"

"Translate it," Trent suggested.

Selby frowned. "Let's see. In law, *carta* used to be a charter. And *vacua* means empty. The Bellman's empty charter—"

"Or chart. Don't you remember?

"He had bought a large map representing the sea,
Without the least vestige of land:
And the crew were much pleased when they found it to be
A map they could all understand.

And in the poem, one of the pages is devoted to the Bellman's empty map."

"Oh! And that tells us—?"

"Why, I believe it tells us to refer to Landell's own copy of the book, and to that blank page."

"Yes, but what for?"

"*Arcana Nieuwillia*, I expect."

"I told you I don't know what *Arcana* means. It isn't law Latin, and I've forgotten most of the other kind."

"This isn't law Latin, as you say. It's the real thing, and it means 'hidden,' Arthur, 'hidden.'"

"Hidden what?" Selby stared at the card again; then suddenly dropped into his chair and turned a pale face to his friend. "My God, Phil! So that's it!"

"It can't be anything else, can it?"

Selby turned to his desk telephone and spoke into the receiver. "I am not to be disturbed on any account till I ring." He turned again to Trent ...

I asked Mr. Trent to drive me down," Selby explained, "because I wanted his help in a matter concerning your husband's estate. He has met you before informally, he tells me."

Mrs. Landell smiled at Trent graciously. "Only the other day he called to see the rock-garden. He mentioned that he was a friend of yours."

She had received them in the morning-room at the Grove, and Trent, who on the occasion of his earlier visit had seen nothing but the hallway running from front to back, was confirmed in his impression that strict discipline ruled in that household. The room was orderly and speckless, the few pictures hung mathematically level, the flowers in a bowl on the table were fresh and well displayed.

"And what is the business that brings you and Mr. Trent down so unexpectedly?" Mrs. Landell inquired. "Is it some new point about the valuation of the property, perhaps?" She looked from one to the other of them with round blue eyes.

Selby looked at her with an expression that was new in Trent's experience of that genial, rather sybaritic man of law. He was now serious, cool, and hard.

"No, Mrs. Landell; nothing to do with that," Selby said. "I am sorry to tell you I have reason to believe that your husband made another will not long ago, and that it is in this house. If there is such a will, and if it is in order legally, it will of course supersede the will made shortly after your marriage."

Mrs. Landell's first emotion on hearing this statement was to be seen in a look of obviously genuine amazement. Her eyes and mouth opened together, and her hands fell on the arms of her chair. The feeling that succeeded, which she did her best to control, was as plainly one of anger and incredulity.

"I don't believe a word of it," she said sharply. "It is quite impossible. My husband certainly did not see his solicitor, or any other lawyer, for a long time before his death. When he did see Mr. Snow, I was always present. If he made another will, I must have known about it. The idea is absurd. Why should he have wanted to make another will?"

Selby shrugged. "That I cannot say, Mrs. Landell. The question does not arise. But if he had wanted to, he could make a will without a lawyer's assistance, and if it complied with the requirements of the law it would be a valid will. The position is that, as his legal adviser and executor of the will of which we know, I am bound to satisfy myself that there is no later will, if I have grounds for thinking that there is one. And I have grounds for thinking so."

Mrs. Landell made a derisive sound. "Have you really? And grounds for thinking it is in this house, too? Well, I can tell you that it isn't. I have been through every single paper in the place, I have looked carefully everywhere, and there is no such thing."

"There was nothing locked up then?" Selby suggested.

"Of course not," Mrs. Landell snapped. "My husband had no secrets from me."

Selby coughed. "It may be so. All the same, Mrs. Landell, I shall have to satisfy myself on the point. The law is very strict about matters of this kind, and I must make a search on my own account."

"And suppose I say I will not allow it? This is all my property now, and I am not obliged to let anyone come rummaging about for something that isn't there."

Again Selby coughed. "That is not exactly the position, Mrs. Landell. When a person dies, having made a will appointing an executor, his property vests at once in that executor, and it remains entirely in his control until the estate has been distributed as the will directs. The will on which you are relying, and which is the only one at present positively known to exist, appointed my partner and myself executors. We must act in that capacity, unless and until a later will comes to light. I hope that is quite clear."

This information appeared, as Selby put it later, to take the wind completely out of Mrs. Landell's sails. She sat in frowning silence, mastering her feelings, for a few moments, then rose to her feet.

"Very well," she said. "If what you tell me is correct, it seems you can do as you like, and I cannot prevent you wasting your time. Where will you begin your search?"

"I think," Selby said, "the best place to make a start would be the room where he spent most of his time when by himself. There is such a room, I suppose?"

She went to the door. "I will show you the study," she said, not looking at either of them. "Your friend had better come too, as you say you want him to assist you."

She led the way across the hall to another room, with a French window opening on the lawn behind the house. Before this stood a large writing-table, old-fashioned and solid like the rest of the furniture, which included three bookcases of bird's-eye maple. Not wasting time, Selby and Trent went each to one of the bookcases, while Mrs. Landell looked on implacably from the doorway.

"*Annales Thucydidei et Xenophontei*," read Selby in an undertone, glancing up and down the shelves. "*Miscellanea Critica*, by Cobet—give me the *Rural Rides*, for choice. I say, Phil, I seem to have come to the wrong shop. *Palæographia Græca*, by Montfaucon—I had an idea that was a place where they used to break chaps on the wheel in Paris. Greek plays— rows and rows of them. How are you getting on?"

"I am on the trail, I believe," Trent answered. "This is all English poetry—but not arranged in any order. Aha! What do I see?" He pulled out a thin red volume. "One of the best-looking books that was ever printed and bound." He was turning the pages rapidly. "Here we are—the Ocean Chart. But no longer 'a perfect and absolute blank.'"

He handed the book to Selby, who scanned attentively the page at which it was opened. "Beautiful writing, isn't it?" he remarked. "Not much larger than smallish print, and quite as legible. Hm! Hm!" He frowned over the minute script, nodding approval from time to time; then looked up. "Yes, this is all right. Everything clear, and the attestation clause quite in order—that's what gets 'em, very often."

Mrs. Landell, whose existence Selby appeared to have forgotten for the moment, now spoke in a strangled voice. "Do you mean to tell me that there is a will written in that book?"

"I beg your pardon," the lawyer said with studied politeness. "Yes, Mrs. Landell, this is the will for which I was looking. It is very brief, but quite clearly expressed, and properly executed and witnessed. The witnesses are Mabel Catherine Wheeler and Ida Florence Kirkby, both domestic servants, resident in this house."

"They dared to do that behind my back!" Mrs. Landell raged. "It's a conspiracy!"

Selby shook his head. "There is no question here of an agreement to carry out some hurtful purpose," he said. "The witnesses appear to have signed their names at the request of their employer, and they were under no obligation to mention the matter to any other person. Possibly he requested them not to do so; it makes no difference. As for the provisions of the will, it begins by bequeathing the sum of ten thousand pounds, free of legacy duty, to yourself—"

"What!" screamed Mrs. Landell.

"Ten thousand pounds, free of legacy duty," Selby repeated calmly. "It gives fifty pounds each to my partner and myself, in consideration of our acting as executors—that, you may remember, was provided by the previous will. And all the rest of the testator's property goes to his nephew, Robert Spencer Landell, of 27 Longland Road, Blackheath, in the county of Kent."

The last vestige of self-control departed from Mrs. Landell as the words were spoken. Choking with fury and trembling violently, she snatched the book from Selby's hand, ripped out the inscribed page, and tore it across again and again. "Now what are you going to do?" she gasped.

"The question is, what you are going to do," Selby returned with perfect coolness. "If you destroy that will beyond repair, you commit a felony which is punishable by penal servitude. Besides that, the will could still be proved; I am acquainted with its contents, and can swear to them. The witnesses can swear that it was executed. Mr. Trent and I can swear to what has just taken place. If you will take my advice, Mrs. Landell, you will give me back those bits of paper. If they can be pieced together into a legible document, the Court will not refuse to recognise it, and I may be able to save you from being prosecuted—I shall do my best. And there is another thing. As matters stand now, I must ask you to consider your arrangements for the future. There is no hurry, naturally; I shall not press you in any way; but you realise that while you continue living here you do so on sufferance, and that the place must be taken over by Mr. Robert Landell in due course."

Mrs. Landell was sobered at last. Very pale, and staring fixedly at Selby, she flung the pieces of the will on the writing-table and walked rapidly from the room.

"I had no idea you could be such a brute, Arthur," Trent remarked as he drove the car Londonwards through the Berkshire levels.

Selby said nothing.

"The accused made no reply," Trent observed. "Perhaps you didn't notice that you were being brutal, with those icy little legal lectures of yours, and your drawing out the agony in that study until you had her almost at screaming point even before the blow fell."

Selby glanced at him. "Yes, I noticed all that. I don't think I am a vindictive man, Phil, but she made me see red. In spite of what she said, it's clear to me that she suspected he might have made another will at some time. She looked for it high and low. If she had found it she would undoubtedly have suppressed it. And her husband had no secrets from her! And whenever Snow was there she was always present! Can you imagine what it was like being dominated and bullied by a harpy like that?"

"Ghastly," Trent agreed. "But look here, Arthur; if he could get the two maids to witness the will, and keep quiet about it, why couldn't he have made it on an ordinary sheet of paper and enclosed it in a letter to your firm, and got either Mabel Catherine or Ida Florence to post it secretly?"

Selby shook his head. "I thought of that. Probably he didn't dare take the risk of the girl being caught with the letter by her mistress. If that had happened, the fat *would* have been in the fire. Besides, we should have acknowledged the letter, and she would have opened our reply and read it. Reading all his correspondence would have been part of the treatment, you may be sure. No, Phil: I liked old Landell, and I meant to hurt. Sorry; but there it is."

"I wasn't objecting to your being brutal," Trent said. "I felt just like you, and you had my unstinted moral support all the time. I particularly liked that passage when you reminded her that she could be slung out on her ear whenever you chose."

"She's devilish lucky, really," Selby said. "She can live fairly comfortably on the income from her legacy if she likes. And she can marry again, God help us all! Landell got back on her in the end; but he did it like a gentleman."

"So did you," Trent said. "A very nice little job of torturing, I should call it."

Selby's smile was bitter. "It only lasted minutes," he said. "Not years."

A Slice of Bad Luck

Nicholas Blake

Nicholas Blake was the name adopted by the poet Cecil Day-Lewis (1904–1972) when he turned his hand to writing detective fiction as a means of supplementing his income. His first novel, *A Question of Proof*, was published in 1935 and introduced Nigel Strangeways. Strangeways appeared in most of Blake's subsequent work, including *The Beast Must Die* (1938), which has been televised and filmed several times over the years; the most recent version is a Britbox TV series first screened in 2021 and very different from the original book. Today, in a twist of fate that the author would not have foreseen (and probably would not have welcomed), he seems to be more highly regarded for his crime fiction than his verse.

Blake's ability as a crime writer was quickly recognised by his peers and he was elected to membership of the prestigious Detection Club in 1937. The Assassins' Club, which features in this story, is a thinly disguised version of the

Detection Club. Herbert Dale, like Blake, has been invited to join this elitist group on the strength of his first two books. This story (subsequently published elsewhere under the title "The Assassins' Club") first appeared in a Detection Club anthology of short stories, edited by John Rhode: *Detection Medley* (1939).

———

"No," thought Nigel Strangeways, looking round the table, "no one would ever guess."

Ever since, quarter of an hour ago, they had assembled in the ante-room for sherry, Nigel had been feeling more and more nervous—a nervousness greater than the prospect of having to make an after-dinner speech seemed to warrant. It was true that, as the guest of honour, something more than the usual post-prandial convivialities would be expected of him. And of course the company present would, from its nature, be especially critical. But still, he had done this sort of thing often enough before; he knew he was pretty good at it. Why the acute state of jitters, then? After it was all over, Nigel was tempted to substitute "foreboding" for "jitters;" to wonder whether he oughtn't to have proclaimed these very curious feelings, like Cassandra, from the house-top—even at the risk of spoiling what looked like being a real peach of a dinner party. After all, the dinner party did get spoiled, anyway, and soon enough, too. But, taking all things into consideration, it probably wouldn't have made any difference.

It was in an attempt to dispel this cloud of uneasiness that Nigel began to play with himself the old game of identity-guessing. There was a curious uniformity amongst the faces of the majority of the twenty-odd diners. The women—there were only three of them—looked homely, humorous, dowdy-and-be-damned-to-it. The men, Nigel finally decided, resembled in the mass sanitary inspectors or very minor Civil Servants. They were most of them rather undersized, and ran to drooping moustaches, gold-rimmed spectacles, and a general air of mild ineffectualness. There were exceptions, of course. That elderly man in the middle of the table, with the face of a dyspeptic and superannuated bloodhound—it was not difficult to place him; even without the top hat or the wig with which the public normally associated him, Lord Justice Pottinger could easily be recognised—the most celebrated criminal judge of his generation. Then that leonine, mobile face on his left; it had been as much photographed as any society beauty's; and well it might, for Sir Eldred Traver's golden tongue had—it was whispered—saved as many murderers as Justice Pottinger had hanged. There were one or two other exceptions, such as the dark-haired, poetic-looking young man sitting on Nigel's right and rolling bread-pellets.

"No," said Nigel, aloud this time, "no one would possibly guess."

"Guess what?" inquired the young man.

"The bloodthirsty character of this assembly." He took up the menu-card, at the top of which was printed in red letters

THE ASSASSINS
Dinner, December 20th.

"No," laughed the young man, "we don't look like murderers, I must admit—not even murderers by proxy."

"Good Lord! are you in the trade, too?"

"Yes. Ought to have introduced myself. Name of Herbert Dale."

Nigel looked at the young man with increased interest. Dale had published only two crime-novels, but he was already accepted as one of the *élite* of detective writers; he could not otherwise have been a member of that most exclusive of clubs, the Assassins; for, apart from a representative of the Bench, the Bar, and Scotland Yard, this club was composed solely of the princes of detective fiction.

It was at this point that Nigel observed two things—that the hand which incessantly rolled bread-pellets was shaking, and that, on the glossy surface of the menu-card Dale had just laid down, there was a moist fingermark.

"Are you making a speech, too?" Nigel said.

"Me? Good Lord, no. Why?"

"I thought you looked nervous," said Nigel, in his direct way.

The young man laughed, a little too loudly. And, as though that was some kind of signal, one of those unrehearsed total silences fell upon the company. Even in the street outside, the noises seemed to be damped, as though an enormous soft pedal had been pressed down on everything. Nigel realised that it must have been snowing since he came in. A disagreeable sensation of eeriness crept over him. Annoyed with this sensation—a detective has no right to feel psychic, he reflected angrily, not even a private detective as celebrated as Nigel Strangeways—he forced himself to look round the brilliantly lighted room, the animated yet oddly neutral-looking faces of the diners, the *maître d'hôtel* in his white gloves—bland and uncreased as his own face, the impassive waiters. Everything was perfectly normal; and yet… Some motive he was never after able satisfactorily to explain forced him to let drop into the yawning silence:

"What a marvellous setting this would be for a murder."

If Nigel had been looking in the right direction at that moment, things might have happened very differently. As it was, he didn't even notice the way Dale's wineglass suddenly tilted and spilt a few drops of sherry.

At once the whole table buzzed again with conversation. A man three places away on Nigel's right raised his head, which had been almost buried in his soup-plate, and said:

"Tchah! This is the one place where a murder would never happen. My respected colleagues are men of peace. I doubt if any of them has the guts to say boo to a goose. Oh, yes, they'd *like* to be men of action, tough guys. But, I ask you, just look at them! That's why they became detective-writers. Wish fulfilment, the psychoanalysts call it—though I don't give much for that gang, either. But it's quite safe, spilling blood, as long as you only do it on paper."

The man turned his thick lips and small, arrogant eyes towards Nigel. "The trouble with you amateur investigators is that you're so romantic. That's why the police beat you to it every time."

A thick-set, swarthy man opposite him exclaimed: "You're wrong there, Mr. Carruthers. We don't seem to have beaten Mr. Strangeways to it in the past every time."

"So our aggressive friend is *the* David Carruthers. Well, well," whispered Nigel to Dale.

"Yes," said Dale, not modifying his tone at all. "A squalid fellow, isn't he? But he gets the public all right. We have sold our thousands, but David has sold his tens of thousands. Got a yellow streak though, I'll bet, in spite of his bluster. Pity somebody doesn't bump him off at this dinner, just to show him he's not the infallible Pope he sets up to be."

Carruthers shot a vicious glance at Dale. "Why not try it yourself? Get you a bit of notoriety, anyway; might even sell your books. Though," he continued, clapping on the shoulder a nondescript little man who was sitting between him and Dale, "I think little Crippen here would be my first bet. You'd like to have my blood, Crippen, wouldn't you?"

The little man said stiffly: "Don't make yourself ridiculous, Carruthers. You must be drunk already. And I'd thank you to remember that my name is Cripps."

At this point the president interposed with a convulsive change of subject, and the dinner resumed its even tenor. While they were disposing of some very tolerable trout, a waiter informed Dale that he was wanted on the telephone. The young man went out. Nigel was trying at the same time to listen to a highly involved story of the president's and decipher the very curious expression on Cripps' face, when all the lights went out too…

There were a few seconds of astonished silence. Then a torrent of talk broke out—the kind of forced jocularity with which man still comforts himself in the face of sudden darkness. Nigel could hear movement all round him, the pushing back of chairs, quick, muffled treads on the carpet—waiters, no doubt. Someone at the end of the table, rather ridiculously, struck a match; it did nothing but emphasize the pitch blackness.

"Stevens, can't someone light the candles?" exclaimed the president irritably.

"Excuse me, sir," came the voice of the *maître d'hôtel*, "there are no candles. Harry, run along to the fuse-box and find out what's gone wrong."

The door banged behind the waiter. Less than a minute later the lights all blazed on again. Blinking, like swimmers come up from a deep dive, the diners looked at each other. Nigel observed that Carruthers' face was even nearer his food than usual. Curious, to go on eating all the time—But no, his head was right on top of the food—lying in the plate like John the Baptist's. And from between his shoulder-blades there stood out a big white handle; the handle—good God! it couldn't be; this was too macabre altogether—but it *was*—the handle of a fish-slice.

A kind of gobbling noise came out of Justice Pottinger's mouth. All eyes turned to where his shaking hand pointed, grew wide with horror, and then turned ludicrously back to him, as though he was about to direct the jury.

"God bless my soul!" was all the Judge could say.

But someone had sized up the whole situation. The thick-set man who had been sitting opposite Carruthers was already standing with his back to the door. His voice snapped:

"Stay where you are, everyone. I'm afraid there's no doubt about this. I must take charge of this case at once. Mr. Strangeways, will you go and ring up Scotland Yard—police surgeon, finger-print men, photographers—the whole bag of tricks; you know what we want."

Nigel sprang up. His gaze, roving round the room, had registered something different, some detail missing; but his mind couldn't identify it. Well, perhaps it would come to him later. He moved towards the door. And just then the door opened brusquely, pushing the thick-set man away from it. There was a general gasp, as though everyone expected to see something walk in with blood on its hands. It was only young Dale, a little white in the face, but grinning amiably.

"What on earth—?" he began. Then he, too, saw...

An hour later, Nigel and the thick-set man, Superintendent Bateman, were alone in the ante-room. The princes of detective fiction were huddled together in another room, talking in shocked whispers.

"Don't like the real thing, do they, sir?" the Superintendent had commented sardonically; "do 'em good to be up against a flesh-and-blood problem for once. I wish 'em luck with it."

"Well," he was saying now. "Doesn't seem like much of a loss to the world, this Carruthers. None of 'em got a good word for him. Too much food, too much drink, too many women. But that doesn't give us a motive. Now this Cripps. Carruthers said Cripps would like to have his blood. Why was that, d'you suppose?"

"You can search me. Cripps wasn't giving anything away when we interviewed him."

"He had enough opportunity. All he had to do when the lights went out was to step over to the buffet, take up the first knife he laid hands on—probably thought the fish-slice was a carving-knife—stab him, and sit down and twiddle his fingers."

"Yes, he could have wrapped his handkerchief round the handle. That would account for there being no fingerprints. And there's no one to swear he moved from his seat; Dale was out of the room—and it's a bit late now to ask Carruthers, who was on his other side. But, if he *did* do it, everything happened very luckily for him."

"Then there's young Dale himself," said Bateman, biting the side of his thumb. "Talked a lot of hot air about bumping Carruthers off before it happened. Might be a double bluff. You see, Mr. Strangeways, there's no doubt about that waiter's evidence. The main switch was thrown over. Now, what about this? Dale arranges to be called up during dinner; answers call; then goes and turns off the main switch—in gloves, I suppose, because there's only the waiter's fingerprints on it—comes back under cover of darkness, stabs his man, and goes out again."

"Mm," ruminated Nigel, "but the motive? And where are the gloves? And why, if it was premeditated, such an outlandish weapon?"

"If he's hidden the gloves, we'll find 'em soon enough. And—" the Superintendent was interrupted by the tinkle of the telephone at his elbow. A brief dialogue ensued. Then he turned to Nigel.

"Man I sent round to interview Morton—bloke who rang Dale up at dinner. Swears he was talking to Dale for three to five minutes. That seems to let Dale out, unless it was collusion."

That moment a plain-clothes man entered, a grin of ill-concealed triumph on his face. He handed a rolled-up pair of black kid gloves to Bateman. "Tucked away behind the pipes in the lavatories, sir."

Bateman unrolled them. There were stains on the fingers. He glanced inside the wrists, then passed the gloves to Nigel, pointing at some initials stamped there.

"Well, well," said Nigel. "H. D. Let's have him in again. Looks as if that telephone call *was* collusion."

"Yes, we've got him now."

But when the young man entered and saw the gloves lying on the table his reactions were very different from what the Superintendent had expected. An expression of relief, instead of the spasm of guilt, passed over his face.

"Stupid of me," he said, "I lost my head for a few minutes, after—But I'd better start at the beginning. Carruthers was always bragging about his nerve and the tight corners he'd been in and so on. A poisonous specimen. So Morton and I decided to play a practical joke on him. He was to 'phone me up; I was to go out and throw the main switch, then come back and pretend to strangle Carruthers from behind—just give him a thorough shaking-up—and leave a blood-curdling message on his plate to the effect that this was just a warning, and next time the Unknown would do the thing properly. We reckoned he'd be gibbering with fright when I turned up the lights again! Well, everything went all right till I came up behind him; but then—then I happened to touch that knife, and I knew somebody had been there before me, in earnest. Afraid, I lost my nerve then, especially when I found I'd got some of his blood on my gloves. So I hid them, and burnt the spoof message. Damn silly of me. The whole idea was damn silly, I can see that now."

"Why gloves at all?" asked Nigel.

"Well, they say it's your hands and your shirtfront that are likely to show in the dark; so I put on black gloves and pinned my coat over my shirtfront. And, I say," he added in a deprecating way, "I don't want to teach you fellows your business, but if I had really meant to kill him, would I have worn gloves with my initials on them?"

"That is as may be," said Bateman coldly, "but I must warn you that you are in—"

"Just a minute," Nigel interrupted. "Why should Cripps have wanted Carruthers' blood?"

"Oh, you'd better ask Cripps. If he won't tell you, I don't think I ought to—"

"Don't be a fool. You're in a damned tight place, and you can't afford to be chivalrous."

"Very well. Little Cripps may be dim, but he's a good sort. He told me once, in confidence, that Carruthers had pirated an idea of his for a plot and made a bestseller out of it. A rotten thing to do. But—dash it—no one would commit murder just because—"

"You must leave that for us to decide, Mr. Dale," said the Superintendent.

When the young man had gone out, under the close surveillance of a constable, Bateman turned wearily to Nigel.

"Well," he said, "it may be him; and it may be Cripps. But, with all these crime authors about, it might be any of 'em."

Nigel leapt up from his seat. "Yes," he exclaimed, "and that's why we've not thought of anyone else. And—" his eyes lit up—"by Jove! now I've remembered it—the missing detail. Quick! Are all those waiters and chaps still there?"

"Yes; we've kept 'em in the dining-room. But what the—?"

Nigel ran into the dining-room, Bateman at his heels. He looked out of one of the windows, open at the top.

"What's down below there?" he asked the *maître d'hôtel*.

"A yard, sir; the kitchen windows look out on it."

"And now, where was Sir Eldred Travers sitting?"

The man pointed to the place without hesitation, his imperturbable face betraying not the least surprise.

"Right; will you go and ask him to step this way for a minute. Oh, by the way," he added, as the *maître d'hôtel* reached the door, "*where are your gloves?*"

The man's eyes flickered. "My gloves, sir?"

"Yes; before the lights went out you were wearing white gloves; after they went up again, I remembered it just now, you were not wearing them. Are they in the yard by any chance?"

The man shot a desperate glance around him; then the bland composure of his face broke up. He collapsed, sobbing, into a chair.

"My daughter—he ruined her—she killed herself. When the lights went out, it was too much for me—the opportunity. He deserved it. I'm not sorry."

"Yes," said Nigel, ten minutes later, "it was too much for him. He picked up the first weapon to hand. Afterwards, knowing everyone would be searched, he had to throw the gloves out of the window. There would be blood on them. With luck, we mightn't have looked in the yard before he could get out to remove them. And, unless one was looking, one wouldn't see them against the snow. They were white."

"What was that about Sir Eldred Travers?" asked the Superintendent.

"Oh, I wanted to put him off his guard, and to get him away from the window. He might have tried to follow his gloves."

"Well, that fish-slice might have been a slice of bad luck for young Dale if you hadn't been here,' said the Superintendent, venturing on a witticism. "What are you grinning away to yourself about?"

"I was just thinking, this must be the first time a judge has been present at a murder."

The Strange Case of the Megatherium Thefts

S. C. Roberts

Sydney Castle Roberts (1887–1966) was a prominent book-man, educated at Brighton College and Cambridge University prior to becoming Secretary to Cambridge University Press in 1922, shortly after publishing a history of the Press. He served in that capacity for more than a quarter of a century before becoming Master of Pembroke College, Cambridge, and Vice-Chancellor of Cambridge University. He chaired the British Film Institute for several years and was knighted in 1958. His publications include books about Dr. Johnson (on whom he was a renowned expert) and Lord Macaulay, as well as *The Charm of Cambridge* and *Adventures with Authors*.

Roberts was a devotee of Sherlock Holmes, and enjoyed meeting the great man's creator, Arthur Conan Doyle, in 1911. In 1929, Roberts published "A Note on the Watson Problem" in the *Cambridge Review*; before long he had established himself as a leading British exponent of Sherlockian scholarship, becoming a member of the first Sherlock Holmes Society of London. "The Adventure of the Megatherium Thefts" was privately printed in 1945 and subsequently included in *Holmes and Watson: A Miscellany* eight years later, as well as in *The Further Adventures of Sherlock Holmes*, edited by Richard Lancelyn Green, who indicates that the story was inspired by a real-life literary crime—the theft of some books from the Athenaeum.

———

I HAVE ALREADY HAD OCCASION, IN THE COURSE OF these reminiscences of my friend Sherlock Holmes, to refer to his liking for the Diogenes Club, the club which contained the most unsociable men in London and forbade talking save in the Strangers' Room. So far as I am aware, this was the only club to which Holmes was attracted, and it struck me as not a little curious that he should have been called upon to solve the extraordinary mystery of the Megatherium Thefts.

It was a dull afternoon in November and Holmes, turning wearily from the cross-indexing of some old newspaper-cuttings, drew his chair near to mine and took out his watch.

"How slow life has become, my dear Watson," he said, "since the successful conclusion of that little episode in a lonely West Country village. Here we are back amongst London's millions and nobody wants us."

He crossed to the window, opened it a little, and peered through the November gloom into Baker Street.

"No, Watson, I'm wrong. I believe we are to have a visitor."

"Is there someone at the door?"

"Not yet. But a hansom has stopped opposite to it. The passenger has alighted and there is a heated discussion in progress concerning the fare. I cannot hear the argument in detail, but it is a lively one."

A few minutes later the visitor was shown into the sitting-room—a tall, stooping figure with a straggling white beard, shabbily dressed and generally unkempt. He spoke with a slight stutter.

"M-Mr. Sherlock Holmes?" he inquired.

"That is my name," replied Holmes, "and this is my friend, Dr. Watson."

The visitor bowed jerkily and Holmes continued: "And whom have I the honour of addressing?"

"My n-name is Wiskerton—Professor Wiskerton—and I have ventured to call upon you in connection with a most remarkable and puzzling affair."

"We are familiar with puzzles in this room, Professor."

"Ah, but not with any like this one. You see, apart from my p-professorial standing, I am one of the oldest members of—"

"The Megatherium?"

"My dear sir, how did you know?"

"Oh, there was no puzzle about that. I happened to hear some reference in your talk with the cabman to your journey having begun at Waterloo Place. Clearly you had travelled from one of two clubs and somehow I should not associate you with the United Services."

"You're p-perfectly right, of course. The driver of that cab was a rapacious scoundrel. It's s-scandalous that—"

"But you have not come to consult me about an extortionate cab-driver?"

"No, no. Of course not. It's about—"

"The Megatherium?"

"Exactly. You see, I am one of the oldest m-members and have been on the Committee for some years. I need hardly tell you the kind of standing which the Megatherium has in the world of learning, Mr. Holmes."

"Dr. Watson, I have no doubt, regards the institution with veneration. For myself, I prefer the soothing atmosphere of the Diogenes."

"The w-what?"

"The Diogenes Club."

"N-never heard of it."

"Precisely. It is a club of which people are not meant to hear—but I beg your pardon for this digression. You were going to say?"

"I was g-going to say that the most distressing thing has happened. I should explain in the first place that in addition to the n-noble collection of books in the Megatherium library, a collection which is one of our most valuable assets, we have available at any one time a number of books from one of the circulating libraries and—"

"And you are losing them?"

"Well—yes, in fact we are. But how did you know?"

"I didn't know—I merely made a deduction. When a client begins to describe his possessions to me, it is generally because some misfortune has occurred in connection with them."

"But this is m-more than a m-misfortune, Mr. Holmes. It is a disgrace, an outrage, a—"

"But what, in fact, has happened?"

"Ah, I was c-coming to that. But perhaps it would be

simpler if I showed you this document and let it speak for itself. P-personally, I think it was a mistake to circulate it, but the Committee over-ruled me and now the story will be all over London and we shall still be no nearer a solution."

Professor Wiskerton fumbled in his pocket and produced a printed document marked **Private and Confidential** in bold red type.

"What do you m-make of it, Mr. Holmes? Isn't it extraordinary? Here is a club whose members are selected from among the most distinguished representatives of the arts and sciences and this is the way they treat the C-club property."

Holmes paid no attention to the Professor's rambling commentary and continued his reading of the document.

"You have brought me quite an interesting case, Professor," he said, at length.

"But it is more than interesting, Mr. Holmes. It is astonishing. It is inexplicable."

"If it were capable of easy explanation, it would cease to be interesting and, furthermore, you would not have spent the money on a cab-fare to visit me."

"That, I suppose, is true. But what do you advise, Mr. Holmes?"

"You must give me a little time, Professor. Perhaps you will be good enough to answer one or two questions first?"

"Willingly."

"This document states that your Committee is satisfied that no member of the staff is implicated. You are satisfied yourself on that point?"

"I am not s-satisfied about anything, Mr. Holmes. As one

who has s-spent a great part of his life amongst books and libraries, the whole subject of the maltreatment of books is repugnant to me. Books are my lifeblood, Mr. Holmes. But perhaps I have not your s-sympathy?"

"On the contrary, Professor, I have a genuine interest in such matters. For myself, however, I travel in those by-ways of bibliophily which are associated with my own profession."

Holmes moved across to a shelf and took out a volume with which I had long been familiar.

"Here, Professor," he continued, "if I may rid myself of false modesty for the moment, is a little monograph of mine: *Upon the Distinction Between the Ashes of the Various Tobaccos.*"

"Ah, most interesting, Mr. Holmes. Not being a smoker myself, I cannot pretend to appraise your work from the point of view of scholarship, but as a bibliophile and especially as a c-collector of out-of-the-way monographs, may I ask whether the work is still available?"

"That is a spare copy, Professor; you are welcome to it."

The Professor's eyes gleamed with voracious pleasure.

"But, Mr. Holmes, this is m-most generous of you. May I b-beg that you will inscribe it? I derive a special delight from what are called 'association copies.'"

"Certainly," said Holmes, with a smile, as he moved to the writing-table.

"Thank you, thank you," murmured the Professor, "but I fear I have distracted you from the main issue."

"Not at all."

"But what is your p-plan, Mr. Holmes? Perhaps you would like to have a look round the Megatherium? Would you care, for instance, to have luncheon tomorrow—but no, I fear I am engaged at that time. What about a c-cup of tea at four o'clock?"

"With pleasure. I trust I may bring Dr. Watson, whose cooperation in such cases has frequently been of great value?"

"Oh—er—yes, certainly."

But it did not seem to me that there was much cordiality in his assent.

"Very well, then," said Holmes. "The document which you have left with me gives the facts and I will study them with great care."

"Thank you, thank you. Tomorrow, then, at four o'clock," said the Professor, as he shook hands, "and I shall t-treasure this volume, Mr. Holmes."

He slipped the monograph into a pocket and left us.

"Well, Watson," said Holmes, as he filled his pipe, "What do you make of this curious little case?"

"Very little, at present. I haven't had a chance to examine the *data*."

"Quite right, Watson. I will reveal them to you." Holmes took up the sheet which the Professor had left.

"This is a confidential letter circulated to members of the Megatherium and dated November 1889. I'll read you a few extracts:

> "In a recent report the Committee drew attention to the serious loss and inconvenience caused by the removal from the Club of books from the circulating library. The practice has continued... At the end of June, the Club paid for no less than 22 missing volumes. By the end of September 15 more were missing... The

*Committee were disposed to ascribe these malpractices
to some undetected individual member, but they have
regretfully come to the conclusion that more members
than one are involved. They are fully satisfied that no
member of the staff is in any way implicated... If the
offenders can be identified, the Committee will not hesitate to apply the Rule which empowers expulsion."*

"There, Watson, what do you think of that?"

"Most extraordinary, Holmes—at the Megatherium, of all clubs."

"*Corruptio optimi pessima,* my dear Watson."

"D'you think the Committee is right about the servants?"

"I'm not interested in the Committee's opinions, Watson, even though they be the opinions of Bishops and Judges and Fellows of the Royal Society. I am concerned only with the facts."

"But the facts are simple, Holmes. Books are being stolen in considerable quantities from the Club and the thief, or thieves, have not been traced."

"Admirably succinct, my dear Watson. And the motive?"

"The thief's usual motive, I suppose—the lure of illicit gain."

"But what gain, Watson? If you took half a dozen books, with the mark of a circulating library on them, to a second-hand bookseller, how much would you expect to get for them?"

"Very little, certainly, Holmes."

"Yes, and that is why the Committee is probably right in ruling out the servants—not that I believe in ruling out anybody or anything on *a priori* grounds. But the motive of gain won't do. You must try again, Watson."

"Well, of course, people are careless about books, especially when they belong to someone else. Isn't it possible that members take these books away from the Club, intending to return them, and then leave them in the train or mislay them at home?"

"Not bad, my dear Watson, and a perfectly reasonable solution if we were dealing with a loss of three or four volumes. In that event our Professor would probably not have troubled to enlist my humble services. But look at the figures, Watson—twenty-two books missing in June, fifteen more in September. There's something more than casual forgetfulness in that."

"That's true, Holmes, and I suppose we can't discover much before we keep our appointment at the Megatherium tomorrow."

"On the contrary, my dear Watson, I hope to pursue a little independent investigation this evening."

"I should be delighted to accompany you, Holmes."

"I am sure you would, Watson, but if you will forgive me for saying so, the little inquiry I have to make is of a personal nature and I think it might be more fruitful if I were alone."

"Oh, very well," I replied, a little nettled at Holmes's superior manner, "I can employ myself very profitably in reading this new work on surgical technique which has just come to hand."

I saw little of Holmes on the following morning. He made no reference to the Megatherium case at breakfast and disappeared shortly afterwards. At luncheon he was in high spirits. There was a gleam in his eye which showed me that he was happily on the trail.

"Holmes," I said, "you have discovered something."

"My dear Watson," he replied, "your acuteness does you credit. I have discovered that after an active morning I am extremely hungry."

But I was not to be put off.

"Come, Holmes, I am too old a campaigner to be bluffed in that way. How far have you penetrated into the Megatherium mystery?"

"Far enough to make me look forward to our tea-party with a lively interest."

Being familiar with my friend's bantering manner, I recognised that it was no good pressing him with further questions for the moment.

Shortly after four o'clock Holmes and I presented ourselves at the portals of the Megatherium. The head porter received us very courteously and seemed, I thought, almost to recognise Sherlock Holmes. He conducted us to a seat in the entrance hall and, as soon as our host appeared, we made our way up the noble staircase to the long drawing-room on the first floor.

"Now let me order some tea," said the Professor. "Do you like anything to eat with it, Mr. Holmes?"

"Just a biscuit for me, Professor, but my friend Watson has an enormous appetite."

"Really, Holmes—" I began.

"No, no. Just a little pleasantry of mine," said Holmes, quickly. I thought I observed an expression of relief on the Professor's face.

"Well, now, about our p-problem, Mr. Holmes. Is there any further information that I can give you?"

"I should like to have a list of the titles of the books which have most recently disappeared."

"Certainly, Mr. Holmes, I can get that for you at once."

The Professor left us for a few minutes and returned with a paper in his hand. I looked over Holmes's shoulder while he read and recognised several well-known books that had been recently published, such as *Robbery under Arms*, *Troy Town*, *The Economic Interpretation of History*, *The Wrong Box*, and *Three Men in a Boat*.

"Do you make any particular deductions from the titles, Mr. Holmes?" the Professor asked.

"I think not," Holmes replied; "there are, of course, certain very popular works of fiction, some other books of more general interest and a few titles of minor importance. I do not think one could draw any conclusion about the culprit's special sphere of interest."

"You think not? Well, I agree, Mr. Holmes. It is all very b-baffling."

"Ah," said Holmes suddenly, "this title reminds me of something."

"What is that, Mr. Holmes?"

"I see that one of the missing books is *Plain Tales from the Hills*. It happens that I saw an exceptionally interesting copy of that book not long ago. It was an advance copy, specially bound and inscribed for presentation to the author's godson who was sailing for India before the date of publication."

"Really, Mr. Holmes, really? That is of the greatest interest to me."

"Your own collection, Professor, is, I suspect, rich in items of such a kind?"

"Well, well, it is not for me to b-boast, Mr. Holmes, but I certainly have one or two volumes of unique association value on my shelves. I am a poor man and do not aspire to first folios, but the p-pride of my collection is that it could not have been assembled through the ordinary channels of trade… But to return to our problem, is there anything else in the Club which you would like to investigate?"

"I think not," said Holmes, "but I must confess that the description of your collection has whetted my own bibliographical appetite."

The Professor flushed with pride.

"Well, Mr. Holmes, if you and your friend would really care to see my few t-treasures, I should be honoured. My rooms are not f-far from here."

"Then let us go," said Holmes, with decision.

I confess that I was somewhat puzzled by my friend's behaviour. He seemed to have forgotten the misfortunes of the Megatherium and to be taking a wholly disproportionate interest in the eccentricities of the Wiskerton collection.

When we reached the Professor's rooms I had a further surprise. I had expected not luxury, of course, but at least some measure of elegance and comfort. Instead, the chairs and tables, the carpets and curtains, everything, in fact, seemed to be of the cheapest quality; even the bookshelves were of plain deal and roughly put together. The books themselves were another matter. They were classified like no other library I had ever seen. In one section were presentation copies from authors; in another were proof-copies bound in what is known as "binder's cloth;" in another were review copies; in another were pamphlets, monographs, and off-prints of all kinds.

"There you are, Mr. Holmes," said the Professor, with all the pride of ownership. "You may think it is a c-collection of oddities, but for me every one of those volumes has a p-personal and s-separate association—including the item which came into my hands yesterday afternoon."

"Quite so," said Holmes, thoughtfully, "and yet they all have a common characteristic."

"I don't understand you."

"No? But I am waiting to see the remainder of your collection, Professor. When I have seen the whole of your library, I shall perhaps be able to explain myself more clearly."

The Professor flushed with annoyance.

"Really, Mr. Holmes, I had been warned of some of your p-peculiarities of manner; but I am entirely at a loss to know what you are d-driving at."

"In that case, Professor, I will thank you for your hospitality and will beg leave to return to the Megatherium for consultation with the Secretary."

"To tell him that you can't f-find the missing books?"

Sherlock Holmes said nothing for a moment. Then he looked straight into the Professor's face and said, very slowly:

"On the contrary, Professor Wiskerton, I shall tell the Secretary that I can direct him to the precise address at which the books may be found."

There was silence. Then an extraordinary thing happened.

The Professor turned away and literally crumpled into a chair; then he looked up at Holmes with the expression of a terrified child:

"Don't do it, Mr. Holmes. Don't do it, I b-b-beseech you. I'll t-tell you everything."

"Where are the books?" asked Holmes, sternly.

"Come with me and I'll show you."

The Professor shuffled out and led us into a dismal bedroom. With a trembling hand he felt in his pocket for his keys and opened a cupboard alongside the wall. Several rows of books were revealed and I quickly recognised one or two titles that I had seen on the Megatherium list.

"Oh, what m-must you think of me, Mr. Holmes?" the Professor began, whimpering.

"My opinion is irrelevant," said Sherlock Holmes, sharply. "Have you any packing-cases?"

"No, but I d-daresay my landlord might be able to find some."

"Send for him."

In a few minutes the landlord appeared. Yes, he thought he could find a sufficient number of cases to take the books in the cupboard.

"Professor Wiskerton," said Holmes "is anxious to have all these books packed at once and sent to the Megatherium, Pall Mall. The matter is urgent."

"Very good, sir. Any letter or message to go with them?"

"No," said Holmes, curtly, "but yes—stop a minute."

He took a pencil and a visiting-card from his pocket and wrote "With the compliments of" above the name.

"See that this card is firmly attached to the first of the packing-cases. Is that clear?"

"Quite correct, sir, if that's what the Professor wants."

"That is what the Professor most particularly wants. Is it not, Professor?" said Holmes, with great emphasis.

"Yes, yes, I suppose so. But c-come back with me into the other room and l-let me explain."

We returned to the sitting-room and the Professor began:

"Doubtless I seem to you either ridiculous or despicable or both. I have had two p-passions in my life—a passion for s-saving money and a passion for acquiring b-books. As a result of an unfortunate dispute with the Dean of my faculty at the University, I retired at a c-comparatively early age and on a very small p-pension. I was determined to amass a collection of books; I was equally determined not to s-spend my precious savings on them. The idea came to me that my library should be unique, in that all the books in it should be acquired by some means other than p-purchase. I had friends amongst authors, printers, and publishers, and I did pretty well, but there were many recently published books that I wanted and saw no m-means of getting until—well, until I absent-mindedly brought home one of the circulating library books from the Megatherium. I meant to return it, of course. But I didn't. Instead, I b-brought home another one…"

"*Facilis descensus…*" murmured Holmes.

"Exactly, Mr. Holmes, exactly. Then, when the Committee began to notice that books were disappearing, I was in a quandary. But I remembered hearing someone say in another connection that the b-best defence was attack and I thought that if I were the first to go to you, I should be the last to be s-suspected."

"I see," said Holmes. "Thank you, Professor Wiskerton."

"And now what are you going to do?"

"First," replied Holmes, "I am going to make certain that your landlord has those cases ready for despatch. After that, Dr. Watson and I have an engagement at St. James's Hall."

"A trivial little case, Watson, but not wholly without

interest," said Holmes, when we returned from the concert hall to Baker Street.

"A most contemptible case, in my opinion. Did you guess from the first that Wiskerton himself was the thief?"

"Not quite, Watson. I never guess. I endeavour to observe. And the first thing I observed about Professor Wiskerton was that he was a miser—the altercation with the cabman, the shabby clothes, the unwillingness to invite us to lunch. That he was an enthusiastic bibliophile was, of course, obvious. At first I was not quite certain how to fit these two characteristics properly together, but after yesterday's interview I remembered that the head porter of the Megatherium had been a useful ally of mine in his earlier days as a Commissionaire and I thought a private talk with him might be useful. His brief characterization put me on the right track at once—"Always here reading," he said, "but never takes a square meal in the Club." After that, and after a little hasty research this morning into the Professor's academic career, I had little doubt."

"But don't you still think it extraordinary, in spite of what he said, that he should have taken the risk of coming to consult you?"

"Of course it's extraordinary, Watson. Wiskerton's an extraordinary man. If, as I hope, he has the decency to resign from the Megatherium, I shall suggest to Mycroft that he puts him up for the Diogenes."

Malice Domestic

Philip MacDonald

Philip MacDonald (1900–1980) was a leading exponent of British Golden Age detective fiction who immigrated to California and became a highly accomplished screenwriter, with the Hitchcock classic *Rebecca* among his credits. He introduced his Great Detective Colonel Anthony Gethryn in *The Rasp* in 1924. Gethryn became a popular character who appeared in an enjoyable series of novels culminating in *The Nursemaid Who Disappeared* aka *Warrant for X* (1938); after a long break, he returned for a final hurrah in *The List of Adrian Messenger* (1958), one of several MacDonald novels to be filmed. His non-series mysteries include *The Rynox Mystery* (1930) and *Murder Gone Mad* (1931), while his pseudonymous work includes *Forbidden Planet* (1956) as W. J. Stuart, a novelisation of a famous science fiction film.

Most of MacDonald's postwar crime fiction was in the short form, and three collections of his mysteries were published. "Malice Domestic" concerns a writer "of some merit, mediocre sales, and—at least among the wordier critics—considerable reputation." The story first appeared in *Ellery Queen's Mystery Magazine* in October 1946, and was included in *Something to Hide* aka *Fingers of Fear* (1952). In 1957, a TV adaptation of the story was screened as part of the second series of *Alfred Hitchcock Presents*.

——

CARL BORDEN CAME OUT OF SEAMAN'S BOOKSTORE INTO the sundrenched, twisting little main street of El Morro Beach. He looked around to see if his wife were in view, and then, as she wasn't, walked to the bar entrance of Eagles' and went in. He was a big, loosely built, rambling sort of a man, with untidy blond hair and a small, somehow featureless face which was redeemed from indistinction by his eyes, which were unexpectedly large, vividly blue, and always remarkably alive. He was a writer of some merit, mediocre sales and—at least among the wordier critics—considerable reputation.

He sat on the first stool at the bar and nodded to the real estate man, Dockweiler, who had once been a Hollywood actor; to Dariev, the Russian who did the murals; then— vaguely—to some people in booths. He didn't smile at all, not even at the barman when he ordered his beer—and Dockweiler said to old Parry beside him, "Catch that Borden, will you! Wonder whatsa matter..."

The barman, who was always called Hiho for some reason everyone had forgotten, brought Carl's drink and set it down before him and glanced at him and said, "Well, Mr. Borden—and how've you been keeping?"

Carl said, "Thanks, Hiho—oh, all right, I guess…" He took a long swallow from the cold glass.

Hiho said, "And how's Mrs. Borden? Okay?"

"Fine!" Carl said. And then again, "Fine!" He put a dollar bill on the bar and Hiho picked it up and went to the cash register.

Carl put his elbows on the bar and dropped his face into his hands; then sat quickly upright as Hiho returned with his change. He pocketed it and swallowed the rest of his beer and stood up. He nodded to Hiho without speaking and walked out into the street again.

His wife was standing by the car with her arms full of packages. He said, "Hey, Annette—hold it!" and quickened his pace to a lumbering trot.

She smiled at him. A brief, wide smile which was just a little on the toothy side. She looked slim and straight and cool and *soignée*, as she always did. She was a blonde Norman woman of thirty-odd, and she had been married to Carl for nine years. They were regarded, by everyone who did not know them well, as an "ideal couple." But their few intimates, of late, had been vaguely unsure of this.

Carl opened the door of the car and took the parcels from Annette's arms, and stowed them away in the back. She said, "Thank you, Carlo," and got into the seat beside him as he settled himself at the wheel. She said, "Please—go around by Beaton's. I have a *big* package there."

He drove down to Las Ondas Road and parked, on the wrong side of the street, outside a white-fenced little building over which a sign announced, "Beaton and Son—Nurseries."

He went into the shop, and the girl gave him a giant paper sack, stuffed overfull with a gallimaufry of purchases. He picked it up—and the bottom tore open and a shower of the miscellany sprayed to the floor.

Carl swore beneath his breath, and the girl said, "Oh, drat!" And whipped around to help him. He put the things he had saved on the counter, then, stooping, retrieved a thick pamphlet called *The Rose-Grower's Handbook* and a carton labelled "Killweed" in white lettering above a red skull-and-crossbones design.

The girl had everything else. Apologizing profusely, she put the whole order into two fresh sacks. Carl put one under each arm and went out into the sunny street again, and saw Doctor Wingate walking along it, approaching the car. Carl called out, "Hi, Tom!" And smiled his first smile of the morning as the other turned and saw him.

"Hi, yourself!" Wingate said. He was a man in the middle forties, a little dandiacal as to dress, and he wore— unusual in a medico—a small, neatly trimmed imperial which some people thought distinguished, others merely caprine. He turned to the car and raised his hat to Annette, wishing her good morning a trifle formally. He opened the rear door for Carl and helped him put the two packages in with the others. He looked at Carl, and for a moment his gaze became sharply professional. He said, "How's the book going?" And Carl hesitated before he answered, "Fine! Tough sledding, of course—but it'll be all right, I think."

"Well," said Wingate, "don't go cold on it. It's too good." Carl shrugged. Annette said, impatiently, "We must get back, Carlo," and he got into the car and started the engine and waved to his friend.

He drove back through the town and then branched inland up into the hills and came in five minutes to the narrow, precipitous road which led up to his house, standing alone on its little bluff. It was a sprawling, grey-shingled building, with tall trees behind it and, in front, a lawn which surrounded a rose bed. Beside the lawn a gravel driveway, with traces of devil grass and other weeds showing through its surface, ran down to the garage.

As he stopped the car, an enormous dog appeared around the corner of the house and bounded toward them. Annette got out first, and looked at the animal and said, "Hallo," and put out her hand as if to fondle it.

The dog backed away. It stood with its head up and stared at her. It was a giant schnauser, as big as a Great Dane, and it was called G.B. because something about its bearded face and sardonic eye had always made Carl think of Shaw.

Annette looked at it; then, with a quick little movement of her head, at her husband. She said sharply, "The dog! Why does he look at me like that?"

Carl was getting out of the car. "Like what?" he said—and then it was upon him, its tail stump wagging madly, its vast mouth open in a wet, white-and-scarlet smile.

"Hi there, G.B.!" Carl said—and the creature rose up on its hind legs and put its forepaws on his shoulders and tried to lick his face. Its head was almost on a level with Carl's.

Annette said, "It is—peculiar. He does not like me lately." She was frowning.

Carl said, "Oh, that's your imagination," and the dog dropped upon all fours again and stood away while the packages were taken out of the car.

Carl carried most of them, Annette the rest. They stood in the kitchen, and Annette began to put her purchases away. Carl stood and watched her. His blue eyes were dark and troubled, and he looked like a Brobdingnagian and bewildered little boy who has found himself in trouble for some reason he cannot understand.

Annette wanted to get to the icebox, and he was in her way. She pushed at his arm, and said sharply, "Move! You are too big for this kitchen!"

But he put his long arms around her and pulled her close to him. He said, "Annette! What's the matter, darling? What is it? What have I done?"

She strained back against his arms—but he tightened their pressure and drew her closer still and buried his face in the cool firm flesh of her throat.

"Carl!" she said. She sounded amazed.

He went on talking, against her neck. His voice sounded almost as if there were tears in it. He said, "Don't tell me there isn't something wrong! Just tell me what it *is*? Tell me what I've *done*! It's been going on for weeks now—maybe months. Ever since you came back from that trip. You've been—different…"

His wife stood motionless. She said, slowly, "But, Carlo—that is what I have been feeling about you."

He raised his head and looked at her. He said, "It's almost

as if you were—suspicious of me. And I don't know what it's about!"

She frowned. "I—" she said. "I—" and then stopped for a long moment.

She said, "Do you know what I think? I think we are two very stupid people." The lines were leaving her face, the colour coming back to it.

"Two stupid people!" she said again. "People who are not so young as they were. People who do not see enough other people—and begin to imagine things…"

She broke off as there drifted through the open window the sound of a car, old and labouring, coming up the hill. She said, "Ah!" and put her hands on Carl's shoulders and kissed him at the corner of his mouth. She said, "The mail—I will get it," and went quickly out of the side door.

He made no attempt to follow her, no suggestion that he should do the errand. Annette had always been very jealous about her letters, and seemed to be growing even more so.

He stood where he was, his big shoulders sagging, the smile with which he had met her smile slowly fading from his face. He shook his head. He drew in a deep breath. He shambled away, through the big living room and through that again into his study. He sat down in front of his typewriter and stared at it for a long time.

He began to work—at first slowly, but finally with a true and page-devouring frenzy…

It was dusk, and he had already switched on his desk light, when there came a gentle sound behind him. He dragged himself back to the world which he did not control and turned in his chair and saw his wife just inside the door. She was very slim, almost boyish, in her gardening overalls. She said, "I do not want to interrupt, Carlo—just to know about dinner." Her face was in shadow, and she might have been smiling.

He stood up and threw his arms wide and stretched. "Any time you like," he said, and then, as she moved to leave the room, "Wait a minute!"

He crossed to her and took her by the shoulders and looked down at her. For a moment she was rigid; then suddenly she put her arms around his neck and moulded her slim strong softness against him and tilted her face up to his.

It was a long and passionate kiss—and it was only broken by the sound of a jarring, persistent thudding at the French windows.

Annette pulled abruptly away from her husband's clasp. She muttered something which sounded like, "*Sacré chien!...*" and went quickly out through the door behind her.

Except for the pool of light upon the desk, the room was very dark now, and after a moment Carl reached out and snapped on the switch of the overhead light. Slowly, he walked over to the windows and opened them and let in the big dog.

It stood close to him, its head more than level with his waist, and he stroked it and pulled gently at its ears. He shut the windows then, and went out of the study and upstairs to his own room, the animal padding heavily beside him. He took a shower and changed his clothes, and when he had finished, could still hear his wife in her own room. He said, "Come on, G.B." and went downstairs again and out of the house.

He put the car away and shut the garage—and was still outside when Annette called him in to dinner.

This was, like all Annette's dinners, a complete and

rounded work of art—and it was made all the more pleasant because, during it, she seemed almost her old self. She
was bright, talkative, smiling—and although the dog lay
directly in the way of her path to the kitchen and would not
move for her, she made no complaint but walked around
him.

As usual, they had coffee in the living room. After his second cup, Carl got up, and stretched. He snapped his fingers at
G.B., who went and stood expectantly by the door. Carl stood
over his wife, smiling down at her. He started to speak—but
she was first, looking up at him in sudden concern.

She said, "Carlo—you do not look well!... You work, I
think, too hard!... You should not go out, perhaps."

But Carl pooh-poohed her. "Feel fine!" he said and bent
over and kissed her on the forehead and crossed to the door
and was gone.

Whistling, and with G.B. bounding ahead of him, he
walked down the steep slant of their own road and on to the
gentler slopes of Paseo Street.

He had gone less than quarter of a mile when his long,
measured stride faltered. He took a few uneven steps, then
stopped altogether. He swayed. He put a hand up to his forehead and found it covered with clammy sweat. He wobbled
to the edge of the road and sat down upon a grass bank.
He dropped his face into both his hands. A vast, black bulk
appeared out of the darkness and thrust a damp nose at him.
He mumbled something and took his hands away from his
face and clapped them to his stomach and bent his head lower,
down between his knees, and began to vomit...

Old Parry was sitting in his living room, a book on his knee, a glass on the table beside him. He heard a scratching at the porch door; then a series of short, deep, demanding barks. He stood up creakily and went to the door and pulled it open. He bowed and said, "I am honoured, Mr. Shaw!"—and then had his high-pitched giggle cut off short as the enormous dog seized the edge of his jacket between its teeth and began to tug at it with gentle but imperious sharpness.

"Something the matter, boy?" said Parry—and went the way he was being told and in a moment found the sick man by the roadside.

Carl had stopped vomiting now, and was sitting straighter. But he was badly shaken and weak as a kitten. In answer to Parry's shocked inquiries he mumbled, "...all right now... sorry...just my stomach upset..." He tried to laugh—a ghastly little sound. "I'm not drunk," he said. "Be all right in a minute—don't bother yourself..."

But Parry did bother himself: he had seen Carl's face— pinched and drawn and of a strange, greenish pallor, shining with an oily film. Somehow, he got the big man to his feet; somehow, under the watchful yellow eye of the schnauser, managed to pilot him into the house and settle him, half seated, half sprawling upon a sofa.

"Thanks," Carl muttered. "Thanks...that's fine..." He sank back on the cushions and closed his eyes.

"Just a minute now—" said old Parry—and went out into his little hallway and busied himself at the telephone to such effect that in less than fifteen minutes, a car pulled up outside and Doctor Thomas Wingate, bag in hand, walked in upon them.

Carl protested. He was much better already, and his face

was pale with a more normal pallor. He was embarrassed and shy. He was grateful to old Parry, and yet plainly annoyed by all this fuss. He sat up very straight, G.B. at his feet, and said firmly, "Look, I'm all right now! Just a touch of ptomaine or something." He looked from his host to the doctor. "Awfully good of you to take so much trouble, Parry. And thanks for turning out, Tom. But—"

"But nothing!" Wingate said. And sat down beside him and took hold of his wrist and felt the pulse. "What you been eating?"

Carl managed a grin. "Better dinner than you'll ever get," he said—and then: "Oh—I had lunch out, maybe *that* was it. Annette and I went to The Hickory Nut, and I had fried shrimps—a double order! Tom, I bet that's what it was!"

Wingate let go of his wrist. "Could be," he said. He looked at Carl's face again and stood up. "That's a trick tummy of yours anyway." He turned to Parry. "I'll just run him home," he said.

Carl got up too. He thanked Parry all over again, and followed Wingate to his car. They put G.B. in the back and he sat immediately behind Carl, breathing protectively down his neck.

Wingate slowed down almost to a crawl as they reached Carl's driveway. He said, with the abruptness of discomfort, "Look now, I know you pretty well, both as a patient and a fellow human being: this—call it 'attack'—may not have been caused by bad food at all. Or bad food may have been only a contributing factor. In other words, my friend, what everyone insists on calling 'nerves' may be at the bottom of it." They were in the driveway now, and he stopped the car.

But he made no move to get out. He looked at Carl's face in the dimness and said, "Speaking purely as a doctor, Carl, have you been—worried at all lately?" He paused, but Carl said nothing. "You haven't seemed like yourself the past few weeks…"

Carl opened the door on his side. "I don't know what the hell you're talking about," he said curtly.

As he stepped out of the car the front door of the house opened and Annette came out on to the porch. She peered through the darkness at the car. She called, "Who is there? Who is it?" Her voice was high-pitched, sharp.

"Only me, dear," Carl said. "Tom Wingate drove me home." He opened the rear door and G.B. jumped out, then followed his master and Wingate up the steps to the house.

Annette stood just inside the door as they entered. Her face was in shadow, but she seemed pale. She acknowledged Wingate's formal greeting with a stiff little bow, and Carl looked harassed and uncomfortable. He tried to stop Wingate from saying what had happened, but to no purpose. Annette was told the whole story, firmly, politely, and incisively—and Annette was given instructions.

She was most distressed. She said that Carl had not looked well after dinner, and she had not wanted him to go out. She was extremely polite to Doctor Wingate, and repeated his instructions carefully and asked for reassurance that the attack had been nothing serious. But all the time she was rigid and unbending, with frost in her manner. Only when Wingate had gone—and that was very soon—did she thaw. It was a most complete thaw, however. She rushed at Carl and fussed over him and got him upstairs and nursed him and mothered him. And when he was comfortably in bed, she kissed him with all the old tenderness.

"Carlo, *mon pauvre!*" she said softly, and then, "I am sorry I was not nice to your doctor, *chèri*. But—but—*eh bien*, you know that I do not like him."

He patted her shoulder, and she kissed him again—and he was very soon asleep…

It was ten days after this that he had the pains again. They struck late at night. He was in his study, working. It was after one, and Annette had been in bed since before midnight.

They were much worse this time. They were agonising. They started with painful cramps in his thighs—and when he stood up to ease this, there was a terrible burning in the pit of his stomach. And then a faintness came over him and he dropped back into his chair. He doubled up, his hands clutching desperately at his belly. Great beads of cold sweat burst out all over his head and neck. He began to retch. Desperately, he swung his chair around until his hanging head was over the big metal wastebasket. He vomited hideously, and for what seemed an eternity…

At last, momentarily, the convulsions ceased. He tried to raise his head—and everything in the room swam before his eyes. Outside, G.B. scratched on the French windows, and a troubled whining came from his throat. Carl pulled a weak hand across his mouth, and his fingers came away streaked with blood. He rested his forehead upon the table top and, with tremendous effort, reached out for the telephone and managed to pull it toward him…

In exactly ten minutes, a car came to a squealing halt in

the driveway—and Wingate jumped out of it and raced up the steps. The front door was unlocked, and he was halfway across the living room when Annette appeared at the top of the stairs. She was in a nightgown and was fumbling to get her arms into a robe. She said, wildly, "What is it? What is the matter?"

Wingate snapped, "Where's Carl?"—and then heard a sound from the study and crossed to it in three strides and burst in.

Carl was on his hands and knees, near the door of the toilet. He raised a ghastly face to Wingate and tried to speak. The room was a shambles—and beside his master, near the leaf of the French window he had broken open, stood G.B.

Carl tried to stand and could not. "Steady now!" Wingate said. "Take it easy…" He crossed quickly to the sick man and half-dragged, half-lifted him to a couch and began to work over him. G.B. stopped whining and lay down. Annette came into the room and stood at Wingate's shoulder. Her hair was in tight braids and her pallid face shone beneath a layer of cream. Her eyes were wide, their pupils dilated. A curious sound—perhaps a scream strangled at birth—had come from her as she entered, but now she seemed in control of herself, though her hands were shaking. She started to speak but Wingate cut her short, almost savagely.

"Hot water," he snapped. "Towels. Glass."

She ran out of the room—and was quickly back with the things he wanted; then stayed with him, an efficient and self-effacing helper, while for an hour and more he laboured.

By three o'clock, though weak and languid and gaunt in

the face, Carl was himself again and comfortable in his own bed. He smiled at Wingate, who closed his bag with a snap.

"Thanks, Tom…" he said—and then, "Sorry to be such a nuisance."

"You're okay." Wingate smiled back at him with tired eyes—and turned to Annette.

"You go to bed, Mrs. Borden," he said. "He'll sleep—he's exhausted." He turned toward the door, stopped with his fingers on the handle. "I'll call by at eight thirty. If he wants anything—don't give it to him."

Annette moved toward him but he checked her. "Don't bother—I'll let myself out," he said—and was gone.

Very slowly, Annette moved back to the bed and stood beside it, looking down at her husband. The mask of cold cream over her face had broken into glistening patches which alternated with islands of dryness which showed the skin tight and drawn, its colour a leaden grey.

Carl reached out and took her hand. He said, "Did I scare you, darling?… I'm awfully sorry!"

Stiffly, she bent over him. She kissed him. "Go to sleep," she said. "You will be all well in the morning…"

And indeed he was, save for a great lassitude and a painful tenderness all around his stomach. He barely waked when Wingate came at eight thirty, and was asleep again the instant he left five minutes later.

At twelve—like a child about to surprise a household—he got up and washed himself and dressed. He was a little tired when he finished—but less so than he had expected. He opened his door quietly, and quietly went downstairs. As he reached the study door, Annette came out of it. She was in her usual houseworking clothes, and carried a dustpan and broom. Under the gay bandanna which was tied around her head, her face seemed oddly thin and angular.

She gave a little exclamation at the sight of him. "Carlo!" she said. "You should not be up! You should have called me!"

He laughed at her tenderly. He pinched her cheek and then kissed it. "I'm fine," he said. "Sort of sore around the mid-section—but that's nothing." He slid his arm around her waist and they went into the study together. She fussed over him, and was settling him in the big chair beside the desk when the telephone rang.

Carl reached out and picked it up and spoke into it. He said, "Hallo?... Oh, hallo, Tom..."

"So you're up, huh?" said Wingate's voice over the wire. "How d'you feel?"

"Fine," said Carl. "Hungry, though..."

"Eaten yet?" The voice on the telephone was suddenly sharp.

"No. But I—"

"Good. Don't. Not until you've seen me. I want to examine you—run a test or two—while that stomach's empty. Can you get down here to the office? That'd be better. Or do you want me to come up?" Wingate's voice wasn't sharp any more: it seemed even more casual than it normally was.

Carl said, "Sure I can come down. When?"

"Right away," said the telephone. "I'll fit you in. G'bye."

Carl hung up. He looked at his wife and smiled ruefully. "Can't eat yet," he said. "Tom Wingate wants to examine me first." He put his hands on the arms of the chair and levered himself to his feet.

Annette stood stock still. "I am coming too," she announced. "I will drive you."

"Oh, phooey!" Carl said. "You know you hate breaking off half-way through the chores." He patted her on the shoulder. "And I'm perfectly all right, darling. Really! Don't you think I've caused enough trouble already?"

"Oh, Carlo—you are foolish!" Her face was very white—and something about the way her mouth moved made it seem as if she were about to cry.

Carl put an arm around her shoulders. "You must be played out, sweet," he said.

"I am very well," she snapped. "I am not tired at all." And then, with effort, she managed to smile. "But perhaps I am," she said. "Do not mind because I am cross. Go and see your Doctor Wingate…"

She hooked her arm in his and walked through the living room with him, and at the front door she kissed him.

"Take care of yourself, Carlo," she said. "And come back quickly." She shut the door behind him.

As he entered the garage, G.B. came racing up—and, the moment Carl opened the car door, leaped neatly in to sit enormous in the seat beside the driver's. His tongue was hanging out and he was smiling all around it.

Carl laughed at him; then winced, as the laughter hurt his sore stomach muscles. He said, "All right, you bum," and got in behind the wheel and started the car and backed out.

He drove slowly, but in a very few minutes was parking outside Wingate's office. He left G.B. in charge of the car and walked around to the back door—entrance for the favoured few.

Wingate was standing by his desk. The light was behind him and Carl couldn't see his face very well, but he seemed older than usual and tired. Even the little beard looked greyer. He waved Carl to a chair and then came and stood over him, feeling his pulse and making him thrust out his tongue to be looked at.

Carl grinned at him. "Goddam professional this morning," he said.

But Wingate didn't answer the smile, or the gibe. He sat down in his swivel chair and stared at Carl and said, "You were pretty sick last night, my friend," and then, after Carl had thrown in a "You're telling me!," added sharply, "you're lucky not to be dead."

Carl's grin faded slowly—and he gave a startled "Huh?"

"You heard what I said." Wingate had taken a pencil from the desk and was rolling it around in his fingers. He was looking at the pencil and not at Carl.

He said, "By the way, there's some property of yours there," and pointed with the pencil to a bulky, cylindrical package, roughly wrapped in brown paper, which stood upon a side table. "Want to take it with you?"

Carl looked bewildered. "What?…" He stared uncomprehendingly. "What are you talking about?"

"That's your wastebasket." Wingate still kept his eyes on the twirling pencil. "From your study. I took it with me last night…"

"Why?… Oh—you mean to get it cleaned…" Carl was floundering. He burst out, "What the hell *is* all this? What're you driving at, Tom?"

Wingate looked at him, and drew in a deep breath. He

said, in a monotone, "You'll find out very soon. Where did you eat yesterday?"

"At home, of course. What's—"

"Be quiet a minute. So you ate at home. What was the last thing you had? Probably around midnight."

"Nothing... Wait a second, though—I'd forgotten. I had a bowl of soup—Annette's onion soup. She brought it to me before she went to bed. But that couldn't—"

"Wait! So you had this soup, at about twelve. And around an hour later, you have cramps in the legs and stomach, faintness, nausea, acute pain in the intestines. And you vomit, copiously. A lot of it, but by no means all, was in that metal wastebasket. And the contents of the basket, analysed, show you must have swallowed at least a grain and a half of arsenic..."

He let his voice fade into silence, then stood up to face Carl, who had jumped to his feet. He put his hand on Carl's arm and pushed him back into his chair. He unconsciously repeated the very words he had used the night before. "Steady now!" he said. "Take it easy!"

Carl sat down. His pallor had increased. He pulled a shaking hand across his forehead and then tried to smile.

"Narrow squeak," he said—and after that, "Grain and a half, huh? That's quite a dose, isn't it?"

"Could be fatal," Wingate said. "And you had more, maybe."

Carl said, "How in hell d'you suppose I picked it up?" He wasn't looking at Wingate, but past him. "Vegetables or something? They spray 'em, don't they?"

"Not in that strength." Wingate went back to his own chair

and sat in it. "And you had that other attack ten days ago. Same thing—but not so much." His voice was absolutely flat. "And you ate at home, both times."

Carl shot out of his chair again. His face was distorted, his blue eyes blazing.

"For God's sake!" he shouted. "Have you gone out of your mind! What are you hinting at?"

"I'm not hinting anything." Wingate's voice was still toneless. "I'm stating something. You have twice been poisoned with arsenic during the last ten days. The second time provably."

Carl flung his big body back into the chair again. He started to speak, but all that came from him was a muffled groan.

Wingate said, "You don't imagine I like doing this, do you? But you have to face it, man! Someone is feeding you arsenic. The odds against accident are two million to one."

Carl's hands gripped the arms of his chair until his knuckles shone white. He said, hoarsely, "If I didn't know you so well, I'd break your neck!" His voice began to rise. "Can't you see the whole thing must have been some weird terrible accident! Don't you *know* that what's in your mind is completely, utterly impossible!" He stopped abruptly. He was panting, as if he had been running.

Wingate sat motionless. His face was shaded by the hands which propped it. He spoke as if Carl had been silent.

"Arsenic's easy to get," he said. "Especially for gardeners— ant paste, Paris green, rose spray, weed killer—"

"God blast you!" Carl crashed his fist down upon the chair-arm. "There *is* weed killer in the house—but *I* told her to get it!"

He got to his feet and towered over Wingate. He said, "I'm going. And I'm not coming back. I don't think you're lying about the arsenic, but I know you're making a monstrous, evil mistake about how I got it—a mistake which oughtn't to be possible to a man of your intelligence!"

He started for the door, turned back. "And another thing," he said. "I can't stop you from thinking your foul thoughts—" his voice was shaking with suppressed passion—"but I *can* stop you from voicing them—and I will! If you so much as breathe a word of this to anyone—I'll half kill you, and then I'll ruin you! And don't forget that—because I mean it!"

He stood over the other man for a long moment—but Wingate did not move, did not so much as look at him—and at last Carl went back to the door and opened it and passed out of the room. He got out into the air again and made his way to the car. He was very white. He opened the car and slumped into the driving-seat. He put his arms down on the wheel and rested his head upon them. He was breathing in long shuddering gasps. G.B. made a little whimpering sound and licked at his master's ear—and two women passing by looked at the tableau with curiosity.

Perhaps Carl felt their gaze, for he raised his head and saw them. He straightened in his seat, and pushed the dog's great head aside with a gentle hand.

He drove home very slowly. Annette heard the car and opened the front door as he climbed up the steps. She said at once, "What did he say, Carlo? Did he know what is the matter with you?" Her haggard, worn look seemed to have intensified.

Carl looked at her—and then he shook his head. He stepped through the door and sank into the nearest chair. He said, slowly, "No... No, he didn't. I don't think he knows much about it..."

He said, "God, I'm tired!... Come and give me a kiss, darling."

She came and sat upon the arm of his chair and kissed him. She pulled his head against her breast and stroked his hair. He could not see her face as she spoke.

"But, *chéri*," she said, "he must know *something*."

Carl sighed. "Oh, he used a lot of medical jargon—all beginning with *gastro*... But I don't think he really knows any more than I do—which is that I happen to have a nervous stomach." He leaned back in his chair and looked up at her. "I tell you—maybe you're right about Tom Wingate. I don't mean as a man—but as a doctor. I think another time—well, I might go to that new man..."

Annette jumped up. "That is quite enough talk about doctors," she said. "And I, I am very bad! Here is my poor man here, white and weak because he has no food! Wait one little moment, Carlo..."

She hurried off to the kitchen. She seemed to have shed her fatigue, her tenseness.

Carl sat where he was. He stared straight ahead with eyes which did not look as if they saw what was in front of them.

In a very little while, Annette came back. She was carrying a small tray upon which were a spoon, a napkin, and a bowl which steamed, gently and fragrantly.

She said, "*Voilà!*—" and set the tray on his knees and put the spoon in his hand and stood back to watch him.

He looked at her for a long unwavering moment—and when she said, "Hurry now and drink your soup!" he did not seem to hear.

He said, very suddenly, "Annette: do you love me?"—and kept on looking at her.

She stared. She said, after an instant, "But yes—but of *course*, Carlo!"

And then she laughed and said, "Do not be a baby! Take your soup—it is not very hot."

He looked at the spoon in his hand and seemed surprised to find it there. He set it down upon the tray and picked up the bowl and looked at his wife over the edge of it.

"*Santé!*" he said—and put the china to his lip and began to drink in great gulps…

He did not have the pains that night.

A week went by and he did not have them—a week in which he had not spoken to, nor seen, nor heard any word of Doctor Thomas Wingate.

It was past eleven at night, and he was walking with G.B. up the last slope of Paseo Street. Behind him, old Parry called a last good night, and he half turned and waved a valedictory hand. He had been returning from a longer walk than usual and had met Parry at the mailbox; a meeting which had somehow led to drinks in Parry's house and a long talk upon Parry's favourite topic, which was that of the world's declining sanity.

He reached his own steep little road and shortened his stride for the climb and whistled for G.B., who came at once and padded beside him.

He was humming as he strode down the drive and up the

steps. He opened the front door and let the dog ahead of him and then went in himself.

He said, "*Oh, my God!*"

He stood motionless for an instant which might have been a century.

Annette was lying on the floor, twisted into a strange and ugly shape—and all around her prostrate and distorted body, the room was dreadfully befouled.

G.B. stared, then pushed through the half-open door to the kitchen. There was a thump as he lay down.

Carl dropped to his knees beside the prostrate woman. He raised her head and it lolled against his arm. Her eyes were closed and her stained and swollen mouth hung open. She was breathing, but lightly, weakly—and when he felt for her heart, its beat was barely perceptible...

Somehow, he was in the study, at the telephone... As if automatically, his shaking fingers dialled a number...

He was speaking to Wingate. "Tom!" he said, on a harsh high note. "Tom! This is Carl. Come at once! *Hurry!*"

His hand put back the phone. His feet took him out into the living room again. His knees bent themselves once more and once more he held his wife in his arms...

He was still holding her when Wingate came.

Wingate examined her and shook his head. He made Carl get up—and took him into the study. He said, "You've got to face it, Carl... She's dead."

Carl was shaking all over—his hands, his body, his head, all of him.

Wingate said, "Sit there—and don't move!" and went out into the living room again.

He looked at the dead woman; at the foulness around her; at everything in the room. He was staring at the two coffee cups which stood on the top of the piano when G.B. came in from the kitchen, paced over to the study and disappeared.

Wingate picked up the cups, one after the other. They were small cups, and each held the heavy, pasty remains of Turkish coffee. He dipped a dampened finger tip into each cup in turn, each time touching the finger to his tongue. The second test gave him the reaction he wanted—and, his face clearing, he strode back to the study.

Carl had not moved, but his trembling had increased. The dog sat beside him, looking into his face.

Wingate put a hand on the shaking shoulder. Carl tried to speak—but his teeth started to chatter and no words came out of him.

Wingate said: "You know, don't you? She tried again… You wouldn't let *me* look after you—but the Fates did!"

Carl mumbled, "I—I—I d-don't understand…"

Wingate said, "She was overconfident. And something went wrong—some little thing to distract her attention." He lifted his shoulders. "And—well, she took the wrong cup."

Carl said, "*God!…*" He covered his face with his hands, the fingers digging into his temples. He said: "Tom—I almost wish it *had* been me!"

"Come on, now!" Wingate took him by the arm. "Stop thinking—just do what I tell you!"

He hauled Carl to his feet and led him out of the study and up the stairs and into his own room. G.B. came close behind them, and lay watchful while Wingate got Carl out of his clothes and into bed and finally slid a hypodermic needle into his arm.

"There!" he said. "You'll be asleep in five minutes…"

He was turning away when Carl reached out and caught his hand and held it.

Carl said, "Don't go…" And then he said, "About what I said in your office—I'm sorry, Tom…"

Wingate did not try to release his hand. "Forget it," he said. "I have."

And then he started talking—slowly, quietly, his casual voice a soothing monotone. He said, "All you have to do now is to go to sleep… I'll see to everything else… In a little while, all this will just be a nightmare you've half forgotten… And don't go worrying yourself about publicity and scandal and things like that, Carl… There won't be any… You see, I was *sure*—and, in spite of what you said, I told Chief Nichols… He and I will explain it all to the Coroner…"

He let his voice trail off into silence—Carl Borden was asleep.

It was three weeks before Carl permitted himself to smile—and then he was not in El Morro Beach. He was in San Francisco—and Lorna was waiting for him.

When he smiled, he was driving up Market Street, G.B. erect beside him.

"Tell you something, boy," he murmured. "I nearly took too much that second time!"

The smile became a chuckle.

A Savage Game

A. A. Milne

The name of Alan Alexander Milne (1882–1956) will forever be associated with his children's stories about a bear called Winnie-the-Pooh, but his range of literary accomplishments was wide. Writing with a light touch, he was equally at home with poetry, plays, essays, nonfiction, and prose fiction in long or short form. His solitary detective novel, *The Red House Mystery* (1922), was an early bestseller during the Golden Age of detective fiction; on the strength of that success, he was elected to membership of the Detection Club.

Milne contributed an amiable introduction to the club's short-story collection *Detection Medley*, in which he mused about the puzzle of the sidekicks to the great detectives—the likes of Captain Hastings, who is apt to regret that Poirot is losing his grip, only to be astounded when the truth is finally revealed: "Will there never come a day when [he] realises that not once has he detected, or his companion failed to detect, the crime and the criminal?" "A Savage Game" is one of Milne's regrettably few short stories and was included in *The Evening Standard Detective Book* in 1950.

———

"Forget the detective story. I'm not saying that because I have written one detective story I am a good detective. What I do say is that any writer who makes his living by creative fiction is well fortified to do what your policeman have to do."

"And what's that?"

"Invent a story which accounts for all the facts and suspicions and discrepancies which the case presents. That's our daily job, inventing stories; making a definite pattern of a number of incidents. Dammit, I could contrive some sort of story out of any assortment of facts: a spot of candlegrease, a badly sharpened pencil, a canary which wouldn't sing anymore, and a man who went to bed one night in his wooden leg." Even as he said this, Coleby began to wonder what the story would be. Better start with the canary...

Colonel Saxe went to his desk and unlocked a drawer. He took out a loose-leaf file of papers and said, "Like to try?" Coleby came back to his surroundings suddenly, and said "Oh—what's that?"

"Our latest murder." The Chief Constable sat down again and began to turn the pages. "You'd better look at this. It shows you the house in relation to the rest of the town. That's important."

Coleby looked at it, and said plaintively, "Can't I have a plan of the room, with X marks the spot?"

"That particular room doesn't matter so much. Still, here you are: bedroom where the body was found, living room where the girl and the man were drugged."

Coleby took them, and said, "Drugs too. I *am* going to enjoy this."

"I'll just give you the set-up. Wavetree—silly name—is a bungalow about three hundred yards outside Easton, which is a small country town in my district. It's got a bit of garden, front and back, and there are half a dozen houses, mostly pretty good ones with a fair amount of land, between it and the town. There were four people at the bungalow that Sunday afternoon. Norris Gaye, the owner, now deceased: elderly, miserly, an invalid, or anyway preferred to live like one, and generally, I should say, a crotchety unpleasant person and a great trial to his niece Phyllida. She is thirty minus, very capable, very good-looking in a big, healthy way, if you know what I mean—Captain of Hockey type—and ran the house and her uncle single-handed. Phyllida's brother, Douglas— hot-tempered, who-the-devil-are-*you* sort of cove, lives in London, test driver for racing cars, generally dashed down to lunch on a Sunday, and dashed off again, but whether from love for his sister or to keep in with his rich uncle, I can't say."

"Did they know he was rich?"

"I think so. Even living as he did, he must have had something to leave. In fact, the girl gets an annuity of £500 and the boy the residue, about £20,000. The fourth person was Mark Royle. You may have come across him: thirty plus, French and German scholar, translates books. Very reliable, I've known his people for ages; very intelligent, Field Security in the war, and did a good job. I say all this, because he is our chief witness."

"You wouldn't let me make him the murderer?"

"That's up to you: you'll see. Personally I have no doubts about him. Well now, there's a confectioner's in the town where people go for coffee in the mornings. A few weeks ago Royle and Phyllida had run into each other, literally, just outside it, and when he had picked her parcels up, and apologised—well, there they were having coffee together, and telling each other their names. And it wasn't surprising, seeing what a good-looking couple they are, that they were doing it again next morning. And so on."

"Both fancy-free at the time?"

"More or less. The girl wears an engagement ring, rather a good one, but the fellow was missing-believed-killed in the war, as Royle was not sorry to hear. I suppose she saw him looking at it and wondering. He seems to have fallen for her rather. And then one Sunday he came to lunch."

"To ask Uncle?"

"Oh no. She wanted him to meet her brother, that's all, or her brother to meet him. Just friendly on her part; probably still thinking of the other man. The three of them lunched together in the dining-room; Uncle was being an invalid in his bed-sitting-room, looking out on to the front garden; and after lunch they went into the living room. Phyllida told her brother to light the fire while she got the coffee. It was a log fire, already laid, and Douglas, when he had got it going, wandered about rather impatiently, looking at his watch. Royle sat down in the armchair on the right of the fireplace as you face it. Phyllida came back with the coffee. She put the tray on the table behind Royle's chair and said, "Pour it out, Douglas. I must just make sure that Uncle's all right.

The cream's for Mr. Royle, special." Apparently they had had some joke about that at the coffee-shop. Of course, it wasn't real cream, just the top of the milk, and only enough for one. You'll see the point of all this directly."

"I'm seeing it now. Who put the sleeping tablets in what?"

"Exactly. Douglas poured out the three cups, put sugar in his own and Phyllida's, pulled up a stool next to Royle, and put on it the third cup, the cream jug, and the sugar bowl. Royle put in the sugar, poured in the cream very gently so that it rested on the top, and left it for the sugar to melt. Apparently this was a little way of his. Douglas drank his straight off, put his cup back on the tray, and, as Phyllida came back, said, 'Sorry, old girl, but I must dash.' She suggested that he should say good-bye to his uncle, and he went out and was back again, Royle says, in a couple of minutes; the door was open and they watched him into his uncle's room and back. Phyllida looked at him a little anxiously when he came back, or so Royle thought, and said, 'All right?' and Douglas said, 'Most genial, but then I wasn't making a touch, and that's all he's afraid of.' They went out to his car, and saw him drive off at a hell of a bat towards the town."

"Exit First Murderer," said Coleby. "Or not?"

"You'll see. The other two went back to the living room. Now then, I'll read Royle's actual statement, starting from there." He drew out the pages and read. Coleby lay back, listening to the words of Royle, imagining the scene.

"I sat down in the chair, and she sat on the sofa, which was on the other side of the fireplace and at right angles to it. She drank her coffee and put the cup down on a little table behind the sofa, and then we talked about her brother.

After a bit she said, 'Oh dear, I do feel so tired, it's very rude of me,' and I said, 'Nonsense! Put your feet up and be comfortable.' So she did. I finished my coffee, and was trying to listen to some story she was telling me, but for some reason I couldn't keep my eyes open. I put my hand up, as if to shield them from the fire, so that she wouldn't notice. Then I suddenly realised that she wasn't talking anymore, and I opened my eyes with an effort, and saw her lying there, utterly still. Her hand drooped to the ground, and the firelight flickered in her ring. She might have been dead. I knew that I ought to do something. I think I knew then that we had both been drugged, but I couldn't take my eyes off that enormous ruby; it got bigger and bigger until it filled the whole room and swallowed me up …and by that time I suppose I had passed out. I woke up to a smell of burning, and thought vaguely of breakfast, and it took me a little time to realise that I wasn't in bed at home. One of her shoes had fallen off, and I suppose a bit of burning wood had shot on to it, and the leather was smouldering gently. Then I knew where I was. I tried to revive her, but she was still completely out. I went into Mr. Gaye's room to find out his doctor's telephone number. He was dead. So I rang up the police. It was just five o'clock."

Saxe returned the statement to the file, and Coleby opened his eyes.

"Very good picture. Or is there too much detail? Oh well, you can take that either way. Now for the body."

"Gaye had been stabbed through the heart by a double-edged knife of some sort, but there was no trace of the weapon. It was an hour before the girl was brought round, and able to make a statement. Wherever it overlapped Royle's, it confirmed him exactly. Of course we analysed all the coffee things. Result: traces of an opiate in the two cups, nothing in the third or in the coffee-pot, cream jug, or sugar basin."

"And the only person who could possibly have dropped anything in the cups was the brother—at least, according to Royle."

"Yes, and the cups were the only possible medium."

"So you sent out an all-station call for Douglas."

"No."

"You surprise me. I should have thought your Inspector would have jumped at it."

"He didn't, for the simple reason that Douglas was already arrested. He was stopped in the town for dangerous driving, lost his temper, laid out a couple of constables, and was now safely locked up. Damned young fool."

"But very convenient for you."

"So we thought. But, you see, we searched him, we searched the car, and there was no weapon!"

"It could have been thrown away anywhere."

"Where? When? The others saw him off, remember, streaking towards the town. Within a minute he was in trouble with the police. We've searched the room and the garden outside the window of the room, we've searched the front gardens on each side of the road, and the dagger is simply not there. But in any case, Coleby, if it was hidden under his coat when he drove off, why should he throw it away at once? By doping the coffee he had given himself at least a couple of hours' start, and could have dropped it in a pond or river a hundred miles away, where it would never be found. Also with a murder behind him, wouldn't he take damned good care *not* to get into the hands of the police?"

"You'd think so. Yes."

"So there we are. I'll bet my last shilling that Douglas drugged that coffee, but I'm damned if I can see how he can have killed his uncle. And I'll put my shirt on Royle as an utterly honest and reliable witness, but that means that the girl couldn't have done it either. So there it is. Now make up a story to account for everything, and I shall believe that you really are an author."

"Dear Saxe, I can give you one straight off. The girl stabbed him when she went to see him after lunch; hid the knife temporarily in the back garden where you never looked, and disposed of it afterwards. To give her a perfect alibi Douglas drugged the two of them, and witnessed that his uncle was alive after Phyllida had left him. To give himself a certain amount of cover, he deliberately got himself arrested. If you'd picked him up two hours later, the absence of the knife wouldn't have been in his favour. Joint murder by the two legatees."

"Good God, Coleby," said Saxe, staring at him. "I believe you've got it."

"Yes, but I don't like it. It doesn't do justice to my creative powers. Any policeman could have thought of it. Also it leaves no alternative suspect, which is bad art, and, from the murderer's point of view, bad management. No, it won't do; there's something damnably wrong somewhere. I was picturing the scene in my delightfully imaginative way—see press cuttings—and something went wrong suddenly. Let me take that plan of the room and Royle's statement to bed with me, and I'll tell you the true story tomorrow."

"Well, got the story?"

"Yes. Your Hockey Captain did it on her own, hoping that her little brother would be hanged, thus scooping the pool. Nice girl."

"Impossible!"

"That's what she hoped you'd think."

"I suppose you mean that, being in love with the girl, Royle made up his story to save her?"

"Who said anything about Royle? Royle is the perfect witness. That's why the girl bumped into him outside the coffee-shop."

"You're suggesting that she deliberately picked him up?"

"Well, you see, he was just what she wanted: good character, observant, and a slow starter with his coffee."

"My dear Coleby, how could she possibly have known beforehand that he drank his coffee slowly—for whatever that's worth?"

"She'd watched him on other mornings. Why not? Now I'll tell you what happened."

"In your story," smiled Saxe, leaving himself free to laugh at it or profit by it.

"In a story," said Coleby firmly, "which may or may not—I haven't decided yet—include a very stupid Chief Constable. Here we go. The morphia was in the cream. Don't interrupt. All went as Royle told you; and there are the two of them sitting by the fire; and in the car, bumping into policemen, which was the last thing she wanted, a witness that the uncle was alive. The plan demands that she shall be the first to drink her coffee, and so now she drinks it. She pretends to feel sleepy, and puts her feet up. Just as he is beginning to fade away, she goes out with a bump, or so it seems; and of course the fact that oblivion, as we novelists say, is descending on him, too, makes it all very convincing. As soon as he is right out, she gets up, and in her quick athletic way stabs that very tiresome uncle. She has a nice little untraceable grave in the back garden waiting for the dagger, and in it goes. She washes out the cream-jug, pours a little undoped cream into it which she has carefully put aside, gives herself a little more coffee, drops in the morphia, stirs and swallows. Then she lies down again on the sofa and—genuinely this time—passes out. And there she is, and there she has been all the time when Royle wakes up, and there is the dope in the coffee-cups and nowhere else. End of story."

"Good Lord, you know," said Saxe in astonishment, "it *could* have happened like that!"

"If there is one thing that Author Coleby prides himself on, it is his realism. It could."

"But that doesn't say that it did. It's just a story." Coleby was silent. "Or have you got any proof? Yes, you said there was something wrong in Royle's statement. Is that it?"

"Not in Royle's statement. Couldn't be more accurate. No; something wrong in my visualisation of the scene. Or so I thought. But on consulting Plan C again in my bedroom I found that there was nothing wrong in my visualisation of the scene. So then I knew that the hockey eleven was going to lose its popular young captain."

"You'll have to explain."

"I insist on explaining. I've been looking forward to explaining ever since 1.30 a.m. When your Inspector arrived on the scene, Phyllida was lying on the sofa with her feet towards the fireplace. Or so I saw her; and I could almost smell the burning shoe—what size does she take, sevens?—which Royle thought was his breakfast. But Royle's last view of her before he passed out included the ruby on her engagement finger, hanging over the side of the sofa. You can only get it there, feet by the fire, if the sofa is on the right of the fireplace. And I'd been picturing it on the left; after, I suppose, a casual glance at the plan."

"But it *is* on the left."

"Exactly. Which means that she was lying in a drugged stupor with her head to the fire at two thirty, and in the same drugged stupor with her feet to the fire at five. Silly girl."

"My God!"

"Yes."

"I think I'll telephone," said Saxe, getting up.

"It may not take you far," said Coleby, "but at least you can dig up the back garden. And you might give Royle a hint, or a French novel to translate, or something, to take his mind off the girl. Quite apart from losing your star witness if he marries her, you don't want to spoil his young life. He wouldn't be happy with Phyllida. Too violent for him. Not hockey; lacrosse, I think, don't you? A savage game."

The Clue in the Book

Julian Symons

Julian Gustave Symons (1912–1994) wrote biographies, military history, poetry, true crime, and fiction, but is today particularly renowned as the author of *Bloody Murder* aka *Mortal Consequences*, a highly influential history of the crime genre. The first edition appeared in 1972 and the final edition twenty years later; Symons is often regarded as unremittingly hostile to traditional detective fiction, but this is an oversimplification of his attitudes. He was, for example, an admirer of Agatha Christie and Anthony Berkeley, but he underestimated the durability of the classic whodunit puzzle. I suspect he would be delighted that some of his own books, such as *The Progress of a Crime* and *The Belting Inheritance*, have enjoyed a new life as British Library Crime Classics, but bewildered by the popularity of authors such as John Bude and E. C. R. Lorac, whose work has reappeared under the same imprint after decades of neglect.

Symons wrote a large number of short, snappy detective stories for newspapers and magazines, essentially for commercial reasons. Typically, these little puzzles, dependent on a single trick, featured the private detective Francis Quarles, who never appeared in a full-length mystery. Almost all of Quarles's cases have been gathered together in collections, but "The Clue in the Book" has escaped the net until now. I'm grateful to John Cooper for drawing it to my attention and sending me a copy of the original from the *Evening Standard* of May 5, 1952. Throughout his life, Symons was a radical, politically on the left, but ideas about what is "progressive" keep changing. The British Library and Poisoned Pen Press wish to acknowledge that outdated language is used with regard to disability in this story.

"YOU'LL FIND THE OLD MAN GREATLY CHANGED," Douglas Brinn said. He turned the car in through the wrought iron gates of Corderley Manor.

Francis Quarles nodded. He had not seen Silas Brinn for five years, at a time when he had helped to clear up a smuggling racket organised within the Brinn Shipping Lines. Like other people, however, he knew of the paralytic stroke that two years ago had turned Silas Brinn from a volcanically active little man with a shrewd, slightly sadistic sense of humour, into an invalid.

"He gets about in a wheelchair but he can't talk—the stroke paralysed his vocal cords. He's lost his sense of smell. And he can only write very shakily with his left hand. Lucky for him he's got Sam Clemens. Secretary, you know. Very good chap. Seems to understand what the old man wants almost by intuition. Don't know how he sticks it. What are these manuscripts you want to look at?"

"I'm giving a talk on criminals' handwriting and among the remarkable things in your father's library is a unique collection of manuscripts written by murderers. I saw them years ago, when I was working on that case. I got in touch with you because I got no reply when I wrote direct."

"Letter got chucked into the wastepaper basket, I expect. The old man made it known he'd be pleased to see you. That's a change, believe me. He's lost interest in everything, even his books and manuscripts."

Before dinner Quarles met the others.

Jacob Brinn was a tall, thin man with a nervous habit of pulling at his cheek. Mary was a plain, aggressive spinster in her late thirties, a few years older than Douglas. Quarles gathered that she acted as housekeeper, and that Jacob Brinn had lived with his brother for years.

The secretary, Sam Clemens, was a fresh-faced, friendly young man with the faint trace of an American accent.

Just before dinner Silas Brinn wheeled himself into the room. Quarles was shocked by the change in his appearance.

This shrunken cripple was unrecognisable as the firm, upright little figure he had known. The hand that touched his wavered and had no strength in it. Only the eyes beneath the thick brows looked with keen intelligence from one face to another.

After he had eaten, the old man manoeuvred his chair away

from the table. Clemens half rose to help him, but Silas shook his head and the secretary sat down again. Silas propelled himself out of the door without a parting glance.

His departure did something to relieve the strain. Jacob rang for a bottle of port and passed it round.

Douglas told some mildly amusing stories of life in the shipping agency, where he had taken on most of his father's work. Three-quarters of an hour had passed when Mary Brinn said: "Father usually likes me to go in about this time, and see if he wants anything."

She left the room. Jacob Brinn said, with his face slightly flushed by port: "She's a good girl, deserves what the old man's leaving her. Let me tell you, Clemens, my lad, if you're trying to curry favour with Silas you're wasting your time."

Clemens said composedly: "I'm just a secretary, Mr. Brinn. I know my place."

"Besides, Uncle Jacob," Douglas said, "you must be careful what you say. You can't be sure that Mr. Quarles isn't here to try to cut you out of the old man's financial affections."

There was an awkward silence. It was broken by the sound of running feet. Then Mary was in the room, her face ashen and her eyes starting with fear. "Quickly," she said.

They ran up a long passage and turned into the library. Silas Brinn lay crumpled in his wheelchair like a crushed spider, his face contorted in agony. On a small writing table by his desk stood an empty glass, with the bitter almond smell of cyanide strong inside it. The bottle of port, which had an ingenious lever device to enable a glass to be poured without handling, smelled equally strongly of cyanide.

Silas Brinn had, it seemed, turned round in his wheelchair after taking the fatal dose. He had stretched out his hand to a book on one of the shelves, pulled it out, and tried to write upon the title-page. All he had been able to do, however, was to score a thick line under the author's name. The book, which remained gripped in his hand, was *Huckleberry Finn*. It was one in a long row of a collected edition of works by the same author. Mark Twain.

"It's a puzzle." Inspector Leeds said to Quarles as they sat in the library next day. "Any one of them could have got at the port. All three of 'em—Jacob, Mary, and Douglas—understood that they came in for a big slice in the will.

"The secretary knew he'd been left out, in the surest way possible, by the fact that he'd been asked to act as witness. Apparently the old man believed money ought to be left inside a family. Solicitor's bringing along the will today, by the way, so we'll know exactly how much each one's been left. And there you are. The old man comes in here, drinks this poison which he can't smell, and dies. We shall try to trace the poison, but if he's covered his tracks on that carefully, it'll be a job."

"There's the question of why he was killed at this particular time," Quarles said. "I can't help feeling that there was some immediate and urgent reason for the murder."

"Perhaps." The Inspector did not sound optimistic.

"Then there's the book. What does that mean? Silas drinks the cyanide. He knows he's been poisoned, and that he's probably got only minutes to live. He pulls a book out of the shelves and underlines the author's name. That means he knew his murderer, and was trying to tell us something about him. What?"

"Lord knows," said the Inspector. "Here's the solicitor."

Mr. Drayton, the solicitor, knew nothing of any plan for a fresh will. The one he produced was dated three years back. It left a sum of £50,000 to Jacob, and divided the rest of his fortune equally between Mary and Douglas ("About £100,000 each after death duties, I should think," said Mr. Drayton).

There was a special clause saying Silas disapproved of gifts in a will being made for long and faithful service since he had paid well for such service, and expected to get it. The will was witnessed by Samuel Langhorne Clemens, secretary, and Arnold Bridgewater West, manservant.

"We're no further forward." said the Inspector, after Mr. Drayton had gone.

"On the contrary." Quarles replied. "The case is solved."

"Silas Brinn was not killed for his money," Quarles said to an attentive group composed of Jacob, Mary, Douglas, and Sam Clemens. Inspector Leeds looked on watchfully. "I'm afraid that I was the indirect cause of his death myself. I said to Inspector Leeds this morning that I felt something had happened to make this murder urgently necessary. Then I realised that what had happened was my visit to look at some valuable manuscripts.

"Some time ago I wrote and asked to look at these manuscripts. I received no reply. Then I got in touch with Douglas here, and he arranged for me to come down. That arrangement was fatal for Silas, for unknown to him, some, or perhaps all, of the manuscripts had been sold by somebody in his confidence."

The secretary said sharply: "Nonsense."

"Will you bring me the manuscripts, Mr. Clemens?"

The secretary crossed the room, unlocked a cupboard, and came back with half a dozen morocco slip cases.

Quarles looked at the papers inside and said: "The thief was really very unlucky. Silas had lost interest in the manuscripts, and the theft might have remained undetected for years. It happens that I examined these manuscripts five years ago, and that these papers are barely a quarter of what was there then. I take it that none of you knows of them being sold since them."

There was a murmur of dissent. Clemens was silent.

"It's hardly surprising that when I wrote asking to look at the manuscripts, I got no reply. When, in spite of that, I came down, Silas must have wanted to see the manuscripts, and have found out that they were stolen.

"Who was the thief who had to act so urgently? It could not have been Jacob or Mary, for they did not know the purpose of my visit. It could not have been Douglas, since he arranged for me to come. That leaves—"

"All right," Clemens said bitterly. "I sold them, and I don't regret it. I had a right to something. That doesn't say I killed him."

"Oh, but Silas left the clearest possible clue to that. Your parents were American, weren't they? And because you had the surname of a famous American writer, they gave you his Christian names as well. Silas's hands were feeble, but his mind was still quick. He underlined the name of his murderer in a book."

"I don't understand," Douglas said. "It was Mark Twain's name he underlined."

"Yes, but Mark Twain used that name as a pseudonym. His real name, as I remembered when I saw a certain signature on a will, was Samuel Langhorne Clemens."

The Manuscript

Gladys Mitchell

Gladys Maude Winifred Mitchell (1901–1983), who also wrote as Stephen Hockaby and Malcolm Torrie, is sometimes ranked as one of the "Queens of Crime" alongside other major women writers who emerged during the Golden Age of detective fiction, such as Agatha Christie, Dorothy L. Sayers, and Margery Allingham. Mitchell was more variable and idiosyncratic than her sisters in crime, perhaps because she wrote so much, but her best work has a distinctive flavour and an appealing wit. Her series detective, Mrs. Bradley, is an unforgettable figure who made an astonishing debut in *Speedy Death* (1929) and proceeded to cackle her way through scores of investigations over the next fifty years or so. The Stone House: A Gladys Mitchell Tribute Site, a website assembled by Jason Half, is a mine of information about this interesting and gifted woman.

Mitchell's ingenuity is most evident in her novels, but she produced a large number of very short stories, many of which are collected in the posthumous volume *Sleuth's Alchemy*, edited by Nicholas Fuller. "The Manuscript" first appeared in the *Evening Standard* on May 11, 1953.

———

"WE'VE GOT TO GET HIM," SAID THE SUPERINTENDENT, "and it's up to you, Rogers. The motive, to a man of his sort, must have loomed up like a mountain. He's a fanatic and almost a recluse, which means he's no sense of proportion.

"After all, it happened to Thomas Carlyle to finish writing a book and then have the manuscript accidentally burned. And that was an important book, mark you, not like this tripe of old Besley's."

"A book about prison life, wasn't it?—Besley's, I mean."

"Yes. He got his stuff direct from the horse's mouth. Used to offer the old lags jobs when they came out and suck them dry. Then he'd write them the whale of a character, sack them gently and politely, and take on another bird of the same kidney."

"Feather, sir. Well, what made him change his habits and kill this girl instead of firing her?"

"Simply that she seems to have taken exception to the circumstances in which she found herself, and chucked the whole manuscript on the fire. She wasn't really an old lag, you see. It appears that he'd finished the big section devoted to men criminals and wanted to put in an extra bit about women. Well, he'd already engaged a woman baby-farmer who'd received a life sentence and had been released on a good-conduct remission, and he wanted a first offender for contrast.

"He picked this girl Angie, who said she was only too ready to go straight, treated her kindly, talked to her about her experiences and, from what we can gather from her relations—all more or less of criminal character, incidentally, he rehabilitated her in her own eyes until she was almost ready to worship him. We've got all this from the letters she used to write home. Then, in accordance with his custom, he gave her the sack. When she protested, the old brute came clean and told her what he had really wanted her for. The idea that her misdeeds were to be handed down to posterity seemed to upset her.

"She sneaked down at night when she knew he had gone to bed, broke open his writing desk, collared the manuscript and stoked the kitchen fire with it. We know all this because she wrote to her parents and told them what she had done."

"And how long after she'd burned the book and written the letter—?"

"Two days. It chanced that he spent the first day fixing up with the next ex-prisoner he wanted, name of Nelly, a girl of Angie's age who was being released after serving a sentence for gang crimes. Besley brought her back with him, and finding Angie still there, inveigled her into the woods outside his house and did her in—in other words, broke her neck.

"She'd been killed where she was found, moreover. That's our difficulty. There's nothing to show that he ever went out of the house, and the new girl, Nelly, can't help us. At least, she says she can't."

"Who found the body?"

"A gamekeeper, out after grey squirrels. It appears they

inhabit those woods and every so often he goes after them with a gun."

"Could it possibly have been an accident?"

"No, I don't see that it could. She'd collected a punch on the jaw."

Detective-Inspector Rogers went off to see Besley. He turned out to be a bearded, crafty-looking gentleman on the threshold of old age. Rogers sized him up but could scarcely see him as the deliverer of murderous blows. He suddenly said: "Do you mind if I look at your hands, sir?"

The recluse stretched them out. Those fine-skinned knuckles had never, unaided, dealt a death-blow to a healthy girl. So much Rogers saw at once.

Rogers went off to look at the place where the girl had been found dead. A local constable was posted just outside the area, which was cordoned off with ropes. Rogers produced his authority, and they chatted.

"Nothing else come to light, I suppose?"

"Nothing at all, sir."

"H'm. Leaf-mould everywhere. That means no identifiable footprints. And no weapon except somebody's fist. All right, constable."

He walked back to the house and found Besley, glasses on nose, bent industriously over his papers. "I've begun my book again, you see. Just like Carlyle, I've kept all my case notes, I find."

"That's very fortunate, sir," said Rogers. This, he regretted, did away with the motive. He inspected the manuscripts from which Besley had been working. So far as he could tell, they were genuine case-notes.

"Were you very angry when you found the girl had burned your manuscript?" he asked.

"I was, indeed," said Besley. "But I simmered down, you know."

"Now, listen, Mr. Besley. You didn't know your book was destroyed when you went to engage this girl Nelly?—No, I thought not. What did you know about Nelly?"

"Well," said Besley, "I knew of course that she had been mixed up with a gang. She was terrified of her old associates, too. She seems frightened out of her life."

"Ah, yes. All right, Mr. Besley. I shan't need to bother you again. Perhaps I could have just a word with Nelly."

"But what gave you the clue?" demanded the Superintendent. "We've picked up Nelly's boyfriend, on your instructions."

"I couldn't believe he killed the girl," said Rogers. "For one thing, with those hands of his, I couldn't see it happening— but, from the medical evidence, he didn't. But it was clearly to the advantage of the rest of her gang that Nelly's activities should remain anonymous. Once her story was down in black and white not one of them felt himself safe. They must have picketed the house, and, as Angie fled from old Besley's wrath, one of them mistook her for Nelly—quite an easy thing in the gloom of the woods at evening."

A Man and His Mother-in-Law

Roy Vickers

Roy Vickers was the main pseudonym of William Edward Vickers (1889–1965), who also wrote as David Durham, John Spencer, and Sefton Kyle. Vickers was prolific, turning out upwards of sixty crime novels, but he is best remembered as creator of the *Department of Dead Ends*, a long series of short stories launched with "The Rubber Trumpet," which originally appeared in *Pearson's Magazine* in September 1934 and was one of the most acclaimed detective short stories of its era.

"A Man and His Mother-in-Law" was included in *Eight Murders in the Suburbs* (1953). On May 31, 1968, a televised adaptation by the Irish dramatist Hugh Leonard aired on BBC1. John Welsh played Inspector Rason and John Wentworth Chief Inspector Karslake. Donald Douglas took the role of Arthur Penfold and Barbara Couper that of Mrs. Blagrove, while Lyn Ashley played Madge. This was an episode in the excellent anthology series *Detective*, which featured many outstanding mystery stories by a wide range of authors; the first series of *Detective*, four years earlier, included another *Dead Ends* story by Vickers, "The Man Who Murdered in Public."

I

IN A LETTER WRITTEN ON THE EVE OF EXECUTION, Arthur Penfold seems to share the judge's astonishment that a man of his calibre should turn to murder to extricate himself from a domestic difficulty. A student of criminology could have told Penfold—if not the learned judge himself—that murder eventuates, not from immediate circumstance, but from an antecedent state of mind.

The murder occurred in 1935. The antecedent state of mind was created five years earlier, on an October evening when Penfold, returning from the office, found a note in his wife's handwriting on the hall table.

Penfold, an only child of very doting parents, was born in 1900. At twenty-five he inherited the family business, a wholesale agency for technical inks—almost any ink except the kind one uses with a pen. His mother had died the previous year. For three years he lived alone in the twelve-roomed house, with an acre of garden, in the overgrown village of Crosswater, some twenty miles out of London. The house was vibrant with memories of a benevolently autocratic father, whose lightest wish became his wife's instant duty—whose opinions on everything she accepted as inspired wisdom. In April 1931 Arthur

Penfold married and eagerly set about modelling his life on that of his father.

Of his bride we need note only that she had been an efficient business girl, a rung or two up the ladder, that she was physically attractive and well mannered—the sort of girl his friends expected him to choose. They had been married six months to a day when he found that note in the hall—six months, he would have told you, of unalloyed happiness. A wife who—*ex officio*, as it were—liked all the things that he liked, lived for the great moment of the day when he returned home, to regale her with small talk of his achievements in business. There was not, he would have asserted, a single cloud in his matrimonial sky.

> *Arthur dear. I am terribly sorry and utterly ashamed of myself, but I can't stick it any longer. It's not your fault—I have no complaint and no excuse. I shall stay with Mother while I'm looking for a job. I don't want any money, please, and I'll agree to anything as long as you don't ask me to come back—Julie.*
>
> *P.S.—There isn't another man and I don't suppose there ever will be.*

Julie remained unattached for three years. Then she wrote Penfold begging for divorce, as she wished to remarry. Penfold chivalrously insisted that he should be the one to give cause, so that she could start again untainted with scandal. He did not hate Julie, but he did hate himself and to a somewhat dangerous degree.

He was the fourth generation of his family to live in that

house. The Penfolds were of the local aristocracy and "knew everybody," meaning fifty or so of the more prosperous families in a largish suburb. Arthur Penfold—though no one claimed him as an intimate friend—was popular, in the sense that no one disliked him nor ever suggested excluding him. He was of medium height, with thin, sandy hair, a little ponderous in manner, self-centred but not boastful. When he was deserted, for no apparent reason, "everybody" agreed that he had been abominably treated and was entitled to sympathy.

While Julie was with him, his own happiness had been obvious to everybody. He had taken for granted that Julie was happy too. How could you have a happy husband and an unhappy wife? But, somehow, you had!

Why had she left him? Too late, he tried to imagine her point of view. It was uphill work, because he knew nothing of her intimate personal history, her tastes, her hopes, her fears. In the sense in which married lovers explore each other's personality and impulse, he knew nothing at all about her—had desired no such knowledge. It escaped him that this might be the reason why Julie had thrown in her hand.

In the sympathy of the neighbours he saw only pity for a man who had some taint or defect, unknown to himself, which made his society intolerable to a normal woman. How could he doubt that behind a mask of friendliness, the neighbours were laughing at him!

There was a certain tragic grandeur in the idea of a man with a taint that baffled definition. In a short time, he began to believe in it.

The desertion was followed by three years of bitter self-contempt, during which every friendly greeting was held to mask a sneer. Irrelevantly, he felt a little better when the divorce was completed. In the summer he accepted an invitation to stay with a cousin who was the vicar of Helmstane. Here he met Margaret Darrington, who became his second wife.

Margaret was twenty-four and a beauty, though she seemed not to know it. Her clothes, expensive but ill-chosen, verged on dowdiness. She lacked the assurance of a girl specially gifted by nature. Her intelligence was adult, but her temperament was that of a prim young schoolgirl with a talent for obedience. At their first meeting, Arthur Penfold, perceiving the talent for obedience, wanted to marry her much more than he had ever wanted anything.

"A very grave young person," the vicar told him. "She lives with an honorary aunt, to whom she is devoted—er— excessively so!" The vicar pulled himself up. "Perhaps that was a mean remark in the special circumstances!" He told a tragic tale. In the 1914 war, when Margaret was six, her mother had been killed in an air raid on London, while the child was in Helmstane with a Mrs. Blagrove. Scarcely had Mrs. Blagrove finished breaking the news to the little girl when a War Office telegram announced that her father had been killed in action. Mrs. Blagrove cherished the orphan, adopted her, and did her best to fill the role of both parents.

"With indifferent success, I fear," finished the vicar. "Margaret is a dear girl—she helps me with the parish chores, which is convenient for me but not really the sort of thing she ought to be doing. She has lost her place in her own generation and shows no desire to find it. I would guess that she is, perhaps, unadventurous—a little afraid of life."

Too afraid of life, in fact, to run away from a husband,

who would stand between her and the world, which she need apprehend only through his eyes. Penfold required no further information about the girl nor her intimate personal history, nor her tastes, nor her hopes, nor her fears. For their first date, he asked her to meet him in London for lunch and a matinée.

For an instant, the schoolgirl personality vanished. The wide-set eyes became the eyes of a vital young woman reaching out for her share of gaiety. But only for an instant.

"I'll ask Aunt Agnes."

Six weeks later, in a punt on the river, he told her that it was in her power to make him extremely happy. He gave instances of so many ways in which she could give him happiness that the idea of marrying him began to take the colour of a moral duty. Whether he could give her a commensurate happiness was a question which was not raised by either side.

Margaret admitted having observed that a girl was expected to marry and leave home—even when her own people were fond of her, which she thought puzzling.

"Then you *will*, Madge?"

"I'll ask Aunt Agnes."

"No, darling!" said Penfold, who had not yet discovered that she was intelligent. "We'll go back at once and I'll tell her myself."

II

Mrs. Blagrove had draped her Victorian furniture in bright chintzes, hung a nude or two on her walls and believed the result to be modern. She believed the same of herself. In the nineties she had considered herself one of the New

Women—had she not smoked cigarettes and read the early works of Bernard Shaw!—though she secretly preferred the output of Miss Ella Wheeler Wilcox, whose sentimental verse was already crossing the Atlantic. She had an income sufficient for all the hobbies and good works with which she fought her dread of lonely old age.

She began by putting Penfold at his ease, which slightly offended him and spoilt his tactical approach.

"I know why you have come, Mr. Penfold." Her smile was elaborately confidential. "I'll say it for you, shall I? You have *asked* Madge, and she has referred you to me. I've felt this in the air for a fortnight. And there was no way of warning either of you."

"But, Mrs. Blagrove! You cannot mean that you refuse your consent?"

"I have no such authority—my guardianship expired when she was twenty-one."

"She would never take an important step against your wishes."

"Nor an unimportant step, either. My moral influence, I admit, is paramount. For that very reason, I shall not exercise it. I shall urge Madge to do whatever she wants to do." Before Penfold could express satisfaction, Mrs. Blagrove added: "I shall simply advise her not to think any more about it. Advice—that will be all!"

Her tone removed insult from her words. Penfold retreated to prepared ground.

"Perhaps you will allow me to give a brief account of myself."

The brevity, however, was not noticeable. Mrs. Blagrove politely refrained from registering inattention.

"In short, you are extremely eligible—the vicar told me all about you." She paused before resuming, on another note. "Mr. Penfold! Have you noticed, as I have, that some women are predestined mothers—you can tell when they're little girls. And some have an obvious talent for wifehood. And some—and Madge is one of these—are predestined *daughters*—daughters in mind and temperament even when they are very old women."

"Old maids, perhaps. But when Madge is married—"

"She'll make her husband more unhappy than herself. Other men have thought they were in love with her, because she's such a pretty thing. But their man's instinct warned them that too much of her would be withheld. Haven't you noticed how she comes to me to ask permission or advice on trifling matters?—and she's twenty-four, remember. It's she who insists on that sort of thing, not I. I flatter myself I'm a modern woman. I believe in complete freedom for women, single or married."

Penfold retained only the impression that "the old lady" intended to keep the girl to herself. He was ready to fight her, tooth and claw. But there was nothing to fight. When Margaret reported back to him, he could hardly take in her words.

"I'm so glad Aunt Agnes doesn't refuse her consent. She just advises us not to. But I think—I'm sure—it's only because she would hate to seem to be glad to get rid of me. It's not reasonable to suppose she really wants me on her hands for ever. So, if you still feel sure that you do, Arthur—"

Penfold expected at best some sulkiness on the part of his honorary mother-in-law. To his amazement, she kept her word to urge the girl to do what she wanted to do. Mrs.

Blagrove was positively co-operative. Pursuing some dimly understood ideal of modernity, she turned her energies to detail, took competent advice in the purchase of a most comprehensive trousseau. Further, she forced the girl into the hands of a beautician for grooming and general instruction.

The result was that Margaret's natural beauty was brought into line with modern requirements. Julie had been ordinarily good looking—Margaret would catch the eye in any community. In Crosswater, the women would be jealous and the men would be envious. They would soon see how wrong they had been in supposing that he could not hold the interest of an attractive wife.

On the last day of their honeymoon in Cornwall, there came a letter from Mrs. Blagrove, jointly addressed and beginning "*My dears,*" announcing that she had sold her house in Helmstane, bought another for the same price in Crosswater and would shortly move in.

"That's almost too good to be true!" exclaimed Margaret. "I can run round every day while you're in London and see that she's all right."

For a few seconds, Penfold hovered on the brink of protest. So that was the game! For all her amiability—for all that really broadminded trousseau—Mrs. Blagrove was hostile and intended to wreck their marriage. She would fail. Margaret's talent for obedience, which had given him such a delightful honeymoon, would prove a two-edged sword, and—and so on!

"I hope, darling," he said, feeling extremely clever, "that Aunt Agnes will stay with us while she is moving in."

Mrs. Blagrove did not stay in their house, but she let

Margaret help her with the move, taking scrupulous care that Penfold's convenience should not be jeopardised. Very shrewd of her, thought Penfold. But he too knew how to wear the velvet glove.

Her house was some half a mile away: visits were constantly exchanged. No man could have been more attentive to his mother-in-law, honorary or otherwise.

In time, they slipped into a little routine. On Wednesday evenings, the Penfolds dined at Dalehurst, Mrs. Blagrove's daily help staying after six. On Sundays, Mrs. Blagrove came for supper to Oakleigh, when Penfold would read aloud a selection from the poems of Miss Ella Wheeler Wilcox who, in Mrs. Blagrove's affections, had never had a rival.

Penfold became aware that on most days of the week Margaret would "run round" to Dalehurst. Many minor domestic arrangements were traceable to Mrs. Blagrove; but they were sensible arrangements, which enhanced his comfort without impinging on his authority. Margaret never quoted Aunt Agnes. It would have been unintelligent to deny that the old lady seemed to be playing no game but an unobtrusively benevolent one. He began to think highly of her, even to enjoy her company, except for the sessions of Miss Ella Wheeler Wilcox. Twice she insinuated a Mrs. Manfried, a fellow devotee. It was his sole grievance.

A year passed, during which Penfold put back the weight he had lost after the collapse of his first marriage. His dream had come true. The women were jealous of Margaret, and the men, within the framework of correct behaviour, registered an envious appreciation of her. No longer did the smile of welcome seem to mask a sneer, tempered with pity.

He could not bring himself to grudge the time his wife spent at Dalehurst, in his absence. Mrs. Blagrove's prophecy that Margaret would make her husband unhappy had been stultified by the event. His life slipped into the pattern of his father's.

The inner history of an egocentric tends to repeat itself. The other half of Mrs. Blagrove's prophecy—the half that was concerned with Margaret's happiness—had slipped from Penfold's memory. He was so happy himself that he had not felt the need to probe into the question of Margaret's happiness—to explore her personality and her impulse. She was an efficient and economical housekeeper. She was of regular, orderly habits. She was lovely to look at and she was obedient in all things. His cup was full.

III

They had been married two years and a month when Mrs. Blagrove fell down in her bedroom and put a finger out of joint. The injury was beginning to be forgotten, when she fell down in the hall, bruising herself painfully. She was not too shaken, however, to come to supper on Sunday—to be whisked back to her girlhood by Penfold, in interpretation of Miss Ella Wheeler Wilcox.

The following week, a trained nurse took up residence at Dalehurst, though Mrs. Blagrove seemed to ignore her presence and to carry on as usual. In the course of a fortnight, Margaret overcame her aunt's reluctance to reveal the facts.

"She falls down because she suddenly loses consciousness," Margaret told her husband. "It's her heart. But Dr. Delmore says her life is in no danger."

Penfold expressed relief. But there was more to come.

"The air here is too bracing, Dr. Delmore says. She will have to sell up and leave. He recommends South Devon."

Some two hundred miles from London! That, Penfold admitted to himself, could be borne with equanimity. He was, in fact, about to say as such.

"I'm sorry, Arthur dear, but I must go with her."

"Yes, darling, of course you must! I'll squeeze a week off, and we'll all go down together and settle her in."

"Dr. Delmore says—" it was as if Penfold had not spoken "—that these little attacks may be frequent. They may come at any hour of the day or night. She might fall in the fire—under the traffic—anything. She must never be alone."

Still Penfold could not see it.

"That means two nurses. Pretty hefty expense—"

"There won't be two nurses. There won't be one. She can't get on with nurses. That nice Nurse Hart has gone, and Aunt Agnes says she won't have another. I must go to her, Arthur. That's what I'm trying to tell you."

There came a moment of stark panic—a long moment in which he again ran the gauntlet of smiles that masked the universal sneer at the man who cannot hold his woman.

"She may live for twenty years or more. Do you want to end our marriage, Madge?"

"It isn't a matter of what I want," she evaded. "Remember, she isn't my aunt, really. She didn't even like me, to start with—I was the horrid child of a young couple she had met on a pleasure cruise. I've never forgotten. All my life I've wondered what I could do in return."

"I'm not belittling her. But what about me? What have I done that I should lose my wife?"

"Nothing. You speak as if I were complaining of you— I'm not—it wouldn't be fair." The unconscious echo of Julie's words made him feel faint. "But you don't *need* me, Arthur—me in particular, I mean."

"Of course I need you! To come home in the evening, with no wife to welcome me—"

"You'll soon find a quiet girl, whose looks appeal to you— you ask so little, Arthur. Then, everything will be the same for you." She spoke without a trace of bitterness. "But Aunt Agnes needs me as *me*!"

He did not understand and would not try. The sense of defeat was numbing him. He went into the dining-room and took a stiff whisky. He would put his case firmly but fairly to Aunt Agnes, with every consideration for her feelings. Velvet glove, in fact. Now he came to think of it, her birthday fell on the day after tomorrow. That could be used to help his opening.

The next day was damp and foggy, increasing his depression, so that he left the office earlier than usual, determined to see Mrs. Blagrove at once.

Now, by chance—good or ill according to one's point of view—a popular publisher had decided to stage a comeback for the poetry of Ella Wheeler Wilcox and was flooding the bookstalls with an initial anthology: *The Best of Wilcox*. There was a double pyramid at one of the bookstalls at Waterloo station, which duly caught Penfold's eye.

The very thing! It would help him to open the interview on a friendly note.

He bought a copy, decided to retain the dust jacket, which carried a design of moonbeams and cupids—"the old lady" reacted to that sort of thing when you steered her into the mood for it.

On arriving at Crosswater at five-three, he reflected that Madge would not be expecting him for another hour—she had said that she would be helping at the vicarage that afternoon. So, instead of going home first, he trudged through the rain and fog to Dalehurst. Mrs. Blagrove was drawing the curtains when he appeared in the front garden. She beckoned and unlatched the French window.

"Come in this way, if you don't mind. It's Bessie's afternoon for visiting her grandmother in hospital. She's supposed to pay me back the time on Saturday, but she always has some excuse. You're home early, aren't you?"

He agreed with enthusiasm—went into the hall to deposit his coat and hat, and returned, flourishing *The Best of Wilcox.*

"This is just out—an anthology. Thought you might like it. Sort of pre-birthday present."

"How thoughtful and kind of you, Arthur! What a perfectly lovely design! I expect I know all the selections—I hope I do!" She lowered herself to the chintz-covered settee and turned over the pages. When Penfold had finished settling himself in an armchair, Mrs. Blagrove was sitting with her hands folded in her lap. The book was not in evidence.

"You've come to talk about Madge, haven't you?"

"And about you and me, Aunt Agnes. It's sheer tragedy that you have to go and live somewhere else. We made a perfect little circle, the three of us. I can safely say that, these last two years, I have been as happy as any man can hope to be."

"Yes!... Yes, I've noticed that you have."

The remark seemed out of focus. Also, Aunt Agnes looked amused, instead of impressed. He reminded himself that he was to be firm as well as fair.

"I have to live near London, of course. That puts Madge in a terrible position. I would not for one moment dispute your claim to a sacrifice on her part—"

"'Sacrifice'!" Mrs. Blagrove laughed somewhat loudly. "Let's see if I've got it the right way round. It would be a sacrifice on *her* part to leave *you* and resume her life with *me*? Sacrifice of what, Arthur?"

While he was groping for a retort, she added:

"There are some things that women cannot conceal from each other, however hard they try."

"What has Madge to conceal from you?" he blustered. "Do I stint her allowance? Do I ask too much of her in return?"

"You ask too little. So that the little you do ask becomes a soul-destroying chore!"

Within him was rising a strange kind of fear, which he did not know to be fear of himself.

"To me, that doesn't make sense. But perhaps it's my fault. Perhaps I have some blind spot—some—taint—of which I am unaware."

"It's nothing so interesting as a taint, Arthur." She was leaning forward on the settee. Her elbows were bent, quivering a little. She seemed to him like a spider about to pounce. "Poor boy!" She was smiling now. "Your egotism protects you from all unpleasant truths—protects you, even, from the hunger for companionship and shared emotion. I'm afraid I must tell you something about yourself—something that's not a bit mystical or dramatic."

"Don't!"

There was an antecedent state of mind, unsuspected by the judge, which made Penfold see in her smile the sneer which he had dreaded to see on the face of his friends, the sneer at the man who cannot hold his woman.

"Your first marriage—" she was saying, though her words now were lost to him "—like your second, failed because you don't want a wife—you want a puppet that can only say 'yes.'"

He had no purpose except that of compelling her to silence, lest she shatter that little world in which he lived so happily with a wife who mirrored his picture of himself. He seized her by the throat—his grip grew in strength while his mind's eye was re-reading Julie's letter: *"I am terribly sorry and utterly ashamed of myself, but I can't stick it any longer."* Madge would leave him, too—and again he would be pitied as the man without a woman of his own. If he had been of a different social type, he might have described his ecstasy as "seeing red and then getting a blackout." He certainly went through a process comparable with that of regaining consciousness, though he was unsurprised when he found that Mrs. Blagrove was dead.

He lurched into the chintz-covered armchair.

"Look what you've done to us *now*, Aunt Agnes!" He whimpered like a child. He was too profoundly shocked to feel fear for himself. This would be the biggest scandal Crosswater had ever known. There was little he could do to avert it, but that little must be done.

With his handkerchief he wiped the chintz of the armchair.

In the hall he wiped the hatstand and the peg on which he had hung his coat. He put on his coat and hat—and his gloves—unlatched the front door, stepped outside and shut it behind him.

He waited a minute or more, listening. He walked down the path to the gate—

"*The Best of Wilcox!*" he muttered. "There'll be my fingerprints on that glossy jacket."

He took off his right glove, found his penknife, opened it, then put the glove on again. With some difficulty he raised the latch of the French windows, slithered round the curtain.

He had left the light burning. In this mild-mannered suburbanite there was no emotion at sight of the woman he had killed—some seven or eight minutes ago. He was concentrated on reclaiming the book—and it was not beside the body, where he had expected it to be. It was not on the seat of the settee nor on the arms nor on the floor.

He was beginning to get flustered, but only because he was always a duffer at finding things. He went down on his knees, looked under the settee—if it had fallen, he might have kicked it there himself. He crawled round to the back of the settee. He stood up, exasperated. The book simply must be in the room somewhere! He took a couple of steps backwards, bumped against the open flap of the escritoire. He wheeled as if a hand had touched him—and stared down at the cupids dancing in the moonbeams.

While he was picking up the book, his eye measured the distance from the back of the settee to the open flap of the escritoire—a good six feet.

How did the book get there? he wondered. She had it in

her hand when she sat down, and he could not remember her leaving the settee. Could someone have entered the room, while he was outside the house? He hurried into the hall, intending to search the house—then abandoned the idea as useless. Anyway, it was much more likely that she had moved while they were talking, without his noticing it. Mustn't start imagining things and giving way to nerves!

He put the book in his overcoat pocket and, leaving the light burning, again left the house by the front door, forgetting to re-fasten the French window. The fog was being thinned out by a rising wind: with the light rain, visibility was still very poor.

He turned up his collar and adopted a slouch—he would be safe from recognition unless he came face to face with an acquaintance. He reached the gate of Oakleigh more than half an hour before his usual time. He observed that the lights were on in the kitchen but nowhere else. Madge, evidently, was still at the vicarage. He must get in without the cook and housemaid hearing him.

He used his latchkey silently, hung up his coat and hat and crept into the drawing-room. He switched on the stove and put *The Best of Wilcox* on an occasional table where Madge would be sure to see it—it would serve as a diversion. Now and again he chuckled to himself, as if he were taking rather sly measures to prevent the club secretary from learning that a friend had broken one of the rules.

He was still alone at five to six when, straining his ears, he could hear the train coming in, then rumbling away. Dangerously soon, he heard Madge's latchkey.

"Why, Arthur! You've beaten me! You must have galloped from the station!"

"I caught the earlier train—miserable day and not much doing at the office. I was dozing off when I heard your latchkey."

She was facing the occasional table—staring at the moonbeams and cupids. She looked disappointed—held the book as if she resented its presence in the house.

"It's not for you!" he laughed. "It's a Wilcox anthology. Out today! I thought Aunt Agnes might like to have it."

"Oh, Arthur, how kind of you!" Her voice was unsteady. With unwonted impulsiveness, she threw her arms round his neck. He was unaware that this was the first time she had volunteered a caress. "Let me take it to her tomorrow morning—please—I want to tell her how you thought of it for her."

Almost reverently, she replaced the book on the little table.

"As you like, dear!" The daily help would arrive at Dalehurst about eight in the morning. The alarm would come, probably, while they were having breakfast.

After dinner Madge slipped away, to reappear in gum boots and mackintosh.

"I promised the vicar I'd take some things to Mrs. Gershaw. I shan't be long."

"It's a filthy night—let me go for you."

"No, thanks! There's a lot of explanation and—and their telephone is out of order."

As soon as his wife had left the house, Penfold became uneasy. It would be all right, he kept telling himself, provided she did not "run round" to Dalehurst with that wretched book. Presently he remembered that she had put it back on the occasional table. He swung round in his chair. The book was no longer on the table.

Gershaw lived less than a hundred yards away. In half an

hour Penfold's nerve began to fail. He had endured an hour and five minutes before Margaret returned.

"What's the matter, Madge?"

"Aunt Agnes is dead. Someone has killed her!"

"Nonsense! How d'you know? Have you been to Dalehurst?" He had to repeat the question.

"Dr. Delmore saw me from his car and stopped. Just now!"

That was all right, then! Sympathy for a bereavement was indicated. He made a suitable exclamation, would have taken her in his arms.

"I want to be alone, Arthur."

She walked past him, up the stairs to her room. She had never behaved like that before. The house suddenly seemed stiflingly hot. He opened the front door and stood in the porch—was there when the police came.

It was soon obvious that they had found nothing that need disturb him. They did not insist on seeing Madge, were content with his account of her movements and his own. They were even chatty, told him that Dr. Delmore, passing in his car, had seen the light in the drawing-room of Dalehurst and the French window swinging in the wind and had gone in to investigate. He had telephoned the police and, on the way home, had spotted Mrs. Penfold in the road and told her. There was, Penfold assured himself, nothing to worry about.

IV

At the inquest, Dr. Delmore testified that death had taken place between five and six o'clock and was due to heart failure caused by partial asphyxia resulting from strangulation. Margaret Penfold stated that she had lunched at Dalehurst, leaving at a quarter to three to go to the vicarage. Mrs. Blagrove had seemed to be in normal health, was expecting no visitor. She was confident that deceased had no personal enemy. Arthur Penfold was not called.

Police evidence revealed that the latch of the French window had been lifted with a penknife, and so clumsily that the woodwork had been chipped. The ground had been too wet to yield footprints of any value. The Coroner was encouraged to believe that an unpractised crook had assaulted the deceased intending to make her disclose the whereabouts of valuables, and had then taken fright—there had been no robbery. The jury returned the obvious verdict and expressed gratification that the local police had been prompt in asking the aid of Scotland Yard.

On taking over, Chief Inspector Karslake ordered an intensive search of the drawing-room for some personal trace of the killer.

"She was on that settee when he attacked her. He must have been leaning well over. Try the folds of the upholstery—between the seat and the back."

The result was disappointing. Between the folds of the upholstery were found three thimbles, two pairs of scissors, nine handkerchiefs, and a book in its dust jacket: *The Best of Wilcox.*

"That's too thick to have slipped down, sir—must've been pushed down."

Karslake examined the book. A new copy—and there was nothing to distinguish it from any other copy in the edition. He opened it in the middle.

"Poetry!" He glanced back at the moonbeams and cupids. "Love stuff. And she was sixty-four! Didn't want to be caught at it. Check on the local booksellers—she probably bought it herself. Try those curtains."

Karslake collected relevant gossip from the local superintendent, then set about eliminating the Penfolds. Margaret was easily disposed of because her movements were checkable up to six o'clock, when the cook and housemaid heard her talking to her husband in the drawing-room.

Penfold's statement that he had arrived at Crosswater station at five three was confirmed by the ticket collector. His servants had not heard him come home, so could not deny that he might have come straight home from the station. This was a negative alibi which left the theoretical possibility that Penfold might have behaved as, in fact, he did behave, but there was no single item of evidence in support. Innocent persons, in the orbit of a murder, often had no alibi.

Moreover motive, in Penfold's case, was apparently lacking. There was no known quarrel, nor conflict of interest. The Penfolds were financially comfortable. Mrs. Blagrove's income had been derived from an annuity. To Mrs. Penfold she had left a sum in cash, her furniture, and her house. But the house had been bought on mortgage and the whole estate would doubtfully yield fifteen hundred pounds.

After the inquest, the feeling of tension passed from Penfold. In so far as he thought clearly about his crime, he reasoned that the police would find evidence against him at once or not at all. For the rest, he had not planned to kill a fellow creature. He had been the unwitting instrument of fate, in whose hand he was soon able to detect a measure of poetic justice.

Madge's general demeanour caused him no unease, though she cut short his not infrequent attempts to express condolence. She spoke hardly at all. However, ten days after the murder—on the evening of the day when Scotland Yard abandoned further work in the locality—she shook off her lethargy.

"I shall not go into mourning for Aunt Agnes," she said, in the drawing-room after dinner. "It wouldn't express anything to me."

"As you please, dear." His voice was low and a little funereal. "I think people will understand—you have been so brave!"

"Oh no! But I have woken up! The shock did it—the shock of learning that some frightened lout who wasn't even a proper criminal had killed that dear, inoffensive woman. But the worst shock was finding that I myself—that I—instead of feeling grief-stricken, I felt as if a huge weight had been lifted off my shoulders.

"The feeling of relief didn't go away after a few minutes, as I thought it would. It stayed—it grew. For a few days I thought myself a low kind of beast with no proper human feelings. Then I began to understand. I had let Aunt Agnes down for years—and myself—by always being so terrifically grateful."

"But my dear!" protested Penfold. "That was a very charming trait in your character."

"It wasn't!" The blunt contradiction made him sure that she was still suffering from shock. She went on: "I let it turn me spiritually into a poor relation, incessantly grateful and ever so anxious to please. Something the vicar had said to me three or four years ago put me on the right track. I loved Aunt Agnes very deeply. I shall love her all my life and shall go on wishing she were alive so that I could tell her I wasn't fair to her nor to myself—nor to my husband!"

"But I have no complaint, Madge, except perhaps—"

"It started our marriage on the wrong foot. I'm ready to start again—I mean, from the beginning—if you are, Arthur. Are you?"

"My darling, how can you ask!"

No, she did not want to be kissed, just then. She was so clear on that point that he felt a little ruffled—it was so unlike her. Almost undutiful.

"We'll take each other on our merits," she said and smiled. "I start at zero—you start one up. I mean—I want to tell you that I was—*stirred*—when you bought that book for poor Aunt Agnes. You'll say it was a trifle. But it pointed in the right direction, Arthur dear."

She was talking, he thought, a little incoherently, letting her tongue run away with her. But she was overwrought, poor child, and he would let it pass without comment.

"I need a change after what's happened," she went on. "We'll have a second honeymoon, Arthur! I want us to shut up the house for a month and stay in a nice hotel in London. You can go to the office, if you have to, but in the evenings we'll have fun."

"Fun" sounded a little ominous, but this was no time to damp her spirits.

"A second honeymoon!" he echoed. "Just what we both need! I know of a quiet little place, one of the old City inns—"

"But I don't want a quiet little place! I want the Savoy or the Waldorf. I know it will cost a huge amount but—listen! I saw the solicitor the other day. He says it will be about eighteen months before probate is granted, but in the meantime his firm is lending me five hundred pounds—in a proper business way, of course. I want you to take two hundred of that. More, if it isn't enough."

He would not take her money because, in the morning, she would modify her plans and they would not go to the Savoy. But they did go to the Savoy and he did take her money, though he earmarked funds to give it back to her when her "mad mood" had passed.

Strangely, he caught something of the mad mood himself. They were both comparatively new to theatre going. And Madge discovered that, after the theatre, you could go to a cabaret. Indeed, there were remarkably few forms of entertainment in London which she failed to discover.

Most of the time he enjoyed himself, while in her company. She could be merry or quietly companionable—provocative sometimes, but never obedient. It was as if there had been some meaning in that high-falutin nonsense she had talked about herself—as if the death of Aunt Agnes had released a coiled spring in her nature. The "second honeymoon" joke was taking on a queer kind of reality. To him it was a revolutionary conception of the relationship of husband and wife. But the month, he reminded himself, would pass. And the coiled spring would have uncoiled itself.

When he was apart from her it seemed a very long month— and a not altogether respectable one, at that—she expected him to treat her as if he had never kissed her before. At the end of the office day, he missed his railway journey and found himself counting the days to be endured before he would slip back into the groove that had become second nature—his way of life, in the protection of which he had killed Mrs. Blagrove.

When the holiday was over they parted at the hotel, he for the office, she for their home. Sitting in the train that evening, he visualised Madge listening for his footstep on the gravel path, opening the door before he could reach it. It did not happen. He let himself in and stopped short in the hall—he smelt the new paint before his eye had taken it in.

The hall, the staircase, the dining-room, the drawing-room—new paint, new wallpaper! He wandered aghast from one room to another. The Landseers had gone from the walls of the dining-room! The Holman Hunt in the drawing-room had been replaced with a modern original! Some of the furniture had been re-upholstered, some banished, and there was a new carpet in the drawing-room.

When she came in twenty minutes later, he was still struggling with his anger.

"Well! D'you like it?" she asked eagerly. She was entreating his approval.

"My dear, I am too astonished to form any opinion. Did it not occur to you, Madge, to consult me before making sweeping alterations in my house?"

"Is it your house, Arthur—or *our* house? Of course I oughtn't to have done it on my own, but I had to take a risk! I had the feeling that everything in the house was practically as it had been when your parents married."

"It was indeed! But what was wrong with it?"

"We have to give ourselves every chance, Arthur—or we shall be slipping back into the old ways."

The last words rendered him speechless. Slipping back into the old ways was precisely what he desired. He could find no means of making her understand. They were in the dining-room. He strode to the sideboard. The tantalus was still there. He took out the whisky decanter—nearly dropped it when she spoke.

"Not whisky for me," said Madge. "Gin and orange, please."

That was another shock. Never before had she taken a drink in the home, except during a party, when she would make a glass of sherry last the whole time. He hesitated, then began to mix the gin. She had turned herself into a different kind of woman and intended to stay so. He was not angry now, only afraid.

"Let's drink to our future, Arthur."

"To our future!" And what sort of future? She no longer interpreted his wishes as her duties—she was compelling him to accept some give-and-take principle of her own. She expected her tastes to be consulted equally with his, and she demanded that he should woo her afresh for every caress.

With a sense of discovery he remembered how he had sat alone in the drawing-room that night, wondering whether she had "run round to Dalehurst with that wretched book." Until he had removed the doubt, there would be nothing for it but abject surrender.

"I'm afraid I've been a bit bearish over the decorations, darling. Sorry! Come and show me everything, and I'll tell you how much I like it all."

She was sweetness itself whenever he made an effort to please her—but the effort had to be successful! Not that she required to be pleased all the time—she was as ready to give as to take. It emerged, however, that the month of madness at the Savoy, shorn of its expensive indulgence, was to be the blueprint for their married life. A kind of marriage which he had never contemplated and did not want.

Most evenings, in the train, he would decide to put his foot down. But when he got out of the train—you could just see the gables of Dalehurst from the arrival platform—other considerations would arise. So he would say nothing when he found a cocktail party in progress at home—nor when Madge was absent, at someone else's party—nor when she said she was sorry but she could never understand stories about business deals.

In June, five months after the Savoy holiday, he contrived to meet Gershaw as if by chance, when the latter was leaving his office for lunch, and enticed him to a drink.

"Madge seems to have got over her bereavement, but the fact is she has had a partial lapse of memory." He brought in an anonymous psychiatrist. "Now, I do remember that she went out after dinner saying that she had a message for Mrs. Gershaw from the vicar and she must go in person, because your telephone was out of order. Can you possibly tell me, old man, how long she was with you?"

"*Phew!* That's a bit of a contract. My wife let her in—I was in the drawing-room, with the door open. I heard them chattering away in the hall and presently I butted in to ask your wife to have a drink, but she said she couldn't stay. I didn't notice the time. Call it three minutes—five, if you like. Best I can do! But I can tell you definitely she's wrong about our telephone. It was on the telephone that we heard that night about the—about Mrs. Blagrove."

That was nearly all that Penfold wanted to know.

"Was Madge carrying anything, Gershaw?"

"Don't think so—oh yes, a book, loosely wrapped in news-paper. The rain had softened the paper and I offered her a satchel. But she found she could get it into the pocket of her mack—I remember pulling the flap over it for her."

So she would have had time to go to Dalehurst and get away, with a margin of minutes, before Dr. Delmore came on the scene. Penfold felt a profound unease and wished he had not tackled Gershaw. After all, there was no proof that she had gone to Dalehurst. The book was not necessarily the Wilcox book. And she might have gone to someone else with another message from the vicar. He decided to let the whole matter drop and found that he could not. The riddle travelled home with him every evening and even intruded on the outward journey, so that his attention would wander from the morning paper.

As he could not shake it off, he tried to stare it out of countenance. Let it be granted that Madge did go to Dalehurst and did know that her aunt was dead before Dr. Delmore stopped her in the road and told her. What did it matter? Was it to be supposed that she went through the open French window and, in a very few minutes—never mind the shock!—saw something, not seen by the highly trained detectives, which told her that he had killed Aunt Agnes? Utterly absurd! Therefore he would put it out of mind.

He did put it out of mind for the better part of a fortnight's holiday in August, which they spent at Brighton. On the last day, the riddle raised its head and he promptly struck at it with a new argument. Would a woman of Madge's character—would anyone but a degraded gun-moll—live with a man whom she believed to have killed a woman who was virtually her mother? She would not! Therefore Madge had no secret weapon and he could be master in his own house.

The obsession was beginning to exist in its own right, as something separate from his desire to change Madge back into a docile and obedient wife. It had an integrity of its own, with no fear outside itself. He did not believe that, if she had proof, she would take it to the police. The terror lay in an imagined moment, in which she would say: "I know you killed Aunt Agnes." Being an imaginative terror, it was more consuming than a reasonable fear.

If she had known before Dr. Delmore had told her, why had she not raised the alarm herself? He could find a dozen contradictory answers. Sometimes in his sleep, and sometimes in a waking dream in the train coming home, he would play the part of Madge entering the room by the French window. "Auntie, I've brought you *The Best of Wilcox*." No, because she would have seen at once that her aunt was dead. In the shock of the discovery she would have forgotten all about the book, which was in the pocket of her mackintosh.

She would have brought the book home.

That night, when Madge had gone to bed, he began his search. In the house there were about a thousand books, some eight hundred of which had been bought by his parents. There were four sectional bookcases—an innovation of Madge's—dotted about the drawing-room. In the section devoted to poetry and novels there was no Wilcox anthology. It was not on the shelves in the morning-room. It had not fallen behind anything. He thought of Madge's mackintosh, which she very rarely wore, found it in the cupboard under the stairs, with the pockets empty.

He had to wait three days before he could be certain that Madge had an afternoon engagement. The strain of waiting preyed on his nerves. Then he came home by the earlier train and made a thorough search upstairs. Finally he was reduced to telling Madge that he had mislaid a technical book urgently needed and, with her able guidance, searched the whole house, without result.

Given that the book was not in his house, where was it? In a week, he was again reconstructing the scene in which Madge was deemed to have entered Dalehurst by the French window. As she walked up the gravelled path she took the book from her pocket. When she entered the room, she flung it from her. In which case it would have been stored with Mrs. Blagrove's furniture, pending probate.

He knew by experience that, for a fixed fee, the depository company would allow detailed examination of goods. On the following Monday, he went to the depository. He had equipped himself with a typewritten letter, purporting to have been signed by Margaret Penfold, which told of one or two rare editions among the comparatively valueless books forming part of the goods deposited. Would they please allow a prospective purchaser to examine? As prospective purchaser, Penfold necessarily adopted a name not his own.

The manager accepted the fee, assured him there would be no difficulty. But, unfortunately, as the goods were awaiting probate, he must obtain formal permission through the solicitor in the case. If it would be convenient to call at the same time on the following day—

Penfold said that it would be quite convenient, and escaped, thankful that he had given a false name.

The solicitor, who was ready to swear that there were no rare editions among Mrs. Blagrove's books, rang Mrs. Penfold during the afternoon to make sure. When Madge said she had never heard of any, he said that evidently some other property was concerned, that he was sorry she had been bothered and that he hoped she was well. It seemed so trivial an incident that Madge did not mention it.

On Saturday morning, as the Penfolds were finishing breakfast, the housemaid brought a card: *Detective Inspector Rason, New Scotland Yard.*

V

The telephone conversation with Margaret Penfold made it obvious to the solicitor that the introductory letter to the depository company was a forgery. He reported the facts to Scotland Yard. The report was passed to the Department of Dead Ends, to which the Blagrove case had drifted.

The impostor had concerned himself with books, so Rason searched the Blagrove dossier for mention of books. With some difficulty he found an unpromising note at the end of a list of gruesome details concerning the settee "...*under seat, misc. articles including newly purchased book: title, 'The Best of Wilcox.' Checked local bookseller (Penting's). Two copies sold, morning, one to Mrs. Manfried, one to Mrs. Penfold (See Penfold, Margaret: movements of).*"

While waiting at the depository for the impostor who did not turn up, Rason inspected the furniture and effects removed from Dalehurst, eventually finding the Wilcox anthology which had been taken from the folds of the settee. He replaced it without feeling any wiser for the effort he had imposed on the warehouseman.

The routine of the Department, constructed by Rason himself, had a certain simplicity. When any object was offered or mentioned, one first checked the object itself. Then one checked the object in relation to the suspects. There were no suspects in this case, unless one counted the Penfolds—so Rason counted them. From the depository, he borrowed the girl who had shown Penfold to the manager's office, and stood her near Penfold's office at lunchtime.

"That's him!" cried the girl, when Penfold came out.

"Don't be silly!" protested Rason. "It can't be. This is only routine."

The girl, however, was quite positive—which presented Rason with a teaser. The only way of squeezing in Penfold as a suspect was to assume he was lying when he said he was in his own drawing-room between five and six, the time of the murder. Nearly a year later he tries to work an elaborate deception on the depository people in order to be able to "inspect" some books, which couldn't have been there. How could all that help him to prove he didn't commit a murder, of which no one suspected him except Rason, who had to, owing to his routine?

Better ask Penfold.

"Renbald's Depository!" he exclaimed when civilities had been exchanged in Penfold's dining-room. Penfold looked ghastly, which was not what Rason wanted. "It's all right, Mr.

Penfold—it's only routine. We don't worry about the forged letter and the fake name. Told 'em you wanted to inspect some books. What did you really want? Tell me, and I can cross it off."

It was an unanswerable question. Penfold remembered the excuse he had used to induce Madge to search for the anthology.

"I did want to inspect the books, though I knew there were no first editions. The truth is, Inspector, I had lost a technical book of my own. I thought it might have got mixed up with Mrs. Blagrove's books—"

"But you could have got your wife to write you a real letter for that—and you could have used your own name?"

"I did ask her. She was unwilling, because she convinced herself that the book couldn't possibly be there."

It was such an unrehearsed, knock-kneed tale that Rason was inclined to believe it.

"Perhaps I can help you," he grinned. "I've inspected those books. Was it called *The Best of Wilcox?*"

"*No!*" The emphasis was not lost on Rason.

"*The Best of Wilcox*—" Rason was mouthing the words, "was found on the settee on which Mrs. Blagrove was killed!"—So Margaret *did* go to Dalehurst, thought Penfold.

"That does not concern me," he said. Playing for his own safety, he added: "The copy of that book which I bought never left this house, so far as I know."

"So *you* bought a copy of that book, Mr. Penfold?"

"I did. I intended to present it to Mrs. Blagrove on the following day, which was her birthday. Wilcox was her favourite author."

"Where did you buy it?"

"In London." He added: "At Waterloo station, before taking the train which arrives here at five three."

Rason felt he was getting somewhere. The note in the dossier said that the book had been bought by Margaret Penfold, from the local bookseller.

"If you've no objection, I'd like to see what Mrs. Penfold has to say about this."

"Certainly! She will tell you that—at around six o'clock that night—she handled the copy I had bought and talked about it—in this house. But I won't have her bullied and frightened."

Penfold did not leave the room. He rang for the housemaid, but it was Madge herself who answered the bell.

"My dear, I'm afraid we have to talk about your poor Aunt Agnes," began Penfold. "Mr. Rason has informed me that on the settee on which she was killed, there was a copy of *The Best of Wilcox*. I have—"

"Oh!" It was a quick little cry of dismay. "I think I can see what has happened. Arthur, I would like to speak to Mr. Rason alone. Please!"

She did go to Dalehurst—Penfold was certain, now. If she had also picked up a clue to his guilt he must try to cope with it before the detective could build it up.

"I am sorry, Madge, but I really feel I have the right to be present."

"Very well, Arthur!" There was a shrug in her voice. "Mr. Rason, on the morning of that day, I bought a copy of that book locally, at Penting's. I lunched with Mrs. Blagrove and gave her the book—not as a birthday present—we were jointly giving her a more elaborate present the next day.

"In the evening I reached home at six. My husband had come home earlier than usual. He showed me a copy of *The Best of Wilcox* which he had bought in London for Aunt—for Mrs. Blagrove." She paused before adding: "I was very greatly surprised—I have to say it!—I thought that my husband was not the sort of man who—who would ever think of doing a kindly little act like that. I did him an injustice, and was ashamed. I was above all anxious not to spoil the whole thing by telling him I had forestalled him. I intended to tell Mrs. Blagrove what had happened and ask her to help me in a harmless fraud. I took the book from my husband and, of course, I had to get rid of it, as Mrs. Blagrove would not want two copies. I had to go out that night to deliver a message to a neighbour, Mrs. Gershaw. I went on to a Mrs. Manfried, who was also a Wilcox fan, and offered her the book. But she had herself bought a copy that morning. The book was published that day and I suppose all the real fans bought it at once. On the way back, Dr. Delmore told me the news and I forgot the book. I found it in my mackintosh a few days later. I dropped the book in the croquet box, under the mallets. It may be there still. If it is, I'll show it to you."

"Don't bother on my account, Mrs. Penfold. I'm glad it's all cleared up," said Rason untruthfully. He had been quite hopeful when he thought he had cornered Penfold over the books. Journey from London for nothing!

"I wish my wife had told me at the time—it wouldn't have hurt my feelings," said Penfold when Madge was out of earshot. "Is it too early for a drink, Inspector?"

"Too early for me, thanks. I—"

Madge burst in.

"Here it is!" The newspaper on which the rain had fallen was crinkled and torn. "Just as I pulled it out of the mack!"

"Well, I can put it on record that I've seen it!" said Rason, as he unwrapped the newspaper. "Cupids, eh! Same as the one I saw at the depository. *The Best of Wilcox!*" With hardly a change of tone, he went on:

"Now let's get this book business straightened out. At lunchtime, Mrs. Penfold, you gave Mrs. Blagrove a copy of this book? So the copy you gave her would still be in her possession at five-three—when Mr. Penfold arrived at the station here? Around six, Mr. Penfold shows you this copy I've now got in my hand—and you take charge of it?"

"Correct!" cut in Penfold, and was echoed by Margaret.

"Somewhere between five-three and six—" Rason turned from Margaret to her husband "—you picked up the wrong copy, Penfold. Look here!"

He opened the book and pointed: *'To dear Aunt Agnes With love from Madge.'*

Grey's Ghost

Michael Innes

Michael Innes was, like several other contributors to this book, an individual who became well-known in another field only to be most widely remembered because of his detective fiction. Innes's real name was John Innes Mackintosh Stewart (1906–1994) and he was an eminent academic who wrote mainstream fiction under his own name. In his memoir *Myself and Michael Innes* he described how he began to dabble in detective fiction, which he had already had the benefit of discussing "with luminaries of the magnitude of Ronald Knox and…T. S. Eliot." As he said, "In one class of polite society writing detective stories had superseded writing ghost stories as an acceptable occupation." Rather like Cecil Day-Lewis and Douglas Cole, he began his first mystery "with the notion of its bringing in a little pocket-money."

Death at the President's Lodging aka *Seven Suspects* (1936) duly launched the police detective John Appleby on what proved to be a long and successful career. Innes wrote a good many short mystery stories featuring Appleby and turning on a single plot twist. Three collections of these little puzzles were published during his lifetime, including *Appleby Talks Again* (1956), from which this story is taken. A posthumous collection, *Appleby Talks about Crime*, appeared in 2010.

———

TEA HAD BEGUN WHILE A PALE SUNSHINE STILL SIFTED through the garden, and animation continued to be lent to the wintry scene by a group of children tirelessly tobogganing on the slopes beyond the village. But now, although the curtains had been drawn a full hour ago, our hostess's tea equipage continued to hold its ground, with the firelight playing agreeably upon its miscellaneous china and silver. The Bishop was the occasion of its lingering. His interest in the handsome Georgian pot was other than merely aesthetic, for he continued to claim cup after cup with a pertinacity that would have done credit to Dr. Johnson. And in the process—but this may have been only my fancy—his complexion changed slowly from ruddy to purple, as if he were concerned to achieve a tint answering harmoniously to the resplendent garments into which he would presently change for the purpose of transacting the serious business of the day.

Yet this business—both dinner itself and our leisured preparations for it—hovered still some time off, and it was possible to feel that a mildly empty interval confronted us. To disperse upon whatever occasions we might severally own—say to attend, as the phrase is, to our correspondence—would have been at so informal an hour, a course of things entirely natural. But in an unpretending country house, little frequented by the great, an ecclesiastical dignitary is a person of consequence; and it was our united sense that our hostess was not minded to a mere breaking apart and drifting away until the episcopal tea-cup had been definitely laid aside. And this was the exigency in which the young woman called Lady Appleby—the wife of an unobtrusive person who had been introduced to me as some kind of Assistant or Deputy Commissioner at Scotland Yard—produced her competition. She produced, that is to say, a weekly paper of the sixpenny species which she had evidently been turning over earlier in the day, together with the proposal that we should collectively endeavour to win the comfortable sum of three guineas.

Our hostess was enchanted—as it was her business to be. "Judith—what a wonderful idea! But is it a *good* competition? I hate the stodgy ones—composing sonnets and *villanelles*. Is it last words? I do adore making up last words for people. Bishop, have you ever tried?"

"Not, dear lady, precisely in the sense we are considering." The Bishop rose and moved implacably forward with his cup. "But I make no objection to the pastime—provided it is not massively exploited for purposes of edification, that is to say... Thank you—two lumps."

"There was such a good one only a few weeks ago. Attributed to King Charles the Second—or was it King Charles the First? That he must apologise for being such a long time in dying."

"Most felicitous." The Bishop offered this comment with gravity, and then turned to Lady Appleby. "But *is* it last words?"

"Not last words—just words. Three enigmatical remarks, accidentally overheard. Elucidations are not required."

There was a pause on this, and I was myself the first person who was prompted to speak. "I think I can supply one straight away. I was once called up on the telephone, rather late at night, by a man's voice announcing, in considerable agitation, that Queen Anne was dead. But he had got the wrong number, and rang off. I never knew what it was about."

I cannot claim that my little anecdote was a great success. Somebody at once pointed out that the truly enigmatical was lacking to it, since what I had accidentally received was plainly urgent intelligence from a kennel or a stable. Oddly enough, this had never occurred to me, and I have to confess that I was a little discomfited. The Bishop I think observed this, and charitably took up the ball.

"There are undoubtedly some snatches of talk which will recur to one teasingly for years. Some of you perhaps knew Charles Whitwell, who was reckoned a barrister of rare promise before his tragic death? We belonged to the same club, and on the occasion which I am recalling I happened to pass close to him in the dining-room when he was entertaining a guest—someone quite unknown to me. And I heard Whitwell utter just four words. I believe they might qualify very well for Lady Appleby's competition. They were these: 'Grey's ghost was black.'"

There was a moment's silence while we absorbed

this—and then our hostess reacted with characteristic dash. "But, my dear Bishop, how marvellously odd! Grey's ghost was black! Did you ever find out what it meant?"

"Never. I had it in mind, indeed, to ask Whitwell one day. I knew him quite well enough to do so. But then, of course, he was killed in the Alps. His guest I never saw again—nor could I very well have tackled him if I had. So there it is: Grey's ghost was black."

"I think it had something to do with heredity." Lady Appleby offered this odd opinion with every appearance of confidence. "Mendelian theory, and so on. Grey's parents had come from either side of the colour bar. And Grey himself was white. But Grey's *ghost* inclined to the other side of the family, and so was black."

"It *might* be heredity. But I think it was trade unions." As our hostess made this strange announcement she looked brightly and largely round. "Strikes, you know. That sort of thing."

"Strikes?" I said. "Trade unions? I don't follow that at all."

"If you are a worker and go against the other workers, aren't you declared black? I'm sure there's some such phrase. Well, as a ghost, Grey had done the wrong thing—worked too long hours, or something of that sort. And so he was black."

There was some laughter at this—I am bound to confess that I myself thought it uncommonly silly—and then the Bishop made a suggestion. "These are rather complicated notions. My own guess is much simpler. Poor Grey had either been strangled or burnt to a cinder. Or perhaps he had been involved in amateur theatricals—say as Othello—at the time of his sudden death. And so his ghost—"

This received general acclamation, in which the speaker's concluding words were drowned. A bishop, as I have said, is a person of consequence in a modest establishment such as I was visiting. And now there was an unexpected contribution to the whole absurd discussion. It came from the Scotland Yard man—Sir John Appleby.

"These are all good speculations. But none of them, as it happens, is correct. I knew Whitwell, and I happen to know, too, the circumstances he was talking about. As a matter of fact, the Bishop was misled by only *hearing* the remark."

This seemed to me nonsense. "By only hearing it? I don't see what difference—"

"He missed the presence—well, of another capital letter. Black ought to be given one, as well as Grey. Grey's ghost was *Black*."

It took me a moment to make any sense of this. "You mean," I presently asked, "that Whitwell was really saying something like 'Robinson's ghost was Smith'?"

Appleby nodded. "Just that."

"Then it appears to me to be quite meaningless."

Appleby smiled. "It depends on what you mean by a ghost."

It was plain that the man intended to tell us a story. From his wife's expression, I guessed that it would probably be of rather a tall order. Whether I was right in this, my readers must judge. I shall simply set down Appleby's words, as well as I can remember them.

"Ghosts—the sort with which, at least in the first instance, I am concerned—appear to be rather unfashionable. One can see why. The cinema and broadcasting and television have all tended to cut down people's reading time, and we no longer call for a prodigious literary output even from very popular writers. Ghost-writers, therefore, don't much flourish except in a few specialised fields. For instance, there is still a small class of persons who believe that their own social or public eminence makes it incumbent upon them to commemorate their activities and persuasions in a book, but who are a little vague about how actually to put the bally thing together. For these to hire some smart fellow with the trick of scribbling is an obvious and quite innocent resource; and there are certainly a few ghosts who are always available for that sort of thing.

"But Grey's ghost was different. He was much closer to the old-fashioned article, employed to amplify the output of a professional author. And yet—at least at the start—he wasn't quite simply that, either. He was called in, one might say, as a specialist. If Grey hadn't begun life as a painter, I doubt whether the notion of his ghost would ever have come to him. For it is the history of painting, of course, that is full of little specialists—dab hands at this or that—being called in to do their stuff in one or another appropriate corner of the canvas.

"I see that some of you have now taken a guess about Grey. And you are quite right. It is Hugo Grey that I am talking about—the powerful and sombre rural novelist who died a good many years ago. By that time, it is true, he had pretty well ceased to be either rural, sombre, or even particularly powerful. But to this I shall presently come.

"Grey's father, as you will no doubt recall, had been a Cumberland shepherd—as indeed all his ancestors had been since long before the poet Wordsworth took to celebrating the monolithic simplicity of that sort of person. Grey himself had monolithic simplicity, and his greatest characters and conceptions—to put it mildly—weren't exactly noted for their complexity. But decidedly his people were above life-size; his secret, as his great admirer Sir Edmund Gosse said, was to give epic proportions to the figures of a pastoral world. That—and perhaps their dark strain of primitive superstition—gave his books their striking individuality. What the younger critics have to say about Grey now I don't at all know. But in those days his rural folk were compared with Thomas Hardy's and George Eliot's. Learned persons earned grateful guineas by comparing his works with the *Dorfgeschichten* of Gottfried Keller. There was no doubt that Grey was going to be an immortal.

"It was doubtless the beautiful directness and simplicity of his mind that led him to hire Black. He read in the reviews, you see, that his peasants were superb, but that he couldn't do the gentry. Perhaps in that case he ought to have done without them. But Grey's plots were always thoroughly old-fashioned contrivances—it was one of the impressive facts about them that the rust positively flaked off his contraptions as the wheels went creaking round—and he always needed at least one gentleman, preferably a baronet, for such matters as seducing shepherds' daughters, foreclosing mortgages, destroying wills, and so on. And the reviewers would declare to a man that these patricians were intolerably wooden.

"Well now, when the patrons, say, of a seventeenth-century Dutch painter declared his cows to be so good that you could hardly restrain yourself from reaching for a milking-pail but his dogs to be such feeble inventions that nobody would think to heave a brick at them, the painter—as I've remarked—simply called in a good dog-man from round the corner. Grey called in Black.

"I doubt whether Walter Black's name will suggest much to any of you. He had begun life in some quite obscure and humble way on the stage. His personality appeared insignificant and perhaps rather effeminate, and it was said to be in an effort to mask this that he wore his large black beard. But Black could write, and he had a flair for polite life. He became a novelist—not perhaps very widely known, but greatly admired by a few for his polished, witty, sophisticated creation. His range was undoubtedly narrow, and it was notorious that his imagination never moved outside Mayfair. Yet there was no question of the purity of his small, carefully husbanded talent. He was always very hard up, and Hugo Grey was probably actuated by genuine benevolence as well as by his own large simple astuteness when he made the arrangement he did. It was not suggested that there was to be anything in the nature of collaboration in a substantial sense. Black was simply to do whatever aristocratic or highly cultivated characters the conduct of Grey's plots required from time to time.

"The arrangement worked very well. The baronets and so forth in Grey's novels became full of life—you might say of really authentic baronial devil and *savoir vivre*—and people who felt they were in the know remarked how wonderfully Grey was assimilating the ways of that higher sort of society to which his literary eminence had gained his admittance.

"Then something rather odd began to happen. I expect

several of you can recall it. The baronets took to spreading themselves over more and more of the picture, and carrying their own world—which was of course Walter Black's elected world—with them. For a time Grey's novels were panoramic representations of English society, the polite and rustic components being mingled about fifty-fifty. Readers were enthusiastic. Professors gave lectures explaining that the English novel had at last recovered the breadth and amplitude of its glorious past.

"In the next few years the balance swung further, and Grey's rural scenes, although still wonderfully realised, became a progressively minor feature of the books. This was a gradual process. But at last something quite sudden and definitive occurred. Grey published *Storied Urns*. It was in many ways a brilliant novel, and some people maintained that the portrait of the old marquis was the most striking thing the author had done. But almost equally notable was something about the few rustic personages who lurked in corners of the story. They were universally described as completely wooden."

Appleby paused on this, and somebody made the not very penetrating remark that it was a case of the wheel having come full circle. And the Bishop interrupted some stout work with his teaspoon to put a question. "It was simply that Grey had been growing increasingly lazy?"

Appleby nodded. "I think it was largely that. No doubt he had been paying Black at so much a line, and it was to Black's advantage to contribute as much as he was let. Grey found that books maintained their popularity with more and more of Black in them, and that his own profits were not seriously diminished by setting Black to do a heavier share of the work."

"Until Grey was really the dog-man himself?" Our hostess offered this with a great air of vivacious intelligence.

"Precisely. He just wrote in his rustics here and there. Eventually, of course, he grew reckless, and didn't bother himself even to do that. The Hugo Grey novels had become, in the old-fashioned sense, one hundred per cent ghost-writing."

"Surely," I asked, "that was extraordinarily immoral—and even positively fraudulent?"

Appleby shook his head. "That, I think, is where the Bishop's friend Whitwell came in. His opinion was sought—and sought by Black. Black had been a party to what, book by book, was without doubt increasingly a deception. But Black felt that he had been ill-used and that he ought to have some redress. The novels were now all his own, but he had to take for them pretty well what Grey chose to give."

This time it was Lady Appleby who broke in. "But couldn't Black simply have started again under his own name?"

"That course was open to him, no doubt. But his own name had dropped into oblivion by this time, and he may have felt that a fresh start was something too formidable to face. He appears not to have been a strong character. Whitwell gave it as his opinion, I imagine, that Black had with full awareness got himself into a mess, that the legal position was quite obscure, and that public reaction to any disclosure could decidedly not be to the advantage of either writer. Black was so disgusted that he shook the dust of England off his feet. That is to say, he collected what may have been his last few hundred pounds from the bank, and went off on one of those aimless cruises that were so fashionable at that time. And the next thing anybody heard about him was that he was dead."

We were all rather startled by this. The Bishop even checked himself in reaching for another lump of sugar. "I hope," he said, "that there was no question of—?"

"It was all quite obscure, and I don't think there was anybody—except conceivably Grey—who was interested. But, of course, we are by no means finished with Walter Black yet."

"Ah!" Our hostess was delighted. "You mean—?"

"Just what you may guess. This is a ghost story, you know—an orthodox Christmas ghost story. Only the ghost in it is just a little out of the ordinary." Appleby paused and looked at us gravely. "As being a *ghost's* ghost, you know."

From Lady Appleby, who was sitting beside me, I thought I heard a resigned sigh. But when she spoke it was briefly enough. "I'm afraid there is nothing for it but to hear John through."

"But, my dear, we are dying to!" Our hostess had every appearance of being enchanted still. And she nodded to Appleby, who resumed his tale.

"You will see that losing Black put the eminent Hugo Grey in rather an awkward position. If he was to continue publishing novels he must either find another ghost-writer or go right back to his own monolithic rural stuff. Very sensibly, he decided to retire. It is not a thing that elderly writers often do—commonly they just can't afford to—but those who manage it sometimes find that its result is greatly to enhance their reputation. They become, so to speak, honorary Grand

Old Men, and are generously praised by those with whom they have ceased to compete.

"This happened to Grey. He became almost at once a venerable leader of the profession of letters, and all sorts of honours were showered upon him. It was on one of those occasions that the trouble began.

"He was being given an honorary degree at one of the provincial universities—Nesfield, I think it was. Just what happened is a bit obscure, largely because there is a tradition up there that the students should create a certain amount of liveliness during the proceedings. But the main fact is clear enough. While one of the big-wigs involved was making old Grey a pompous speech, telling him what a large whack of our glorious cultural heritage he was, Grey gave a sudden nasty sort of howl and bolted from the hall.

"Well, even in a Grand Old Man that sort of thing takes a bit of living down, and it seems that thereafter the unfortunate novelist thought it wise to lie rather low. It is true that some months later he did attend an authors' international congress and make a speech. But halfway through he was unfortunately and unaccountably taken ill, and was obliged to spend a week or two in a nursing home. There was a bulletin, I seem to remember, saying that he required rest. People naturally said that the old boy was breaking up.

"And now I can tell you his own story—for the simple reason that it ended in a small abortive police investigation which came to my notice. What Grey conceived to have happened upon both the occasions I have mentioned was a horrid supernatural visitation. The phantasm of Black had appeared apparently from nowhere, advanced upon him through the assembled company in a threatening manner, and then disappeared. And Grey—like Macbeth confronted by the ghost of Banquo—had been unable to take it.

"That was bad enough—but there was a second phase to the haunting that was much worse. Black's ghost settled in with Grey at home. This was naturally unnerving, and its calamitous effect upon its victim was the greater upon several accounts. Grey, you remember, had that strong streak of primitive superstition in him. Moreover he had retired to his native fells, and was living in some isolation about a mile from the nearest village, alone except for two or three elderly female servants. And—yet again—the uncanny visitation took place during a particularly hard winter, while Grey was totally without visitors from week's end to week's end.

"At first the ghost's behaviour was rather colourless. It just came and went, without seeming to be aware of Grey, and without any suggestion of intent. Well, that is how ghosts *do* behave. I mean, of course, *real* ghosts as distinct from storybook ones. And Grey, who was quite well up in psychical research, became convinced that he was dealing with what the textbooks call a veridical phantasm of the dead. That, in a way, ought to have eased his mind, since there is abundant evidence that real ghosts are almost pathetically harmless. But it is plain that, in point of fact, the thing steadily wore him down. And then Black's ghost *did* begin attending to him, and *did* seem to be cherishing some design. Grey would wake up to find the phantom glaring at him over its great beard—and it would then raise an arm, point, and glide from the room. On one occasion he plucked up courage to get out of bed and follow it—only to have the embarrassment of finding himself tumbling into the arms of his cook. As he was dressed only in pyjamas, and as she was a comparatively new employee, this upset him very much. Apparently—quite without knowing it—he had taken to giving a bit of a yelp as soon as the apparition showed up, and on this occasion the woman had heard him and come to investigate.

"The climax came on Christmas Eve. Hitherto the ghost had only appeared to Grey when he was in his bedroom. He was quite unprepared, therefore, for the experience that befell him shortly after dinner. He commonly finished the day, it seems, in his study—a long, low, book-lined room on the ground floor. Although he had given up writing in any large way he still produced an occasional Grand Old Man's review, and for this purpose he kept a typewriter on a table at the far end of the room.

"He was surprised, as he entered, to hear the sound of this machine in operation. He was more surprised still when, by the light of a small lamp standing on the table, he saw nothing but an empty chair—and the typewriter at work under the plain impulsion of a supernatural agency. For there could be no doubt of it: the keys were flicking up and down, the carriage moving to and fro, and the little bell going *ping*, although there wasn't a soul in the room but himself.

"Grey had just grasped the full horror of this when the machine stopped, and at the same time he heard a low laugh behind him. He swung round—and there was Black's ghost practically at his elbow. The ghost pointed down the room towards the typewriter, paused for a moment, and then vanished behind a window curtain.

"It seems that Grey was almost hypnotised. He moved

dully down the room, took the paper from the machine, and read it. Of what he read, all I need give you is the heading. 'A full and free confession by me, Hugo Grey, of my evil profiting by the genius and labour of Walter Black.' There followed a detailed statement and a space for a signature. The phantasm, it appeared, had a thoroughly businesslike side.

"Grey felt his reason deserting him, and he dragged himself off to his bedroom with some notion of lying down and composing himself. I needn't tell you that the spectre was waiting for him. But this time there was a difference. Hitherto its appearances had been fleeting, and had always obeyed whatever normal optical conditions the actual lighting of the room might be expected to impose. This time it remained steadily in evidence, but in a fluctuating light which Grey felt to be quite unnatural. And now as he stared at the apparition something unprecedented happened. The form and features of the ferociously bearded Black melted, faded, and re-formed—re-formed themselves into the very figure and lineaments of Grey himself. He was confronting his own image—confronting a hideously ingenious commentary, one might say, upon his own ambiguous relationship to another man. Once more—does it not?—the wheel comes full circle. We began with the proposition that Grey's ghost was Black. And here, finally, Black's ghost is Grey."

Appleby paused on this—as well he might. The Bishop—and it was with an air of finality at last—put down his cup. "A pretty tableau, Sir John. But one seeming to require for its resolution a decided *coup de théâtre*."

"And that is precisely what turned up. You remember it was Christmas Eve? Well at this identical agonising moment there came a burst of singing from outside the house. It was a group of carol singers who had made their way with some pertinacity to Grey's remote dwelling. Theirs was the first incursion of an outer world there for weeks—and it broke a spell. Grey found himself reaching for the first object he could lay his hand on—I believe it was a hairbrush—and hurling it with all his might at that spine-chilling simulacrum of himself. There was a crash of glass and the image vanished. And at that Grey fainted away.

"He came to in the presence of his housekeeper and his cook—and plainly delirious. They sent for a doctor. And the housekeeper, who appears to have been a shrewd woman, sent also for the police. When they arrived they found the cook rather hastily packing her trunk. Or rather—need I say it?—*his* trunk."

"Black—the living Black!" Our hostess, having achieved this powerful feat of mind, delightedly clapped her hands.

"Precisely. Black's supposed death had been the beginning of an ingenious plot which he was peculiarly well-fitted to carry out. You will remember that beneath his great beard he was an effeminate little man, and his early training had made impersonation easy. Moreover that obscure theatrical start had, it seems, been as a magician, and the trick typewriter had been one of his most successful properties."

"But the business of the dissolving ghosts?" Our hostess was all acuteness.

"It required nothing more elaborate than a couple of

lamps, a dimmer controlling them, and the large mirror on Grey's own wardrobe."

"And so the truth came out?"

"Dear me, no. An *éclairissement* would still have been to the advantage of nobody, and so the whole odd business was hushed up. That is how I came into it myself. My opinion was asked about whether the local police might reasonably drop their inquiries."

"And poor Black remained entirely obscure?"

"Entirely." Appleby smiled blandly. "That is apparent from the fact that none of you has ever heard of him."

"But of course we have all heard of the eminent Grey." It was Lady Appleby who delivered herself of this—and I fancied she gave her husband rather a grim look. "We have all—at least tacitly—acknowledged our familiarity with his works. My own favourite, I confess, is *Storied Urns*. Bishop, what is your favourite Grey?"

There was a second's silence. It was brilliantly broken by our hostess. "My dears!" she cried—and once more clapped her hands. "My dears—just look at the clock!"

Dear Mr. Editor…

Christianna Brand

Christianna Brand (1907–1988) published her first novel, *Death in High Heels*, in 1941. Her third, *Green for Danger* (1944), is a superb wartime whodunit which was memorably filmed, while the impossible crime puzzle *Death of Jezebel* (1948) brought together her two principal investigators, Inspector Cockrill and Inspector Charlesworth. Although she belonged to a younger generation than the "Crime Queens" who were so prominent during the Golden Age, essentially she worked in the Golden Age tradition, specialising in tricky plots with a closed circle of suspects and multiple false solutions. After 1955, she turned away from crime fiction, but her final novel, the unusual and underestimated *The Rose in Darkness* (1979), brought Charlesworth back almost forty years after his first appearance.

Brand's ingenuity is evident in her polished short stories, including "Dear Mr. Editor…" It first appeared in 1958 under the title "Dear Mr. MacDonald" in an anthology edited on behalf of the Mystery Writers of America by John D. MacDonald, *The Lethal Sex*. To say much more might be a spoiler.

———

DEAR MR. EDITOR,

I'm so sorry but your letter asking me to write something for your proposed anthology, was delivered to the wrong address—as you'll see from the enclosed; and I've only just found out about it, too late to send you a story, I'm afraid. I thought, however, that you personally might be interested in this document (though I hope you won't blame yourself— you can see that the poor creature was quite mad). It is only a copy, of course. The original, which the dead woman was clutching, is in handwriting, very illegible and blotchy and what the trick. cycs. call "disturbed." The police have it now. This has been very much tidied up and made readable—as it stood it really was hardly sense.

Don't bother to return it.

Yours sincerely,
Christianna Brand

Enclosure:

DEAR MR. EDITOR,

I am writing this in the kitchen while I wait for the kettle to boil and also of course because of the gas in the sitting-room. And anyway, Helen's in the sitting-room and making dreadful noises, sort of snoring. She's lying all hunched up and queer and her face is scarlet. Last time she was as white as a fish but drowning's different: not that she *was* drowned because they interfered and got her out. Now I've got to kill her all over again, this time with the gas, because of the story.

This time it's because of you, writing and asking me to do a short story for this anthology of yours. I found the letter on the table in the hall this morning, half out of the envelope—I don't know what's become of the envelope. There was another bit of paper there too, I didn't notice what that was about, a small slip of green paper. Was it something to do with the story? The letter starts "Dear Girl" so it couldn't be for Helen, she's nearly forty although she's still quite pretty. (I see now that you say it's a sort of joke, starting the story "Dear Girl"—all the people writing in the book are to be women; so perhaps it was for Helen, but it's too late now.) Anyway, you say you want a nice creepy sort of story full of colour and horror and all the rest. I don't know why you should ask me to write a story or Helen either, if it was meant for Helen; unless of course you know about that other time, about the drowning? Naturally *I* immediately thought of the drowning, because that was creepy and horrible enough, Helen and me alone out there in the mist on the edge of the canal; and Helen's face when she saw the little gun in my hand. But on the other hand, I thought it might not do for the story because she was saved, so it wasn't a proper murder.

And then I thought suddenly: you can't be punished twice for the same crime—can you?

And I've already been punished once for killing Helen, I've done my sentence, I've been in prison, and I didn't even actually kill her. So I thought I might as well kill her again, for the story.

So after breakfast I got the little gun.

Helen was terribly frightened when she saw the little gun. In fact I think she was frightened before she saw it, just when she saw my face. She cried out: "Oh, darling, oh, Minna, no, no! Oh God, not again, it hasn't begun again!" It was like a kind of prayer. It was after that that she saw the gun. Then the fear changed; at first I think it was more for me, in some strange way; now it was for me, but for herself as well. But she was angry too. She said, "Where did you get that gun?"

I said, "I had it all the time."

She said, "You told me it had fallen into the canal. I didn't tell them about it because you said it was in the canal."

"I hid it," I said.

"You promised me," she said. "You swore to me. And all this time you've been deceiving me. I didn't tell the police, in case it should make things even worse for you; and all this time—"

"You might as well have," I said. "They punished me, they sent me to prison."

She went into the old spiel. "Oh, darling, it wasn't punishment, it wasn't prison, do try to believe, do try to understand! It was only to make you better. And it did make you better, didn't it, darling?"

It did make me better!—locked up in that place with all those criminals, that Mrs. Whosit who killed her baby, that woman who called herself Gloria Swanson, but *I* knew she wasn't Gloria Swanson, what would Gloria Swanson be doing in a place like that?—that girl that was always dreaming and moaning for "one little shot." Well, Helen was going to get one little shot now; but not the same kind of shot.

I told her this joke.

She started to be kind and sweet and try to wheedle me. She said she hadn't made things "even worse" for me that last time by telling about the gun. She'd trusted me. Now for me to trust her and give her the gun. "I'll give you the gun all right," I said. I couldn't help laughing. The jokes seemed to keep coming into my head. I went on and on laughing.

She didn't try to run away or anything. She just stood with her hands over her face. I think she was crying. She kept saying, "Oh, my poor Minna! My poor little Minna!"

"What's poor about *me*?" I said. "They can't punish me twice for killing you, can they? And they punished me last time and you hadn't even died. So I'll kill you now."

"If you kill me," she said, "who will you have left? Who will look after you?" And she pleaded: "Darling, if you kill me, they'll think you aren't better after all and they'll—they'll take you back, they'll have to, darling, do try to understand it—"

"They can't," I said. "Not twice."

"Oh, God!" she said. "Oh, God, help her to understand, make her understand…!" But she gave it up. She tried again, a different way. "Minna," she said, "if you kill me, who will look after you, darling?—who will there be to take care of you, to fight for you? There'll be nobody, they'll have to take you back to—to that place because there'll be nothing else for you." I think she really meant it, I don't think she was troubling about her own danger a bit: not then. It was all for me. She's always looked after me as though I were a child, even before Father died—our mother was never there, she was away somewhere in some hospital, nobody ever seemed to talk about her. I think Helen knew, but she wouldn't tell me. "Don't worry, darling, I'll look after you," she used to say. Why? Why should I need looking after? It used to make me angry, it still does when I think of it, it's one of the things that makes me want to kill her sometimes. Once she got angry herself and blurted out that just to look after me she'd given up marrying Jimmy Hanson, she'd condemned herself for ever to… She broke off then and said she was sorry. I should think so! So did I give up marrying, one great love after another I gave up, I could have been rich and courted beyond the dreams of ordinary woman, the King of Roumania was at my feet in those days, and other men, other kings, wonderful, splendid men…

I think I sort of dropped off to sleep for a moment then. When I woke up I went in and looked at her again. She's still lying there. Her breathing's quieter. She must be nearly dead.

In the end of course, I didn't shoot her. She kept pleading with me not to. I felt more kind to her. After all, it's hard to die just so that someone can write a story; though I keep explaining to her that you've asked me to write one, you've sent me this letter—and I simply don't *know* any other story; and it seems such a good plot, how if you've been punished for killing a person you can't be punished again so you may as well kill them anyway. So I said, "Well, how would you rather die?" because after all it didn't matter to me, no clues to hide, nothing—I wouldn't care who knew I'd done it. I said, "I could make you walk along the canal again and push you in like the last time." She said, "Yes—yes, you could do that," but too eagerly. I realised she knew that we'd meet hundreds of people, they'd see me with the gun pointed at her, forcing her to go there. (Last time of course she had no suspicions till we got there: we were just going for a walk.) "A knife?" I said. "Or I could make you drink some poison?"

This time she tried not to seem so eager. "Poison can be painful," she said.

"I don't want you to suffer," I said. "I don't even *want* you to die. It's only for my story."

She looked at me, very sadly. I suppose she was sad at having to die just for the story. She said, still not as though she were eager about it: "Couldn't we make up a story together?"

"Of course not," I said. "It has to be my story. The man says so, he says he wants an original story..."

She gave that one up. She went back to the poisons. She said, still not eagerly, more as though she were a bit doubtful: "Of course *all* poisons aren't painful." Then she suddenly said: "There's some rat poison in the kitchen. They say that that one doesn't make the rats suffer."

"I don't remember it," I said.

"I don't think you knew about it," she said. "It's on the shelf. In a little tin, a white powder."

I made her pass in front of me, keeping apart from her so that she couldn't jump at me and get the gun away (but I would have shot her if she had. She knew that.) She went to the shelf and sure enough there was a little tin. On the way back I picked up a glass of water. I made her empty the powder into the water, all of it. She stood there with the empty tin in her hand and I stood and faced her, holding the gun. I heard the church clock strike; it was half past eleven in the morning, three hours since I'd read your letter beginning "Dear Girl." "This is your last moment, Helen," I said. I felt quite sad but I knew I had to do it. "Now drink the poison," I said.

She took up the brimming glass with her left hand. She was trembling and the poison slopped over the side. "Use your right hand," I said. "You're trying to spill it."

She had to do it. She had to put down the little tin. I saw then *Bicarbonate of Soda* on the label.

It made me terribly angry. I do sometimes lose my temper. I don't think I ever lost it worse than then. I don't remember it very well, I went a sort of blank like I did just now when I was writing about the King of Roumania and all my lovers; but I know that I screamed and raged at her and afterwards I had to rub my hands to get the torn hair away from my fingers and there was some blood on my nails; and I remember that her face was absolutely white, as white as when they got her up out of the water that other time, and streaked with my nail marks; I remember her being backed up in a corner, one arm over her face, and she was sort of gibbering, shaking all over, and gibbering like a monkey, making frantic little dabs at me with the other arm, trying to fend me off. She kept praying, "Oh, God, no more, no more! Oh, God help me, God pity me, oh God don't let me die like this, not like this...!" All for herself now! Not for me any more, not a word about what will become of my poor little Minna and all the rest of it... When at last I left her, I was shaking too and I went and sat in a chair, only still pointing the gun, and she was still crouched in the corner with her white, streaked face and her eyes half closed, taking great sobbing, gasping breaths. We stayed like that for a long time, even when she had grown quiet. I have only twice seen Helen afraid—really afraid, for herself alone.

Once was in the split moment between my pushing her and her falling into the water; and the other was now. I think she gave up then. I think she saw at last that the time had come and she really was going to die.

At last I said: "I'm sorry. I think I lost my temper. You shouldn't try to trick me. Now, Helen, this time you really have got to die. I have to write the story."

She said in a sick voice: "Minna, I've decided. Will you do it by gas?"

"No more tricks," I said.

She said wearily: "No. I can't struggle any more." And she said it again, "I can't struggle any more." She said, "I'll lie down here and you can turn on the gas and I'll put my face close to it. You can keep the gun pointed at me." And she said again in that weary, desolate, hopeless kind of voice, "I'm not fighting you, Minna. I give up. If I die—I'd rather die. God knows what will happen to you, but I couldn't go through—that—again. I'm finished. And the gas will be merciful." She added: "To you as well as to me."

"What do you mean?" I said, sharply again.

"Oh, I don't mean that," she said. "You'll be safe enough from the gas if you keep well away from it, in a room of this size. I only meant that if you shoot me—it could be so ghastly. For me; but for you too."

"You'd be dead," I said.

"I might not be dead. You couldn't come close because you'd be afraid of my getting the gun away; and supposing you missed killing me, suppose I was just wounded, horribly, dreadfully, in—in the face or something..." She closed her eyes against the thought of it as though she felt sick. After all, she was talking about her own death and it was coming soon. I suppose she thought death by gas was a beautiful, peaceful affair. Well, it isn't. That awful breathing, and that scarlet face...

So she lay down and I told her to turn on the gas tap and she did; and she put her mouth close to the leak and just lay there, drinking it in. But after a moment she sat up. She shook her head as though she were already a little bit muzzy. She said: "Minna, I had better write a message."

"Another trick?" I said.

"It will hardly help *me*," she said bitterly. "It's for your sake. Give me a piece of paper and a pencil and let me write a message."

"How do I know what you would write?"

"I thought you'd say that," she said. "Well, write it yourself and then just give it to me and I'll hold it in my hand. If you die holding a thing, you hold it tight. They'll find the message there, when they find me dead."

So to please her I wrote the message on a scrap of paper and gave it to her to hold and she lay down again, quite quietly and I went back myself and sat near the window, leaving it open just a crack, and kept the gun pointed at her. I won't describe it, I don't like horrors, but anyway it didn't take long. Soon she was unconscious. I went over to her and rolled back her eyelids—I didn't want her fooling me, nudging off the gas or something, the moment my back was turned; and just to make sure I pulled back her sleeve and dragged my nails down her arm. But she never moved, she just lay there heaving with those awful snoring breaths. She was out all right. She didn't look pretty now. She looked horrible. And the smell of gas was getting very strong so I closed the window and the door and came into the kitchen. I don't know how long they take to die.

Before I left her, of course, I took away the bit of paper with the message. It wasn't going to do any good, she simply couldn't see that I don't need "saving," I can't be punished a second time. But it was kind of her; and typical of her, poor Helen—she was always trying to "protect" me.

"I am taking my own life," she'd made me write. She was going to lie there with it in her hand.

It's here on the kitchen table in front of me: a scrap of green paper with the message written on it.

I see now that it's the bit of paper that was lying on the hall table when the letter came.

It says on the other side…

It's nothing to do with your story after all. It says…

It's some sort of a "Warning Notice." It says…

It says that at noon today "for some hours"—*our gas will be cut off at the main.*

And now that I think of it—that kettle's never boiled.

She knew! Helen knew! It was just another trick. All this time I've been writing here, she's been lying there—with the gas turned off. All this time—to recover from those first few inhalations before it failed…

Can she even have been shamming after all? When I bent down over her, when I felt so sure she was unconscious, that she was going to die…?

When I took away…

When I took away from her this note: this note that says, "I am taking my own life."

This note—in *my* handwriting.

Someone is stirring in the next room.

The gun! The little gun! I have left the little gun in that room—with Helen...

P.S. I hope I didn't unintentionally mislead you? I did say it was the dead woman who was clutching this letter.

C.B.

Murder in Advance

Marjorie Bremner

Marjorie Bremner (1916–1993) is by some distance the most obscure writer to feature in this anthology. She only published two crime novels, *Murder Most Familiar* (1953) and *Murder Amid Proofs* (1955), the latter being set in a magazine office. Information about her is not easy to come by, but she was born in Chicago and, according to the invaluable Golden Age of Detection Wiki, studied psychology and social sciences at the University of Chicago and Columbia University. In 1946, she moved to London to work on a doctorate in political science. She became a researcher for the Hansard Society and also lectured and worked as a journalist and reviewer.

She became a member of the Crime Writers' Association in its early days, and contributed "Murder in Advance" to *Choice of Weapons*, a CWA anthology edited by Michael Gilbert and published in 1958. At around the same time, she became the third wife of David Graham Hutton, an economist and author who shared her interest in politics, and after this she seems to have published very little. Her husband predeceased her and she was still living in London at the time of her own death.

———

"Now who," said Dacre, who was an inspector of Scotland Yard, "would want to murder a playwright?"

He was a dark, lean young man. At the moment, he was relaxing comfortably in the study of his good friend, Dr. Allerton, a benign, grey-haired man in his sixties, with whom he often discussed his cases—Allerton had, long ago and briefly, been a police doctor. The study had panelled walls, and was bright with firelight. The two men were at ease, sipping whisky-and-soda. Violent death seemed a world away.

Allerton grinned. "*I* would. Plenty of playwrights. When I think of some of the evenings I've spent watching plays in which the charwomen turn out to be symbols of Mother Earth and in which—"

"They wouldn't have been by Lewis Maynard. He was a damned good playwright. Everyone liked him—public *and* critics."

"Have you anything to go on at all?"

"Almost nothing. Maynard was alone in his house in Chelsea all evening. The doctor says death took place any time between six and eight o'clock at night. He was shot at close range through the back of the head, while he was bending over the liquor cabinet—presumably to get out a bottle and some glasses. No useful fingerprints."

"No clues at all?"

"Two cigarettes in an ashtray. One was tipped—Maynard's; he only smoked tipped cigarettes. The other was a standard brand."

"If there was no lipstick on it, you know it wasn't a woman."

"Unless it was a woman who didn't wear lipstick."

Allerton smiled. "A perfect crime, then?"

"So far, at any rate. At this stage, I don't even know where to begin. I can't see who would *want* to kill Maynard."

"His rivals."

Dacre snorted. "Playwrights don't go around murdering their more successful rivals. Wouldn't do them any good. You haven't got a better chance of having your play put on just because there's one less writer in the world."

"A jealous woman. Someone due to inherit money from him. His producer. Someone whom he'd injured. A stray burglar who lost his head."

Dacre sighed. "Maynard was a very nice fellow. He's been very happily married to the same woman for fifteen years—she was in Switzerland with her parents when he was killed. His money—with the exception of a few charitable bequests—all goes to his wife and son. The same man's produced his plays for years, they're very good friends, and besides, the producer was at a party surrounded by a dozen people when the murder took place. There's no evidence Maynard ever injured anyone—his life's an open book, no secret years in South America or anything like that. Finally— the killer knew him. There were no signs of a forced entry, so Maynard must have opened the door himself. And he'd hardly invite a burglar to smoke a cigarette and have a drink."

"Then the solution's obvious."

"What?"

"He wasn't murdered."

Dacre smiled reluctantly. "It isn't funny, though. Maynard was an important chap, in his way. Very popular. If we don't learn who killed him, the police are going to have a rough time. And all you can do is to make wisecracks."

"Well, you've produced the portrait of a man no one would have murdered. What else can I say? No, I've got another suggestion: he wasn't murdered for anything he'd done, he was murdered for something he was going to do."

"If that's all you—" Dacre stopped suddenly. The two men looked at each other. Then Allerton said, "You see—even wisecracks may have their uses."

"They may," agreed Dacre, thoughtfully. "It's possible."

A week later, Dacre told the story to Allerton.

"Your remark was the key," said Dacre. "D'you remember saying Maynard might have been murdered *not* for something he'd done but for something he was *going* to do? Well, there's one thing a playwright's always going to do—and that's to write another play. So I went to see Mrs. Maynard again..."

"Well, yes," said Mrs. Maynard, who was a very attractive woman in her late thirties. "Lewis *was* working on a new play—or at least, starting to think about one. But the first I heard of it was at a dinner party, the night before I went to Switzerland..."

It had been a very pleasant dinner, given by a couple called Rowle—Donald Rowle was in the Foreign Office, and they had just returned from several years abroad. The dining-room of the house in Westminster was spacious and high-ceilinged. Silver and crystal glasses shone against the dark, brightly polished table. In the background, a large looking-glass reflected the white shirtfronts of the men, and the gayer colours worn by the women. Conversation had been light and easy. And then Lewis Maynard had begun to talk about Henry Waterman: Waterman, the rising young M.P., who had suddenly and without explanation thrown up his seat in the Commons, and a year later died in an airplane crash, along with his sister, brother-in-law, and a dozen others. "It'll make a good play," said Maynard.

Edward Linhope, a dark, aquiline-featured man who edited one of the most influential morning newspapers, said, "But you haven't *got* a play, Maynard. All you've got is a short story—unless, of course, you're going to do a philosophic discussion of the death of ambition."

Maynard laughed. "No," he said. "No. But no one's ever solved the problem of *why* Waterman left public life. *That's* the play."

"But no one ever knew why." That was John Sherwood, a member of the Cabinet, a man—like Linhope—in his middle forties, with a quiet face and a gentle voice. "Of course, *you* were a very close friend of his. Perhaps he gave you some idea?"

The question sounded innocent enough. But something changed in the easy, pleasant atmosphere for a moment. Some hint of anxiety entered the air, and clung there.

Maynard did not answer the question directly. He said, "Well, I'm not a playwright for nothing. You're right, I was a close friend of his, and—like everyone else—I was puzzled. And I can use my imagination—in fact, if you come to think of it, it's a situation that might stimulate *any* writer's imagination."

"And how does your imagination solve it, Mr. Maynard?" It was the hostess, diverted by the turn of the conversation, who spoke.

"Oh, various ways. But I suppose the best assumption— for a play, let's say—is that Waterman gave up his seat because he was blackmailed."

"*Blackmailed!*" Several voices spoke at once.

"Yes. I don't mean money, you understand. But—say someone disliked Waterman. For the sake of argument, assume it was a political rival. The rival knows something Waterman wants kept quiet. He says, you get out of public life and I'll *keep* it quiet—otherwise, I shan't. Waterman does. End of story."

There was a brief pause—a pause long enough for the earlier tension to deepen into something like menace. But Roger Adams, the highly efficient head of a nationalised industry, said lightly, "Not only the end of the story, the end of the play after Act One."

Maynard smiled. "You're being severe. I've got at least one and *a half* acts."

Sherwood had objected. "But I *knew* Waterman. He didn't seem the sort of chap—what *could* he have done that needed to be kept quiet?"

"Oh, anything. Perhaps he resigned to save someone else, not himself. Someone he was fond of. A woman."

Linhope, the editor, said, "Well, I'll see your play,

Maynard—I always do. But I'm damned if I can see how you'll end it."

"Easy." Maynard's good-looking face was alight with amusement and intelligence. "This chap—X—blackmails Waterman out of public life. Then the woman he's been protecting dies."

"Well," said the hostess, thoughtfully, "I suppose the woman he was protecting could be his sister. She was killed in that air crash with him, of course—but in a play, you needn't stick to reality, need you? If that were so and she died—he'd be free to speak up."

"It's one possibility," said Maynard. "Suppose Waterman—or whatever I call him in my play—had kept some proof of the blackmail. As long as his sister was alive, his hands were tied. Once she was dead, it was another story. *That'd* make a play, you know—revenge, and how it works out. But to tell you the truth, I haven't got that far yet. I haven't decided yet how it ends."

Dacre broke off his narrative. "Of course," he said to Allerton, "you can see what sticks out a mile."

"That Maynard knew the truth about Waterman—and was threatening someone at that dinner party. Yes. He certainly dropped enough hints, didn't he? 'Maybe he was protecting a woman.' 'Revenge, and how it works out.' 'I haven't decided yet how it ends.'"

"Yes—he'd as good as told the whole story: that Waterman was blackmailed out of public life, that he allowed himself to be driven to protect his sister, that he'd told Maynard the whole story. Maynard would *never* have talked that freely about a play he was just beginning to write, if he hadn't had a reason. His wife said she was surprised. She'd never known him do anything like that before."

"It's a very public way to do it, though. Why not threaten the chap in private?"

"I don't know. My *guess* is that he was trying to make the chap squirm a bit. Waterman had been his friend, after all. I think Maynard was getting Waterman's revenge for him—and this was a part of it. He may have been wanting poetic justice. I mean, by writing a play about the episode, so it would be possible for everyone to guess *who* the blackmailer had been, Maynard may have been meaning to drive *him* out of public life, just as Waterman himself had been driven earlier."

"Very dramatic. But I suppose you ought to expect drama from a playwright. What did you do then?"

"Well, first of all, I narrowed down my list. There'd been six couples at that dinner. I thought I could eliminate the women—none of them was in public life. And I could eliminate, besides Maynard himself, two of the men: the host, who'd been abroad when all this had happened, and another chap, who was a visiting Canadian." He paused. "That left Adams, Linhope, and Sherwood."

Allerton whistled. "The head of a nationalised industry, an influential editor, and a Cabinet Minister! What a trio of suspects!"

"Yes, indeed. I couldn't afford a mistake, of course—not with people like that. I was morally certain it *was* one of them, it *had* to be. But I still didn't know how to move. I was still trying to think of a way, when Mrs. Maynard rang me up and asked me to come and see her…"

"I'm sorry to bother you," said Mrs. Maynard to Dacre, "since it's probably all for nothing. But you said I was to tell you if anything at all out of the way struck me—"

"Of course. What is it?"

"This." She held out a copy of an evening newspaper, and Dacre took it. He said, glancing at the date, "But this is from the day your husband was killed."

"Yes. I was just sorting out some papers in that rack—" she nodded toward a wicker rack in the corner of the room— "and I found it."

"But what makes you think it might be important?"

"Just that my husband never bought an evening paper in his life."

Dacre felt a rising excitement. It wasn't much of a clue, but it was the first tangible one he'd had. He said, "You have a maid?"

"A daily woman. She comes at nine-thirty and leaves at two-thirty. *She* never reads *anything*. But I asked her, to make sure. She said she didn't buy it. She remembered finding it in the study the day after Lewis was—was killed. She put it in the rack."

Dacre mentally damned the unusual tidiness of the maid. When first examining the room, he had asked her if everything had been left untouched and been told it had. Putting a newspaper in a rack apparently did not count as touching anything.

He said, cautiously, "Well, of course, it could have been left by a casual caller."

Mrs. Maynard shook her head. "No. Lewis never had casual callers. He couldn't bear to be interrupted when he was working. He sometimes made appointments ahead to see people. But he'd never stop his work to see a casual caller."

"I see."

"I don't suppose it'll be of much help," said Mrs. Maynard, diffidently. "They must sell a million of those a day. But I thought—"

"You were quite right. And it may turn out to be useful, after all. One can never tell about these things."

"I certainly *hope* it is. Have you made any progress yet?"

"I'm not sure," said Dacre. "I've been thinking about that dinner party though—there may be a line there."

"You mean about Henry Waterman?"

"Yes. You knew him fairly well, didn't you?"

"Fairly. Lewis knew him much better, of course—they were very good friends."

"D'you think there *could* have been anything in that idea— that he was protecting his sister, I mean?"

Mrs. Maynard hesitated. "I'm not sure. There *may* have been. Lewis never said anything to me directly, you understand. But he did say one or two things some time ago, and I've come to think they *might* have referred to Arabella—that was the sister's name, you know."

"What sort of thing?"

"Oh, nothing very definite. But I got the idea she might have had an affair with an American during the war."

Dacre considered it. "But would that have been so very damaging, even if it *had* come out? After all, plenty of people—"

Mrs. Maynard smiled faintly. "Plenty of people weren't married to Arabella's husband. He was a terrible prig. He'd have left her on the spot, if he'd even heard a *rumour* of anything like that. And she was very unstable. She'd probably have gone off her head. She might even have killed herself."

"She was *that* unstable?"

"I think so. There's a streak in that family, you know."

"I didn't know it was that serious," said Dacre. "And I still—Well, I should have thought, even if you're right, that to sacrifice your career for something like that would be carrying brotherly devotion rather far."

"Yes—except that it wasn't an ordinary relationship. Arabella and Henry had been brought up by distant relatives whom they loathed. As a result, they were *very* close. He'd have done anything for her."

"I see. He still sounds rather a quixotic type to me."

"Oh, he was. It was one of the most charming things about him. I think that's why everyone liked him so much."

"Someone didn't," said Dacre, grimly. "Not if your conjecture's right, I mean. You never met anyone who disliked him?"

"No." Mrs. Maynard paused. She said, "You know, Henry was a very lucky man. He was handsome, charming, well-liked, well-connected. Someone who hadn't had that kind of luck—who'd had a harder time of it—might have resented him: particularly a rival."

"Put that way," said Dacre, slowly, "I can see that someone might. Well, thank you very much, Mrs. Maynard. You've been very helpful—and I don't just mean finding this newspaper for me. I'll let you know what happens."

"I didn't expect much from that newspaper," Dacre told Allerton. "But I took it back to the office and went over it inch by inch. There were fingerprints, of course, but they were much too blurred to be of any use. However, I found something else."

"What?"

"Someone—whoever had had the paper—had marked several stories in it. He'd used green ink—and a regular *manuscript* pen. You know, those pens they sell nowaday for script writing."

"I know," said Allerton. "People who want to write the beautiful hand of their ancestors, as it says in advertisements. Myself, I'm satisfied with an ordinary scrawl."

"No one except a chemist expects to be able to read a doctor's writing," said Dacre, with a grin.

"True. What kind of stories had been marked—and how?"

"An item in a gossip column about the nationalised industry. A story on the rising cost of living. And an account of some Oxford—Cambridge athletic event. All the stories had a ring around them. And on two of them, there was a mark like this."

He took a pencil and paper from his pocket, made a mark like this ↗, and handed the paper to Allerton.

Allerton studied it a minute. Then he said, "But that means—"

"Not necessarily. I know what *you* mean. But there's more to it than that. It depended, in part, on how those three men had spent their lives. I knew what they were doing now, of course. But I had to know everything they *had* done. *Who's Who* wasn't good enough, for my purpose. No one puts in *Who's Who* that he spent three months in a pickle-bottling factory when he was nineteen. But you can pick up habits from such experiences that'll last a lifetime. Look at people who've had a year in the Navy—they go around for years carrying packages in their left hand, to keep the right free for saluting, long after it's not necessary."

"So you had to talk to the men themselves?"

"Yes. It wasn't too easy to arrange, but I did. First of all, I went to see Sherwood, in his office in Whitehall. He was very gracious—said the Commissioner had told him it was important and that it had something to do with Lewis Maynard..."

The office was quiet, large, and somewhat austere. Sherwood's desk was neat and tidy, the "In" and "Out" trays almost empty of papers. Sherwood himself sat behind the desk, quiet, poised, and authoritative. He was young for Cabinet rank.

Dacre said, "Yes, it's about Lewis Maynard. More specifically, it's about that dinner party when he talked about Henry Waterman. I suppose you remember that?"

"Of course I do. It was the last time I saw Maynard. But d'you mean to say you think that had something to do with his death?"

"I honestly don't know at this stage, sir. Did Maynard say anything special about Waterman?"

"Special? I don't think so. Of course, as you'll have heard, he advanced the theory that Waterman had been blackmailed out of public life—to protect some woman, I believe he said."

"His sister?"

"Yes, someone suggested it might have been."

Dacre took out a cigarette and offered one to Sherwood, who took one and lighted both his and Dacre's. Dacre noted that the Minister was left-handed. He said, his eyes on his glowing cigarette-end, "What did you think of the theory, sir?"

"Frankly, not much. Maynard was a very imaginative type. He could have made a good *play* out of it. But as to the chances of its being true—of Waterman actually having allowed himself to be blackmailed in that fashion—I wouldn't give you much for them!"

"I don't suppose *you* had any idea why Waterman acted as he did, sir?"

Sherwood paused. Then he said, "Well, between the two of us, Inspector, *all* the Watermans have been very unstable. D'you know that portrait of his grandfather in the National Portrait Gallery—fair, tall, fine-featured, highly strung? Henry was just like that—even looked like that. Arabella was worse, I may add, though that's by the way. I think what Henry did was just an example of that instability coming out. I wouldn't have been surprised to hear he regretted it later—resigning his seat on some odd impulse or other, I mean."

"I see," said Dacre. "That's very interesting, sir. Perhaps you wouldn't mind also telling me what you thought of Maynard?"

"Not at all. I liked him. Nice chap. Very intelligent. Lively. Unconventional thinker. But he'd never have done as a Civil Servant."

Both men smiled. Dacre said, "I'd rather be a playwright than a Civil Servant, myself."

"Would you? *I* wouldn't. I hate paper work and any kind of writing. Even make my wife do all the family letters. The Americans have the right idea there—type, dictate, use a dictaphone, get a secretary—but get out of writing some way."

Dacre glanced at the empty "In" and "Out" trays, and the clear desk. "You seem to do fairly well in that line yourself."

"Not too badly."

Dacre returned to the subject of Waterman. "D'you think he'd have had much of a future—Waterman, I mean? A political future?"

"If he could have learned to master that instability, I think so. We were all in the House together at that time, you know—he, Linhope, Adams, and I. No reason why he shouldn't have done as well as any of us."

Linhope's office was very different: the office of a newspaper editor. There were papers all over the large desk and in untidy piles on the shelves. There were also three telephones, which rang intermittently while Dacre and Linhope were talking.

Linhope was very different from Sherwood—taller, thinner, and giving an impression of dynamic energy. But he, too, had the authority of the man to whom success has come relatively young in life. He agreed willingly to let Dacre look through the newspaper's files for stories about Waterman and Maynard, and added with a smile that there should be plenty about both men. Dacre, offering a cigarette and noting that the editor was right-handed, led him to speak of Maynard's theory that Waterman had been blackmailed out of public life. "D'you think it's possible, sir?"

"I don't know," said Linhope, slowly. "I don't have to tell you that there's much more blackmail going on than most people realise. Of course, those being blackmailed *ought* to go to the police. Again, I don't have to tell *you* that they very often don't."

"You're quite right. Then you think Maynard *may* have been on to something?"

"That's hard to say. It's a very big thing—to let yourself be blackmailed out of your career. *I* should have thought he had more guts: that he was more of a fighter. But of course, I could be wrong."

"Perhaps he was, if it only concerned himself. But if he was protecting someone else—"

"Oh, yes. It's *possible*. But I don't see why anyone would have *wanted* Waterman out of public life."

"Someone might just have loathed him—or sensed in him a rival."

Linhope looked sceptical. "I never met anyone who loathed him, or even disliked him. He was a nice chap. As to rivals—we all have 'em. But we don't go around blackmailing them out of their careers."

"No. Well, it was only *Maynard's* theory, of course. Still—at that dinner party, did anyone seem to take it seriously?"

"I don't *think* so. But let me understand the theory. Waterman was blackmailed out of public life, Maynard knew about it—"

"And was going to make it clear in his play who it had been, and so finish the blackmailer's public career. A matter of private justice."

Linhope shook his head. "Well, Inspector, *you* know your business. *I* don't. I'm a newspaperman—a mere hack writer. I always have been, even when I was in the House. But—well, frankly, to me it sounds fantastic."

"Frankly," said Dacre, "it does to me, too. But fantastic things *do* happen, particularly in murder cases. Incidentally, since you knew Waterman, did you know anything about his plans—before he resigned?"

"Plans?"

"Yes. I mean, did he want to stay in politics and possibly get in the Cabinet? Or would he have left it, as *you* did when you became editor, or as that other chap did when he went into the aircraft industry?"

"Oh, I see. Well, I think his main interest was politics. But he was interested in education, too—he might have wanted to head one of these so-called Red-brick Universities, that sort of thing."

"Really? I'd not heard that before."

"Oh, we used to talk about it a bit in the bar. I think he mentioned it once or twice."

"I see. Pity, isn't it? We haven't got so many good men we can afford to lose them."

"A great pity."

Adams was a stocky, rugged man, who had been a Rowing Blue and a Boxing half-Blue. His manner was easy and friendly, when Dacre explained the purpose of his call. He refused Dacre's proffered cigarette, saying he had never smoked in his life, pushed forward a large glass ashtray, and invited the inspector to ask whatever he liked.

"Well, I'm interested in your impressions of that dinner party at the Rowles, sir. You remember—they talked about Henry Waterman."

"Of course I remember," said Adams. "But you mean—are you suggesting that had something to do with *Maynard's* death?"

"I don't know, but I think it's possible. Anyway, it interests me. Can you tell me what was said at the time?"

"Certainly. It was Maynard himself who began to talk about Henry Waterman—"

"Did you know him well, sir?"

"Waterman? Fairly, yes. We were at school together—in the same form. He always beat me, though. Nice chap. He'd have gone a long way."

"In politics?"

Adams seemed surprised. "I imagine so. Why not? That's what he was interested in!"

"Was he at all interested in the nationalised industries?"

"You mean, would he have liked a job like mine? Yes, he might have. He'd have done well at it, too."

Dacre drew on his cigarette. "I see. But I'm sorry, sir, I interrupted you. You were telling me about that conversation—"

"Yes. But there wasn't anything much to it." He proceeded to give Dacre a succinct and accurate account of the entire conversation. When he had finished, Dacre said, admiringly, "You've got a remarkable memory, sir."

Adams smiled. "Only for the spoken word. Not for anything else. I can repeat a conversation almost *verbatim*. But my memory for print isn't very good."

"If you've got an ear for *words*, you ought to write plays—like Maynard."

"No." Adams laughed. "No imagination. I might have liked journalism, though. I even thought of taking it up, once—when I was at school. But then I went to the University, and more or less forgot about it."

Dacre nodded. "Sherwood and Linhope weren't at school with you and Waterman by any chance, were they?"

Adams shook his head. "No. I think Sherwood went to Harrow. Linhope—I don't know, I don't think he went to a public school."

"D'you think that sort of thing still matters?" asked Dacre, curiously. "The school one went to, I mean?"

"Oh, it helps." Adams smiled. "I have an idea it always will—in this country, anyway. Reformers tell us it's a mistake, and they may be right. But there it is."

"So," said Dacre to Allerton, "I knew who'd killed Maynard. They'd as good as told me—the three of them."

"I know." Allerton spoke soberly. "Very clever of you—all without a really direct question. It's—I find it staggering. But you hadn't actual proof, you know."

"No. Just the outline of a personality. A man who was envious of Waterman; a right-handed man; a man who smoked—"

"What did you do?"

"Well, I'd already learned that that newspaper had been sold between five-thirty and six o'clock, near Victoria Station. And I'd shown a photograph to a few people. Then I went to pay a call. It was a bit unorthodox. But we didn't want an open scandal, and it seemed the only way. Officially, of course, the Commissioner had no idea…"

Dacre went to see the man who had killed Maynard, the man who in his mind he had called X. He was pleasantly received, and given a drink and a cigarette. Dacre, though he was convinced of the man's guilt and appalled at what he had been willing to do, found himself sad at the waste of such ability and personality. But patiently and painstakingly, he outlined the way he had been thinking about Maynard's death; and equally patiently, his host listened.

"You see," said Dacre, "I was almost certain from the start that Maynard was murdered as a consequence of what he had said at that dinner party. He had been openly threatening someone to reveal—in a play—what had happened to Waterman, and who had done it."

"Very interesting."

"As you no doubt remember, there were six men present—of whom I could eliminate three: Maynard himself, the host, and the visiting Canadian. That narrowed down my suspects to three."

"Three," said his host, politely, "is rather a lot of suspects."

"Except," said Dacre, "that I had two clues. Whoever had done it had left a cigarette stub—there were two, Maynard's and another; and had also left a newspaper which he'd marked in green ink with a manuscript pen."

"You sound like Sherlock Holmes," said the voice. It sounded amused.

"Do I? Anyway, *that's* what solved the case. One of the three suspects didn't smoke. The other was left-handed."

"I follow you about the smoking," said the courteous voice. "But the reference to the left hand baffles me."

"Well, you see, the marks had been made with a manuscript pen. Now, as you know, they make special manuscript pens for use with the *left* hand. Anyone who cared enough about his handwriting to buy a manuscript pen would certainly have bought a left-handed one—*if he'd been left-handed.*"

"All very speculative and inconclusive," said X, lightly.

"Perhaps. There was more, though. Of the three, only *one* had *real* reason to envy Waterman—or thought he had. Only *one* claimed not to know him well, but seemed to know rather a lot about him."

"Really?"

"Really. Finally, only *one* had the kind of experience that would lead him to mark a paper in a *certain way.*"

"You're being very mysterious." The voice was mocking. "*What* way?"

Dacre ignored this. "So I took along a photograph of you," he said. "I showed it to various people who worked at or near Victoria Station. That's where you bought that evening paper, you remember."

"In fact, I *don't* remember."

"It doesn't matter. I found a newspaper seller who *thinks* he remembers you. Says he *thinks* you bought a paper from him once, and it could have been the day of the murder."

X laughed. "As a trained policeman, are you suggesting that's *evidence*?"

"Not by itself, perhaps," said Dacre, steadily. "But I also found a porter who *thinks* he remembers you crossing Victoria Station that night. And a neighbour who *thinks* he saw you on the street where Maynard lived."

"*Really*, Inspector—"

"You were at a conference near Victoria that day," added Dacre. "You could easily have bought the paper there."

"Altogether," said X, with another laugh, "you haven't enough straw to make even a *very small* brick."

"I'm not so sure," said Dacre, evenly. "I might—with a bit more evidence—get an indictment. But even if I didn't—"

He paused. After a moment, the voice said, a bit edgily, "Well?"

"Well, there's nothing to prevent one of Maynard's friends doing what *he* was going to do, is there? Writing the play *Maynard* was going to write? *I* can give him the plot. It'd be clear enough to finish you in public life, even if I couldn't get you indicted for murder."

"You may have noticed," said the voice, still edgily, "that not every play that's written gets produced."

"This one would. Mrs. Maynard would *pay* to get it put on, if she had to. Maynard's friends would see it got talked about and written about in the papers. Waterman's friends would help—he had a lot of them, you know."

There was a silence. Then the voice said, "You're a very determined man, Inspector. You might even be called a bit unscrupulous. I suppose you realise this is a form of blackmail?"

"Certainly I do. But *you* won't complain to anyone about *that*, will you? And it seemed to me the best way out— considering everything, I mean."

When the voice spoke again, it had lost its edge, and sounded weary and resigned. "Yes. I see. You're not only a determined man, Inspector, you're a very clever one, too. I see I must think this over. Incidentally, since you can't *prove* anything and we're alone—*what* did I put on that paper?"

Dacre took out a pen and a piece of paper, made a mark on it, and handed it over. The other man glanced at it. Then he smiled. "A delete sign," he said. "A sign that there's an extra letter or word that shouldn't be there. Of course. I do it automatically. Trained to it. I told you I never was anything but a newspaperman."

Edward Linhope was killed later that same evening, when his car crashed over a cliff not far from Dover.

A Question of Character

Victor Canning

Victor Canning (1911–1986), born in Plymouth, left school
in his teens and soon turned to writing fiction, beginning
with short stories and publishing his first novel in 1934.
After serving in the army during the war (training in the
Royal Artillery alongside the distinguished thriller writer
Eric Ambler), he concentrated increasingly on crime fiction
of various kinds. *The Golden Salamander* (1949) was filmed
with Trevor Howard in the lead, while *Venetian Bird* (1950)
was also turned into a movie, this time starring Richard Todd,
as well as being reinvented in the 1970s as an episode for
the American TV series *Mannix*. Canning's vivid style of
writing continued to attract film and television interest; *The
Limbo Line* (1963) was adapted for the big screen, while
Alfred Hitchcock's final film, *Family Plot*, was a much-changed
version of Canning's thriller *The Rainbird Pattern* (1972), a
novel with an extremely chilling finale. As well as spy and

thriller novels, Canning wrote a series featuring private eye Rex Carver.

Canning's short stories tend, by comparison, to be overlooked, but the posthumous collection *The Minerva Club* is an enjoyable set of mysteries in the classic vein. "A Question of Character" appeared in *Suspense* magazine in the UK in July 1960.

——

THE REAL REASON WHY GEOFFREY GILROY DECIDED TO murder his wife was not just that he wished to marry another woman with whom he had fallen in love. No, that may be the kind of motive which forces a man to the point of thinking about murder. But to take him over the edge into action it needs more than that. Plenty of men would like to murder their wives—and the other way round, I suppose. But that's so far as it gets. No, the thing which determined Gilroy was his vanity.

The thing happened at a cocktail party when he was introduced to a woman who said brightly, "Oh, yes, you must be Martha Gilroy's husband. I do think her books are marvellous, don't you? Tell me, what is it like having a novelist for a wife?"

He didn't tell her, he just saw red, gulped his martini, and got out of the room as fast as he could. He walked all the way back to Sloane Street with his mind in a murderous fog. Martha Gilroy's husband. The bestselling novelist. He'd married Martha ten years before, when she had been a private secretary to an industrial consultant. Not a good secretary, either. Married her when already he was Geoffrey Gilroy, bestselling writer of thrillers and detective novels. Although he still turned out his one book a year, was still a good seller, her name had eclipsed his. He was just Martha Gilroy's husband. He went up to their flat and fixed himself a large whisky. Martha was out, and to ease his feelings he picked up a copy of her latest book—*The Hydra-Headed Answer*—and slammed it against the far wall.

He sat down with the whisky decanter and the siphon close to hand and forced himself to consider the situation.

Ten years. He'd married Martha when she was twenty; a quiet, dark-haired, pleasant girl with little personality. She was good about the flat, she was in love with him and she was dominated by him. At first she typed his manuscripts. She took an interest in his work, which he encouraged. As a writer he knew his own weaknesses. There was no one who could touch him at devising plots, no one who could so deftly twist the sequence of actions to achieve devastating surprise…but he was bad at characters. Fundamentally, he wasn't interested in what made people do things. He was only interested in what they did, and how they did it.

Thinking it over now, he couldn't remember how Martha had gradually come to take a bigger part in his work. But they had soon reached a point when it was normal practice for him to discuss his plots and characters with her while he was in the process of planning a book. And she came up with good ideas. Made suggestions that brought his people to life. He was grateful to her, but he didn't show it too much.

And then, without telling him, she had written a book of her own. He knew nothing of it until the proof copies arrived at the flat. *The Broken Link* by Martha Gilroy. He thought the title was poor, uncompelling, and he thought she might have used her maiden name and not traded on his, but he said nothing and was even a little sorry for her when the book faded to a quiet death two weeks after its publication. But her second book went away with a bang. The serial rights were sold in America and England. Hollywood bought the film rights for 20,000 dollars and within a month it had sold 80,000 copies. It had taken him ten years to reach that figure with his own books. Her third book had been an explosion!

He helped himself to more whisky. He was going to murder her. There was no doubt of that. In a way it was ironical because he could see that he himself had created her, watched her first steps in all those things in which she had eventually outshone him…things which he had suffered in silence because, whatever else he might be, he was not ill-mannered. He'd taught her to play bridge and now she could leave him standing. Whatever she tried to do it seemed she could do with an effortless ease. They had a little cottage in Kent and, as a bachelor, he had enjoyed working in the garden, been in fact quite a competent gardener and knowledgeable about rock plants and roses. When he first took her there as his wife, Martha hadn't known a viburnum from a lilac. Within a year she knew more about gardening than he did, and was taking prizes at the local flower show… What a woman, what a damnable woman. He tossed his whisky back and glowered at her book lying by the skirting.

He'd almost reached the murder point over golf. There was a golf course not far from the cottage and at the weekends he played around with a men's four, happily slicing and shanking to a handicap of eighteen. Martha had taken lessons from the pro and within two years could beat him level. He gave up golf.

And now, while his sales were slipping, her damned *Hydra-Headed Answer* was everywhere, and he was being referred to as Martha Gilroy's husband. And he was in love with another woman, Evelyn Marks. Martha knew about that, though they had only once discussed it. She wouldn't divorce him because she loved him still and felt that eventually he would come back to her. They went on living together, but not as man and wife, and she was content to wait for him, confident that he would come back. That had been two years ago.

He got up and went into his bedroom and began to pack a bag. Well, this was the end. He was going to get rid of Martha Gilroy. But it had to be thought out. No mistakes.

He left a note for her to say that he was going down to Kent to work out the plot of his next murder mystery. So he was.

The drive, going easily, took about an hour and a half. On the way he calmed down, but his resolution to get rid of Martha was unshaken. For once he was planning a murder—not for the benefit of his sales and his readers—but for himself. And it had to be good. It had to be foolproof. One thing was certain, Evelyn must know nothing about it. She lived in Kent, about twenty miles from the cottage.

For the next two days he kept to the cottage, thinking about Martha, thinking... He went over in his mind all her habits, all her mannerisms, all the customary movements she had when she was at the cottage—for he had decided that the murder must take place here. Here, where she kept her golf clubs, where he had dealt her her first hand of bridge, and where she had first started gardening. It took him three days to get it all worked out. And when it was worked out he examined his plan and tried to fault it. He couldn't.

He would have liked to have put the plan into operation at once. But Martha was busy finishing a book and wouldn't be at the cottage for a month yet. In July, though, there was the village Flower Show and always they came down to the cottage a week before and stayed over for the Show. Meanwhile, he arranged to give a lecture in Watford on the day they would be coming down to the cottage. That made it easy. Martha would come down on her own in the afternoon. He would send a telegram saying he had been delayed in town after the lecture and would be down the next morning. By midnight Martha would be dead.

He stayed on at the cottage for another two days and most of that time he spent in the cellar. The cellar was full of junk furniture, a great pile of winter logs, packing-cases and straw bottle covers from the little store of whisky which he kept there. The whisky would have to be sacrificed.

On one wall of the cellar was a forty-eight hour clock. It hung about five feet from the ground and had two heavy lead weights on chains that regulated the pendulum. The weights and the pendulum swung free of the clock. Over the two days he carefully checked the movements of the weights to determine how long ahead he would have to start the clock in order for the falling weight to reach a height of two feet from the ground. When he had determined this, he substituted for the weight a plastic bottle which had contained hand lotion and which he filled with petrol. He had a little trouble adjusting the amount of petrol in the bottle to the exact weight. There was an electric point in the cellar into which they occasionally plugged an electric fire to dry out the place. He put the fire, which had two unguarded bars, under the weighted bottle.

It would take, he discovered, fourteen hours for the weight to fall from its top position to be within a couple of inches of the electric fire bars when the fire was raised on a packing-case. Once the plastic bottle was within an inch or so of the fire it would melt and the petrol would cascade on to the elements. He didn't leave this to chance. He carried out the full experiment with petrol, standing by with a bucket of water. The bottle didn't melt and release the petrol, he discovered, until it was actually touching the two elements. And it took him a few anxious moments to get the flames under control. The electric fire was ruined. He threw it away going back to London. There was another fire in the house he could use. He also bought another bottle of hand lotion and emptied it.

All he would have to do was to set the clock going at ten o'clock on the morning of the day Martha was due at the cottage. She never went down to the cellar. But he would lock it to make sure. At midnight the fire would start. And she would sleep through the conflagration. He would make sure of that. The burning cottage would collapse on top of the cellar and there would be no trace found of clock or electric fire. Ten o'clock. That would give him time to motor easily to Watford for his afternoon lecture.

On his way back to London he called on Evelyn and had coffee with her. At least with Evelyn he knew there would be no recurrence of the trouble he'd had with Martha. She was the widow of a naval officer, a tall, slim blonde with very little brain. But gay and good company. Already they had spent holidays together and not once, refreshingly, had he ever seen her reading a book. *Vogue* and *The Tatler* were her only literary interests.

Living with Martha from then on was not easy. The best course he found was to spend as little time as possible with her. He used his club more than he had done and, whenever he felt that they might be alone in the evenings, he invited people in; and he kept counting the days to July and the week before the Flower Show. In the meantime he saw his doctor and complained of insomnia. He grumbled that the first prescription did nothing for him and got the doctor to write a stronger one. But for three weeks he took none of the sleeping tablets.

When the day came, there was no hitch. He left the flat at half-past eight, telling Martha that he was going to spend the morning at the London Library. He drove down to the cottage, which stood on the edge of a wood out of sight of other houses. He parked his car on the far side of the wood and walked through it to the back of the cottage. He went up into the bathroom and took down a bottle of health salts from the cabinet. Martha was a neat, orderly person. Her bathroom at the flat was duplicated here to save her carrying unnecessary things to and fro. Every night before going to bed she took a glass of health salts. He crushed up his sleeping tablets into a fine powder and tipped this into the bottle, mixing it slightly with the surface layer of salts. In the effervescence Martha would notice nothing. He had no fears that she would not take her dose. He had never known her miss a night.

At five minutes to ten he was in the cellar and set the

clock going with the petrol-filled bottle as its master weight. He fixed up the electric fire on its packing-case at the foot of the wall below the bottle and piled around it straw bottle cases and junk that would burn easily. The cottage itself was mostly wood and had a reed thatch. It would go up like a torch. He switched on the fire, watched the lazy swing of the pendulum for a moment or two, and then went out, locking the cellar door. Martha Gilroy's husband...the husband who had taught her what a split infinitive was, taught her the difference between a primula and a polyanthus, taught her her first bridge convention, taught her... He went out and tucked the door key under the white stone by the rockery.

He was in Watford by one and had a drink and some sandwiches in a pub. At half-past two he gave his lecture. At six o'clock he was back in London and went straight to his club. He had dinner and then went to a theatre with a club friend. After this, he sent a telegram which, since the cottage wasn't on the telephone, he knew wouldn't be delivered until the morning post, explaining that he was staying in London the night and coming down in the morning.

At eleven o'clock he went back to the flat for the night—and got the surprise of his life.

Martha was in bed with the light on, reading.

Gilroy stood in the doorway staring at her in amazement.

"What the devil are you doing here?"

She put her book down slowly and looked at him.

"Why aren't you at the cottage?" she asked.

"I had dinner at the club and felt too damned tired to make the drive. I sent a telegram to you there. Why aren't you there?"

Martha lit a cigarette slowly before she replied. She looked tired and when she answered there was a spiritlessness in her voice.

"Because I'm never going there again, Geoffrey. Never. And tomorrow I'm moving out of here. You can have your divorce."

"What is this?"

For a moment she managed a smile. "You don't understand? No, perhaps not. But then you were never very good at character, were you? For years I've thought that this thing between you and Evelyn wouldn't last. That you'd come back. I've clung to that. But I was wrong. In this last month I've seen it so plainly. You've gone right away from me. So far that you can never come back. I can't fight the inevitable. So I give up. You're free."

Gilroy stood there, saying nothing. In his imagination he could see the pendulum swinging and the lead weight now so far down the wall. Damn the woman, why couldn't she have come out with this before? Even when she did something for him she had to spoil it. He was fond of the cottage and now it would burn to no purpose.

"Aren't you going to say anything?" she asked.

"What can I say? Thank you?"

"I suppose not..." She picked up her book and went on, "It's a pity you haven't gone down to the cottage. I made a big gesture for you... You might almost call it my last love gift."

"What do you mean it's a pity I didn't go down?"

"I took the liberty of sending a telegram to Evelyn. I signed it as though from you, saying that I'd agreed to give you a divorce and asking her to come over to the cottage to stay. If I know her, she'll be sitting up in bed waiting for you."

For a moment Gilroy stared at her, his face a mask of anguish.

"No! It can't be!" he cried.

"But it is. She's waiting for you—probably asleep. Geoffrey, what—"

But Gilroy wasn't there. He had turned and rushed from the bedroom.

He didn't take the lift. It was quicker to go down the steps at this time of night. His car was parked in the street outside. He was in it and driving hard south towards the river within half a minute. It was gone eleven. The petrol bomb would go off at twelve, maybe a few minutes before. And God! Oh God! Evelyn, he remembered, sometimes took health salts. They were slimming and she always fussed about her figure.

An hour and a half driving normally. An hour, at this time of night, if he stepped on it and wasn't held up. He had an hour of hell ahead of him. Evelyn would be there, he knew that. This was what she had always wanted. His divorce. She had stayed at the cottage with him before. Knew all about the key under the stone. He dare not telephone the fire brigade. There was nothing he could do that would save Evelyn and keep him safe except get there before the worst could happen.

As he came round the corner of the wood road, he saw the flames, licking up on the outside of one wall towards the thatch roof. He roared by two or three men who were running up the road and he stopped and leaped from the car. He sprinted up to the door and flung it open. A great wall of flame and smoke surged outwards, sweeping across the hall. He put his hands over his face and ran through it to the stairs.

On the cellar side they were alight. He went up feeling the terrible heat biting at his hands and face. For a moment The there was fresh air at the top of the stairs. He sobbed with the relief of being able to breathe, and then flung open the door of the bedroom. The whole window side of the room was blazing with flames and he could see them spurting and twisting across the room towards the bed. Already some of the hangings on the fourposter were showing little tongues of flame. The framework of the window was burnt away and the glass gone. The draught drove in, fanning the flames.

She was lying half uncovered, her arms and shoulders bare, her blonde head pillowed on one hand.

"Evelyn!"

He ran to her and shook her. Her head fell back and he heard her breath, thick and drugged. He wrapped the bed cover about her head and shoulders, gathered it round her, and lifted her. The window and its wall was a great sweep of flame and the air was full of the sound of wood and thatch as it crackled and spat. Through the open door a great roll of smoke and flame barred his way. He lowered his head and rushed towards the window, shouting, screaming. As he reached it he raised her and saw for a moment the flame-lit figures of men below. He leaned forward and flung her from him, saw her falling ...and then he staggered back as the flames beat into his face and eyes. He collapsed to the floor and as he fell the ceiling above him came down in a great spread of roaring, grinding fire, bringing to an end the last work of Geoffrey Gilroy.

The Book of Honour

John Creasey

John Creasey (1908–1973) was a natural storyteller whose determination to become a published novelist was such that he overcame hundreds of rejections before achieving his goal. Once he'd seen his work in print, there was no stopping him, and he became one of Britain's most prolific published novelists. Not only is it easy to lose count of how many books he wrote, it is also hard to keep track of the many pen-names he used. Creasey was not a sophisticated prose stylist, but his industry and inventiveness ensured that his books sold by the million. Several were filmed, and there were TV versions of his series featuring the policeman George Gideon and also John Mannering, alias "The Baron."

Even if he had not been such a successful author, Creasey would deserve the gratitude of his fellow writers for the efforts he made to establish the Crime Writers' Association, of which he became the first chairman. There was a *John*

Creasey Mystery Magazine and a series of *John Creasey Mystery Bedside Books*, which evolved into a long series of Crime Writers' Association anthologies. "The Book of Honour" first appeared in the sixth *Mystery Bedside Book* in 1965.

———

THERE CAN BE NO GREATER TRAGEDY THAN FOR A MAN to be hated by his son. For a good father it carries a daily hurt, thrusting deeper each day. So it was with Baburao Munshi, my oldest friend in Bombay. I say friend, but we were closer than that or I would not be able to tell this story of how his son Krishna hated him, and how they fought each other. It was not a physical struggle; I have never heard of a Hindu laying a hand upon his own father. It was a war of attrition.

When I first saw Baburao, I thought he was a beggar. I hadn't been in Bombay long enough to tell the difference between the simply poor and the destitute; between the man who works and the man whose work is begging.

I was twenty-three at the time, and had come from England to assist an ageing Irishman who represented several large English publishing houses. I loved books and wanted to trade in them...

One January morning a softening haze spread over the unrippled water of the harbour, so that the white sails of small yachts and the dark sails of native boats and Arab dhows were etched against the serene blue of sky and sea. I walked from my hotel near Apollo Bunder. Across the road, the Gateway of India stood dark and massive.

Most of the beggars, the itinerant chiropodist with his

little black case, the sellers of foreign stamps and crude post-cards, knew and did not accost me. Two tiny boys, black hair long and matted, faces filthy, bodies clothed in rags, each thrust a hand in front of me, rubbed a thin stomach, and chanted: "Me no eat, me no eat, me no eat." I dropped a paisa on to each palm, and they beamed and bobbed and hurried off.

As I walked to the sea wall to watch the shapes emerging from the haze, I saw a Hindu about my own age, a few yards away. He was very slim, with rather sharp features, and had the familiar, drawn look of hunger. His jacket had once been black but was now green and shiny, with holes at the elbows and one shoulder. His dhoti was tied round his waist and pulled up between his legs, looking like a pair of loose-fitting pantaloons. It was snowy white, like the twist of his turban.

He moved towards me, carrying a few picture-postcards. Obviously he was too diffident to have much success importuning tourists. He held the postcards out and spoke in better English than most. "Sahib want postcards?" he asked.

I didn't, really. They were cheap pictures of the Gateway, Bombay Castle, the Rajabai Tower, the Hanging Gardens. He didn't speak again, but his eyes talked eloquently; fine, clear brown eyes, at once proud and appealing in that hungry face. I thrust my hand into my pocket, and the first note I pulled out was a five-rupee.

I gave it to him. He hesitated, almost embarrassed. "I cannot change, sahib."

"Never mind the change," I said, and took half a dozen of the postcards. "Thanks. Good luck!"

When I hurried away, I wondered whether I had been a fool, whether he would pester me every morning. I found myself expecting him next day, but he wasn't there.

———

He did not reappear for several weeks but, when he did, I recognised him on the instant; a remarkable fact, since every day I saw thousands of men dressed like him.

The Irishman I was working for had gone home on leave, and I had been extremely busy. The staff was well-trained, Hindus and Anglo-Indians who worked conscientiously, and I was planning a long trip, north to Delhi and across to Calcutta, to meet customers whom I hadn't yet seen.

On the day before I left, I saw Baburao—my postcard seller—again. He was selling newspapers at a corner of Phirozeshah Meta Road, near the little hole-in-the-wall shops which offered everything from a needle-and-thread to a tiger-skin. I bought a paper. Obviously he recognised me, but neither of us spoke.

A month later, I came back from a long, wearisome, dusty, harassing trip by train with enough orders in my pocket to make it worth while. Baburao was at the same corner, dressed exactly the same; but he had added to his stock. As well as newspapers there were a dozen or so thin paper books.

Books always loosen my tongue. "Hallo," I said. "Going into the book trade?"

"That is so, sahib."

"When you run out of stock, come and see what I have," I said, and told him where my office was.

He gave a little, secret smile. "I know well where it is, sahib. Thank you."

About a month after this, I was sitting in my office with the door open and the fans whirring; the April heat was as oppressive as a blast from a brick kiln, for the rains hadn't yet broken.

I looked up and saw Baburao. He looked hot and damp, but as always, his clothes were clean, if old. And the hungry look was gone. There was something else different, too—he looked as if he were lit up by a flame that sprang from great joy.

"Good morning, Baburao," I greeted, "how are you?"

"Today is a great day, Mr. Graham, for my first-born is a boy."

"I'm delighted," I said. "May it be the first of many."

"It will be," said Baburao confidently. "There will be many mouths to fill, and so I must increase my business. That is another reason why I am here. I wish to sell more books. I think that I could sell some of these." His gaze roamed round my shelves. "I would like to try, sir."

He was implying that he could not afford to buy stock and wanted credit, but would never ask for it.

I said: "Look around, select what you want, and I will send you a bill in a month's time. If you want me to take any back, please protect them against the weather." I had an eye on the coming rains.

"That is already done," said Baburao. "When I have selected and arranged them, you will see. Thank you."

He wasn't surprised by my offer, but was pleased. He left with a carton of books, mostly paper-backs but with a few cloth-bound volumes. I wished he hadn't been so ambitious, for these were likely to get dirty. But obviously he was confident.

At the end of the day I went out into the street, where he was squatting by his stand. He had built a kind of bookcase with a wide, overhanging top, against the wall of the stone building where he had his pitch. It was on the right side of the road, where the rain, when it came, was likely to be blown the other way; he also had a canvas canopy.

"You're really working at this," I said with admiration. "It looks fine. Good luck!"

"Thank you, Mr. Graham."

"By the way," I said, "what is the name of your first-born?"

"Krishna," Baburao told me. "Krishna Munshi."

There was joy in his eyes—then.

I was astonished when Baburao appeared next morning, selected three cloth-bound books and several paper-backs, took these to the trade counter and paid in cash. I went to find out what he'd bought.

"Repeats of titles he took before," said Mary Lewis, my counter-clerk, a bright, business-like Anglo-Indian with a very fair skin. "He wanted three others, but we're out of stock."

That night I noticed that his shelves were packed so tightly that he couldn't squeeze another book in. I mingled with the colourful, noisy crowd of home-going clerks, and watched. Baburao sold two books while I was there and promptly replaced them from a wooden box, which he used afterwards as a chair.

He came for a little stock most days, always repeating popular titles, and gradually built up a steady business. He improved the appearance of his stand, but never of his clothes.

He paid in cash for everything he bought, but nothing off the first bill. Mary Lewis told me that she had put it into his hand, but he had blandly ignored it.

"Don't worry," I said, "he'll pay one day."

My interest stimulated by Baburao's great pride in his son, I began to understand the strength of Hindu family loyalty, with its always fanatical influence, and to respect my friend's love for his first-born. Whenever I asked about Krishna, I was told he was a strong, healthy, and intelligent boy; just the son to take over his father's business one day.

That was Baburao's dream…

By Krishna's first birthday the bookstand was twice its original size and Baburao had to step on to a stool to reach the top row. He was turning over several thousand rupees a month—not big money by western standards, but none the less impressive for a Hindu who had started from nothing.

As I became more familiar with Indian ways and customs, I learned that Baburao was of high caste, had come to Bombay with a flood of refugees from a famine area, and now lived in a shelter against an old wall of a dismantled building. The roof and walls were of banana fronds, his wife cooked on bricks outside the tiny entrance, and washed their clothes on the stones at the water's edge nearby.

Hundreds of thousands lived like them in poverty which bred fatalism and despair—but, in Baburao, hope…

Mary Lewis reminded me of Krishna's next birthday, and added tartly that although he paid cash for everything he bought now, Baburao hadn't paid that first bill. I ought to remind him, she said.

I went into the street to congratulate Baburao, and caught

him stepping down from the box—not with a book but a hammer in his hand. Above the stand was a painted sign:

BABURAO MUNSHI & SON
BOOKS

I didn't speak about that old account...

Three months or so later he told me that his second son, Rama, had been born. He was pleased but not overjoyed. He was changing in some ways, and had become a brisk, confident business man with a flair for knowing which books would sell. He acquired many regular customers and ran accounts for them. Hindus, Moslems, Sikhs, Parsees, and Europeans, students, business men, and clerks all patronised him, and Baburao made friends with them all.

His English was now almost perfect. He dressed a little better, but it was noticeable that, whenever he needed an assistant, he took him from among the destitute. There were more and more fugitives in the city from famine areas.

Just before Krishna's third birthday, Baburao asked me to have lunch with him. We went to an ordinary little restaurant in Hornby Road, not far from Crawford Market. With its rioting colours and contrasts, its variety of tiny shops, the insistent pleading of the sidewalk pedlars and the beggars, the Chinese with their paper lanterns, the district always fascinated me. The food, served in little metal bowls and eaten with the fingers, was spicy and sweet.

"Mr. Graham, I will be grateful for your advice," Baburao said when we had finished. "I wish to open another stall or shop. I wish to employ one or two men who are not ignorant of books and who can be trusted. You can tell me of those who are not ignorant, and I will judge their loyalty." He smiled at me, modestly. "You do not think I am foolish?"

I said: "I think I could recommend one or two men, but there's something I ought to have said to you long ago, Baburao."

His smile was gentle. "That old bill, perhaps?"

"No—I shall leave that to your conscience. It's about your business. You buy all your books from me, and I represent only a few English publishers. You should buy from the other agencies in Bombay, and stock all books which have a ready sale."

He leaned across the little table and touched my arm. "You are generous and a good friend, Mr. Graham. Perhaps I will do that. I do not think you will sell less because of it.

"And now I will tell *you* something. *I* am making a book." He was obviously highly amused. "It will be a big book, and when it is finished I shall give it to you. All the time I worked on it, I remind myself of some postcards on the Apollo Bunder, and also of the day when you first allowed me credit. It is—what is the phrase?—a labour of love."

"Don't be too long finishing it," I said.

"Look forward to the day when Krishna begins to work with me," he answered…

It was at a period of great crisis, when Gandhi was at the height of his power, that I met Baburao and Krishna near Crawford Market. The boy was nearly ten. I had never taken to him, but exerted myself to be friendly.

"Hallo, Krishna," I said, after greeting his father. "How are you?"

He stared at me with great, dark eyes; and he said, slowly and deliberately: "Bloody Englishman."

The pain in Baburao's eyes gave me my first hint of his tragedy. It was a long time before I realised the truth: that his son had been born evil, as Baburao had been born good.

Nevertheless, Baburao was flourishing. He had moved from the banana-frond hut, first into a flat and then into a big, rambling old bungalow near the museum. Occasionally I spent an evening there, but the atmosphere was never really happy. Krishna, young though he was, spoiled it by sitting and staring at me as if in contempt. So, more often, Baburao came to me.

He no longer needed advice about books; he had five shops and as many stands, and was one of the biggest booksellers in the city. Practically all of his assistants came from the famine camps, and he spent much time and money in relief work.

The only time I really saw him angry was when he discovered dope pedlars busy in a camp. The hungry and the hopeless were easy victims of dope traffickers, and money desperately needed for food, clothes, and children was spent on the vile stuff, which gave an illusion of happiness and yet sent men to hell...

And then the nightmare came—partition.

Hordes of refugees, turned out of Pakistan, strained the resources of Bombay and brought a plague of disease and despair. It was horror.

Day after day, Baburao worked until he dropped. By now, Krishna was working in the business, and showed his remarkable maturity by taking his father's place when Baburao was out on relief work. He was studiously polite to me, but I was sure that his dislike was as bitter as ever. His eyes still had a burning defiance which mingled with arrogance. Against his father's wishes he had given up the dhoti—which Baburao always wore—for western clothes.

Rama, the second boy, was very different. Willing, eager, and gay, he made up in friendliness what he lacked in experience. I came to know him well enough to ask him: "What doesn't Krishna like about me, Rama?"

The boy hesitated before answering quickly: "It is not you alone, Mr. Graham. It is any friend of our father."

Then he went on to talk freely, worriedly. Krishna was bitter and aloof with his father, he had a cruel streak, and loved to hurt—animals, insects, his brother, his servants. Rama gave depth to the picture I had always imagined of Krishna. I feared…well, I don't know what I feared for Baburao.

I did not fear the worst, but it came.

In business, Krishna soon proved his brilliance. More and more was left to him. While Baburao worked for the refugees, his son became master of the complex working of a firm with thirty branches, mostly in Bombay, but some in Delhi, Calcutta, and Madras. His father could take pride in him, yet be afraid.

One evening, Baburao came to me, relaxed in a long chair, and watched me drink my whisky—he himself neither drank nor smoked. Obviously he was happier than he had been for a long, long time, and I felt reassured.

"I think I shall be able to finish the book before long," he told me. "I shall soon have more time. A miracle is happening,

Malcolm. At last Krishna has seen what urges me to work for the poor. You will never guess what he has started to do."

"I won't try," I said.

"Imagine this, then—he has started libraries. Travelling libraries, which go to the camps and lend books to those who can read. Malcolm—" Baburao sat up, almost excited—"you know and I know that the greatest evil we have to fight is that of drugs. Can the people be blamed for taking refuge in them when their life is such a misery? Can they?"

"We've agreed about that before," I said, "but how does Krishna's new idea affect that?"

"But it is obvious. Those who can will read aloud to their families, there will be something new to fill their minds, a fresh interest, a great distraction. First a few and gradually many will be wooed away from drugs. Many who would start taking them will never do so. Why, this could be the weapon to attack illiteracy, to begin a thirst for knowledge."

I had never seen him so pleased—and, oddly, I had never been filled with such disquiet. But I could not say a word to spoil Baburao's dream.

Soon afterwards I was called unexpectedly to London, and was away for two months. I would have stayed longer, but a letter from a mutual friend in Bombay worried me.

"Baburao looks as if he is going mad," he wrote. "He hasn't said a word to any of us, but I'm sure he would talk to you."

I flew back to Bombay. Within an hour, Baburao was with me, looking old and broken, and with the shadow of dread in his eyes.

"But what is it?" I demanded. "What's done all this?"

"It is Krishna," he said brokenly. "It is my first-born, born also of the Devil."

He could hardly bring himself to tell me the truth—that Krishna was using the travelling libraries, the bookstands, and some of the shops for distributing cocaine and heroin to the people of the crowded camps.

Baburao had proof, and Krishna admitted it.

"Help me, Malcolm," he begged. "Tell me what I must do. He hates me. Understand, he hates me. He has no shame."

I could find nothing to say. He stood gazing down at me, and I wished I could not see into his eyes.

"You say nothing, but you think much—and I know what you think," he said. "That I can defeat this by going to the police. I can betray my son as he has betrayed me." He clenched his fists. "They are the thoughts in your mind, Malcolm. Admit it."

I said, slowly, painfully: "Yes, Baburao. You would spend a fortune hounding down anyone else who did this. Will you let Krishna undo everything that you and others have done?"

He whispered: "He is my son. I cannot betray my son."

The hurt went almost as deep with me as with him. But I had to say: "The one certain thing is that you must stop it. Not soon—but now!"

I took him home and as I turned away and walked blindly towards the gate, another car pulled up. Light from a lamp fell on Krishna's face.

He watched me, gloating. I could strike him, and it would be senseless. I could shout at him, and it would add to his sadistic triumph.

But I could not go away without trying to hurt him. As I approached, I asked: "Why?"

He said: "I am myself and he is himself."

"I am his friend," I said, "and I can do what he cannot—I can go to the police."

Krishna's expression did not change. He said: "Go to them, by all means. They will find that everything I have done has been approved—by my father. Without reading them, he has signed many letters which I have placed before him, and so I have made sure that he cannot drag me down without dragging himself down. I am going to tell him that now. Be good enough to let me pass."

I waited outside when he had gone. There would be awful despair when he faced his father, and I did not believe that Baburao's wife, or Rama, or his other son could help. So I had to go to Baburao. I went back to the house and rang the bell, and waited for a long time before the door opened.

Rama stood there. "Mr. Graham…" His voice was hoarse and frightened. "They are together, now."

"I'll go in," I said. "Tell no one."

He stood aside. Baburao's room was on the left of a narrow hall, and there was a light under the door. I heard voices as I opened the door softly and stepped in.

Baburao echoed the question I had asked in a voice so quiet that I thought his spirit was already dead. He said, in a voice that was little more than a whisper: "You have not told me why, my son."

"I am myself and you are yourself, that is why," Krishna said. "But I am not here to talk of that. I tell you again that if you go to the police, you will bring ruin on yourself. It is done so that both of us must be free or both must be damned. There is no way out, and you will do as I do."

His voice held no expression, he was so sure of himself. As they stood there, Krishna in western clothes, his father in his long black jacket and dhoti, they looked strangely alike.

"So there is no way out," said Baburao, and he smiled.

"Therefore I shall not seek a way out," he went on. "You are right, my son. I have wasted too much energy on attempting the impossible. I shall not do that again." He moved, turning away from me, and neither knew that I was there. He went to a low table by the books and picked up the telephone, standing erect and smiling at Krishna.

Krishna moved, and his voice lost its calm. "What are you doing?"

"Can you not guess?" asked Baburao softly. "I am calling the police, my son. I could not and would not betray you alone, but I can confess for both of us. We have never really been together, but we shall be together now. Your crime is mine from now on; my punishment will also be yours."

For a moment, Krishna was stunned to silence. So was I. But the sublime expression on Baburao's face could not last; exaltation would surely die.

Then Krishna moved. "Come away." He moved forward, hand outstretched, shouting. "You old fool, that won't help either you or me, it—"

"I would like to talk to Mr. Patel—the Mr. Patel in the Unlawful Drugs Division, please," Baburao said into the telephone. "Tell him that—"

Krishna reached out and wrenched the telephone away, but I moved, too. I struck Krishna a blow that knocked him off his feet, sent him crashing against the bookcase and then on to the floor. It was a golden moment.

Baburao recognised me as he backed away in alarm. He began to smile again, retrieved the telephone and said: "*You* won't try to stop me, Malcolm."

"I won't stop you," I said. "Just go ahead…"

I told the police what Baburao and Krishna had said to me. That was easy. I made Rama and another son break the vow of silence that their father had imposed on them. That was with the help of priests, and was much more difficult.

But perhaps my only true victory, won without help and over the mind of a man, was in my struggle with Baburao. I broke through the barrier of his absurd but noble folly, and when he came to trial his plea was "not guilty." So was the verdict of the jury. But there was no mercy for his son…

Outwardly, after that, Baburao looked much older, but also more serene. I was never quite sure that he knew peace, and even wondered if he felt that I had made him betray himself, until the day, not long ago, when he brought the book.

It was a heavy book, bound in fine leather and with much beautiful scrollwork and heavy parchment pages. Without speaking he handed it to me, and without speaking I opened it at the first page.

Fastened to it was an old, yellowing sheet of paper; the unsettled account of many years ago. I turned the page. The next was headed: "To remind you of trust you showed without good reason."

At the bottom, 200-rupee notes were fastened. Two more were on the next page, dated three months later. Two more on each succeeding page at three-monthly intervals; many, many thousands of rupees, with entries in Baburao's own hand, telling of some talk between us, recording the history of nearly thirty years, not only of Baburao Munshi & Son, but of our friendship.

The last sentence explained the years of waiting.

"This is prepared for you as a record of our abiding friendship, and of my love; and a token of the love of all my family."

We Know You're Busy Writing,

But We Thought You Wouldn't Mind If We Just Dropped in for a Minute

Edmund Crispin

Edmund Crispin (1921–1978) enjoyed conspicuous success in two distinct careers under two different names, an achievement all the more impressive because he was plagued by ill-health, and in later life, alcoholism. Born Robert Bruce Montgomery, he became a highly regarded composer of light music, writing the scores for nearly forty films as well as a number of orchestral concert works. He adopted the Crispin name for his detective fiction, which again was written with a light touch. By the time he was thirty, he'd published eight novels featuring the Oxford don Gervase Fen. After a gap of twenty-six years, a ninth book appeared; this was *The Glimpses of the Moon* (1977), which was published in the year before his death.

Crispin's short stories were usually short and snappy, dependent on a single trick. Fen featured in many of them, but is absent from "We Know You're Busy Writing," an ironic tale about the troubles of the writing life which has appeared under a variety of titles over the years since first publication in *Winter's Crimes 1*, edited by George Hardinge in 1969. It reflects Crispin's own long-term struggle to rediscover his writing flair, and is in many ways the most personal piece of crime fiction that he wrote. In this centenary year of his birth, it also offers a pleasing reminder of his gift for entertaining the reader.

I

"After all, it's only us," they said.

I must introduce myself.

None of this is going to be read, even, let alone published. Ever.

Nevertheless, there is habit—the habit of putting words together in the most effective order you can think of. There is self-respect, too. That, and habit, make me try to tell this as if it were in fact going to be read.

Which God forbid.

I am forty-seven, unmarried, living alone, a minor crime-fiction writer earning, on average, rather less than £1,000 a year.

I live in Devon.

I live in a small cottage which is isolated, in the sense that there is no one nearer than a quarter of a mile.

I am not, however, at a loss for company.

For one thing, I have a telephone.

I am a hypochondriac, well into the coronary belt. Also, I go in fear of accidents, with broken bones. The telephone is thus a necessity. I can afford only one, so its siting is a matter of great discretion. In the end, it is in the hall, just at the foot of the steep stairs. It is on a shelf only two feet from the floor, so that if I had to crawl to it, it will still be within reach.

If I have my coronary *upstairs*, too bad.

———

The telephone is for me to use in an emergency. Other people, however, regard it differently.

Take, for example, my bank manager.

"Torhaven 153," I say.

"Hello? Bradley, is that Mr. Bradley?"

"Bradley speaking."

"This is Wimpole, Wimpole. Mr. Bradley, I have to talk to you."

"Speaking."

"Now, it's like this, Mr. Bradley. How soon can we expect some further payments in, Mr. Bradley? Payments out, yes, we have plenty of those, but payments in…"

"I'm doing everything I can, Mr. Wimpole."

"Everything, yes, everything, but payments in, what is going to be coming in during the next month, Mr. Bradley?"

"Quite a lot, I hope."

"Yes, you hope, Mr. Bradley, you hope. But what am I going to say to my regional office, Mr. Bradley, how am I going to represent the matter to them, to it? You have this accommodation with us, this matter of £500…"

"Had it for years, Mr. Wimpole."

"Yes, Mr. Bradley, and that is exactly the trouble. You must reduce it, Mr. Bradley, reduce it, I say," this lunatic bawls at me.

I can no more reduce my overdraft than I can fly.

I am adequately industrious. I aim to write 2,000 words a day, which would support me in the event that I were able to complete them. But if you live alone you are not, contrary to popular supposition, in a state of unbroken placidity.

Quite the contrary.

———

I have tried night-work, a consuming yawn to every tap on the typewriter. I have tried early-morning work.

And here H. L. Mencken comes in, suggesting that bad writing is due to bad digestion.

My own digestion is bad at any time, particularly bad during milkmen's hours, and I have never found that I could do much in the dawn. This is a weakness, and I admit it. But apparently it has to be. Work, for me, is thus office hours, nine till five.

I have told everyone about this, begging them, if it isn't a matter of emergency, to get in touch with me in the *evenings*. Office hours, I tell them, same as everyone else. You wouldn't telephone a solicitor about nothing in particular during his office hours, would you? Well, so why ring me?

I am typing a sentence which starts *His crushed hand, paining him less now, nevertheless gave him a sense of...*

I know what is going to happen after "of": *the appalling frailty of the human body.*

Or rather, I did know, and it wasn't that. It might have been that (feeble though it is) but for the fact that then the doorbell rang.

(I hope that it might have been something better.)

The doorbell rang. It was a Mrs. Prance morning, but she hadn't yet arrived, so I answered the door myself, clattering down from the upstairs room where I work. It was the meter-reader. The meter being outside the door, I was at a loss to know why I had to sanction its being scrutinised.

"A sense of the dreadful agonies," I said to the meter-reader, "of which the human body is capable."

"Wonderful weather for the time of year."

"I'll leave you, if you don't mind. I'm a bit busy."

"Suit yourself," he said, offended.

Then Mrs. Prance came.

Mrs. Prance comes three mornings a week. She is slow, and deaf, but she is all I can hope to get, short of winning the Pools.

She answers the door, but is afraid of the telephone, and consequently never answers that, though I've done my utmost to train her to it.

She is very anxious that I should know precisely what she is doing in my tatty little cottage, and approve of it.

"Mr. Bradley?"

"Yes, Mrs. Prance?"

"It's the HI-GLOW."

"What about it, Mrs. Prance?"

"Pardon?"

"I said, what about it?"

"We did ought to change."

"Yes, well, let's change, by all means."

"Pardon?"

"I said, Yes."

"Doesn't bring the wood up, not the way it ought to."

"You're the best judge, Mrs. Prance."

"Pardon?"

"I'm sorry, Mrs. Prance, but I'm working now. We'll talk about it some other time."

"Toffee-nosed," says Mrs. Prance.

Gave him a sense of—a sense of—a sense of burr-burr, burr-burr, burr-burr.

Mrs. Prance shouts that it's the telephone.

I stumble downstairs and pick the thing up.

"Darling."

"Oh, hello, Chris."

"How are you, darling?"

"A sense of the gross cruelty which filled all history."

"What, darling? What was that you said?"

"Sorry, I was just trying to keep a glass of water balanced on my head."

A tinkle of laughter.

"You're a poppet. Listen, I've a wonderful idea. It's a party. Here in my flat. Today week. You will come, Edward, won't you?"

"Yes, of course, I will, Chris, but may I just remind you about something?"

"What's that, darling?"

"You said you wouldn't ring me up during working hours."

A short silence; then:

"Oh, but *just this once*. It's going to be such a lovely party, darling. You don't mind *just this once*."

"Chris, are you having a coffee break?"

"Yes, darling, and oh God, don't I need it!"

"Well, I'm *not* having a coffee break."

A rather longer silence; then:

"You don't love me any more."

"It's just that I'm trying to get a story written. There's a deadline for it."

"If you don't want to come to the party, all you've got to do is say so."

"I do want to come to the party, but I also want to get on with earning my living. Seriously, Chris, as it's a week ahead, couldn't you have waited till this evening to ring me?"

A sob.

"I think you're beastly. I think you're utterly, utterly *horrible*."

"Chris."

"And I never want to *see* you again."

...*a sense of treachery*, I typed, sedulously. *The agony still flamed up his arm, but it was now*

The doorbell rang.

—*it was now less than—more than—*

"It's the laundry, Mr. Bradley," Mrs. Prance shouted up the stairs to me.

"Coming, Mrs. Prance."

I went out on to the small landing. Mrs. Prance's great moonface peered up at me from below.

"Coming Thursday next week," she shouted at me, "because of Good Friday."

"Yes, Mrs. Prance, but what has that got to do with *me*? I mean, you'll be here on Wednesday as usual, won't you, to change the sheets?"

"Pardon?"

"Thank you for telling me, Mrs. Prance."

One way and another, it was a remarkable Tuesday morning: seven telephone calls, none of them in the least important, eleven people at the door, and Mrs. Prance anxious that no scintilla of her efforts should lack my personal verbal approval. I had sat down in front of my typewriter at 9:30. By twelve noon, I had achieved the following:

His crushed hand, paining him less now, nevertheless gave him a sense of treachery, the appalling frailty of the human body, but it was now less than it had been, more than, indifferent to him since, after, because though the pain could be shrugged off the betrayal was a

I make no pretence to be a quick writer, but that really was a very bad morning indeed.

II

Afternoon started better. With some garlic sausage and bread inside me, I ran to another seven paragraphs, unimpeded.

As he clawed his way out, hatred seized him, I tapped out, enthusiastically embarking on the eighth. *No such emotion had ever before—*

The doorbell rang.

—Had ever before disturbed his quiet existence. It was as if—

The doorbell rang again, lengthily, someone leaning on it.

—as if a beast had taken charge, a beast inordinate, insatiable.

The doorbell was now ringing for many seconds at a time, uninterruptedly.

Was this a survival factor, or would it blur his mind? He scarcely knew. One thing was abundantly clear, namely that he was going to have to answer the bloody doorbell.

He did so.

On the doorstep, their car standing in the lane beyond, were a couple in early middle age, who could be seen at a glance to be fresh out from The Duke.

The Duke of Devonshire is my local. When I first moved to this quiet part of Devon, I had nothing against The Duke: it was a small village pub serving small village drinks, with an occasional commercialised pork pie, or sausage-roll. But then it changed hands. A Postgate admirer took over. Hams, game, patties, quail eggs, and other such fanciful foods were introduced to a noise of trumpets; esurient lunatics began rolling up in every sort of car, gobble-mad for exotic Ploughman's Lunches and suavely served lobster creams, their throats parched for the vinegar of 1964 clarets or the ullage of the abominable home-brewed beer; and there was no longer any peace for anyone.

In particular, there was no longer any peace for me. "Let's go and see old Ted," people said to one another as they were shooed out of the bar at closing time. "He lives near here."

"Charles," said this man on the doorstep, extending his hand.

The woman with him tittered. She had fluffy hair, and lips so pale that they stood out disconcertingly, like scars, against her blotched complexion. "It's Ted, lovey," she said.

"Ted, of course it's Ted. Known him for years. How are you, Charley boy?"

"*Ted*, angel."

I recognised them both, slightly, from one or two parties. They were presumably a married couple, but not married for long, if offensive nonsenses like "angel" were to be believed.

"We're not interrupting anything," she said.

Interested by this statement of fact, I found spouting up in my pharynx the reply, "Yes, you sodding well are." But this had to be choked back; bourgeois education forbids such replies, other than euphemistically.

"Come on in," I said.

They came on in.

I took them into the downstairs living room, which lack of money has left a ghost of its original intention. There are two armchairs, a chesterfield, a coffee table, a corner cupboard for drinks: but all, despite HI-GLOW, dull and tattered on the plain carpet.

I got them settled on the chesterfield.

"Coffee?" I suggested.

But this seemed not to be what was wanted.

"You haven't got a drink, old boy?" the man said.

"Stanislas," the girl said.

"Yes, of course. Whisky? Gin? Sherry?"

"Oh, Stanislas darling, you are *awful*," said this female. "Fancy asking."

I had no recollection of the name of either of them, but surely Stanislas couldn't be right. "Stanislas?" I asked.

"It's private," she said, taking one of his hands in one of hers, and wringing it. "You don't mind? It's sort of a joke. It's private between us."

"I see. Well, what would you like to drink?"

He chose whisky, she gin and Italian.

"If you'll excuse me, I'll have to go upstairs for a minute," I said, after serving them.

One thing was abundantly clear: Giorgio's map had been wrong, and as a consequence—

"Ooh-hooh!"

I went out on to the landing.

"Yes?"

"We're lonely."

"Down in just a minute."

"You're doing that nasty writing."

"No, just checking something."

"We heard the typewriter. Do come down, Charles, Edward, I mean, we've got something terribly, terribly important to tell you."

"Coming straightaway," I said, my mind full of Giorgio's map.

I refilled their glasses.

"You're Diana," I said to her.

"Daphne," she squeaked.

"Yes, of course, Daphne. Drink all right?"

She took a great swallow of it, and so was unable to speak for fear of vomiting. Stanislas roused himself to fill the conversational gap.

"How's the old writing, then?"

"Going along well."

"Mad Martians, eh? Don't read that sort of thing myself, I'm afraid, too busy with biography and history. Has Daphne told you?"

"No. Told me what?"

"About Us, old boy, about Us."

This was the first indication I'd had that they *weren't* a married couple. Fond locutions survive courtship by God knows how many years, fossilizing to automatic gabble, and so are no guide to actual relationships. But in "Us," the capital letter, audible anyway, flag-wags something new.

"Ah-ha!" I said.

With an effort, Stanislas leaned forward. "Daphne's husband is a beast," he said, enunciating distinctly.

"Giorgio's map," I said. "Defective."

"A mere brute. So she's going to throw in her lot with me."

Satisfied, he fell back on to the cushions. "Darling," he said.

As a consequence, we were two miles south-west of our expected position. "So what is the expected position?" I asked.

"We're eloping," Daphne said.

"This very day. Darling."

"Angel."

"Yes, this very day," said Stanislas, ostentatiously sucking up the last drops from the bottom of his glass. "This very day as ever is. We've planned it," he confided.

The plan had gone wrong, had gone rotten. Giorgio had failed.

"Had gone rotten," I said, hoping I might just possibly remember the phrase when this pair of lunatics had taken themselves off.

"Rotten is the word for that bastard," said Stanislas. Suddenly his eyes filled with alcoholic tears. "What Daphne has suffered, no one will ever know," he gulped. "There's even been…beating." Daphne lowered her lids demurely, in tacit confirmation. "So we're off and away together," said Stanislas, recovering slightly. "A new life. Abroad. A new humane relationship."

But was his failure final? Wasn't there still a chance?

"If you'll excuse me," I said, "I shall have to go upstairs again."

But this attempt aborted. Daphne seized me so violently by the wrist, as I was on the move, that I had difficulty in not falling over sideways.

"You're with us, aren't you?" she breathed.

"Oh yes, of course."

"My husband would come after us, if he knew."

"A good thing he doesn't know, then."

"But he'll guess. He'll guess it's Stanislas."

"I suppose so."

"You don't mind us being here, Charles, do you? We have to wait till dark."

"Well, actually, there is a bit of work I ought to be getting on with."

"I'm sorry, Ted," she said, smoothing her skirt. "We've been inconsiderate. We must go." She went on picking at her hemline, but there was no tensing of the leg muscles, preliminary to rising, so I refilled her glass. "No, don't go," I said, the British middle class confronting its finest hour. "Tell me more about it."

"Stanislas."

"H'm, h'm."

"Wake *up*, sweetie-pie. Tell Charles all about it."

Stanislas got himself approximately upright. "All about what?"

"About Us, angel."

But the devil of it was, if Giorgio's map was wrong, our chances had receded to nil.

"To nil," I said. "Nil."

"Not nil at all, old boy," Stanislas said. "And as a matter of fact, if you don't mind my saying so, I rather resent the 'nil.' We may not be special, like writer blokes like you, but we aren't 'nil,' Daphne and me. We're human, and so forth. Cut us and we bleed, and that. I'm no great cop, I'll grant you that, but Daphne—Daphne—"

"A splendid girl," I said.

"Yes, you say that now, but what would you have said five minutes ago? Eh? Eh?"

"The same thing, of course."

"You think you're rather marvellous, don't you? You think you've...got it made. Well, let me tell you one thing, Mr. so-called Bradley: you may think you're very clever, with all this writing of Westerns and so on, but I can tell you, there are more important things in life than Westerns.

I don't suppose you'll understand about it, but there's Love. Daphne and I, we love one another. You can jeer, and you do jeer. All I can tell you is, you're wrong as can be. Daphne and I, we're going off together, and to hell with people who…jeer."

"Have another drink."

"Well, thanks, I don't mind if I do."

They stayed for four whole hours.

Somewhere in the middle, they made a pretence of drinking tea. Some time after that, they expressed concern at the length of time they had stayed—without, however, giving any sign of leaving. I gathered, as Giorgio and his map faded inexorably from my mind, that their elopement plans were dependent on darkness: this, rather than the charm of my company, was what they were waiting for. Meanwhile, with my deadline irrevocably lost, I listened to their soul-searching—he unjustifiably divorced, she tied to a brutish lout who unfortunately wielded influence over a large range of local and national affairs, and would pursue her to the ends of the earth unless precautions were taken to foil him.

I heard a good deal about their precautions, registering them without, at the time, realising how useful they were going to be.

"Charles, Edward."

"Yes?"

"We've been bastards."

"Of course not."

"We haven't been letting you get on with your work."

"Too late now."

"Not really too late," lachrymosely. "You go and write, and we'll just sit here, and do no harm to a soul."

"I've rather forgotten what I was saying, and in any case I've missed the last post."

"Oh, Charles, Charles, you shame us. We abase ourselves."

"No need for that."

"*Naturally* we abase ourselves. We've drunk your liquor, we've sat on your...your sofa, we've stopped you working. Sweetie-pie, isn't that true? Haven't we stopped him working?"

"If you say so, sweetie-pie."

"I most certainly do say so. And it's a disgrace."

"So we're disgraced, Poppet. *Bad,*" she said histrionically. "But are we so bad? I mean, he's self-employed, he's got all the time in the world, he can work just whenever he likes. Not like you and me. He's got it *made.*"

"Oh God," I mumbled.

"Well, that's true," Stanislas said, with difficulty. "And it's a nice quiet life."

"Quiet, that's it."

"Don't have to do anything if you don't want to. Ah, come the day."

"He's looking cross."

"What's that? Old Charles looking cross? Angel, you're mistaken. Don't you believe it. Not cross, Charles are you?"

"We *have* stayed rather long, darling. Darling, are you awake? I say, we *have* stayed rather long."

"H'm."

"But it's special. Edward, it's special. You do see that, don't you? Special. Because of Stanislas and me."

I said, "All I know is that I…"

"Just this once," she said. "You'll forgive us just this once? After all, you *are* a free agent. And after all, it's only us."

I stared at them.

I looked at him, nine-tenths asleep. I looked at her, half asleep. I thought what a life they were going to have if they eloped together.

But "It's only us" had triggered something off.

I remembered that on just that one day, not an extraordinary one, there had been Mrs. Prance, the meter-reader, Chris (twice: she had telephoned a second time during working hours to apologize for telephoning the first time during working hours), the laundry-man, the grocer (no Chivers Peas this week), my tax accountant, a woman collecting for the Church, a Frenchman wanting to know if he was on the right road to The Duke.

I remembered that a frippet had come from the National Insurance, or whatever the hell it's called now, to ask what I was doing about Mrs. Prance, and if not, why not. I remembered a long, inconclusive telephone call from someone's secretary at the BBC—the someone, despite his anxiety to be in touch with me, having vanished without notice into the BBC Club. I remembered that undergraduates at the University of Essex were wanting me to give them a talk, and were going to be so good as to pay second-class rail fare, though no fee.

I remembered that my whole morning's work had been

a single, botched, incomplete paragraph, and that my afternoon's work, before this further interruption, had been little more than 200 words.

I remembered that I had missed the post.

I remembered that I had missed the post before, for much the same reasons, and that publishers are unenthusiastic about writers who keep failing to meet deadlines.

I remembered that I was very short of money, and that sitting giving drink to almost total strangers for four hours on end wasn't the best way of improving the situation.

I remembered.

I saw red.

A red mist swam before his eyes, doing the butterfly stroke.

I picked up the poker from the fireplace, and went round behind them.

Did they—I sometimes ask myself—wonder what I could possibly be doing, edging round the back of the chesterfield with a great lump of iron in my hand?

They were probably too far gone to wonder.

In any case, they weren't left wondering for long.

III

Eighteen months have passed.

At the end of the first week, a detective constable came to see me. His name was Ellis. He was thin to the point of emaciation, and seemed, despite his youth, permanently depressed. He was in plain clothes.

He told me that their names were Daphne Fiddler and Clarence Oates.

"Now, sir, we've looked into this matter and we understand that you didn't know this lady and gentleman at all well."

"I'd just met them once or twice."

"They came here, though, that Tuesday afternoon."

"Yes, but they'd been booted out of the pub. People often come here because they've been booted out of the pub."

Lounging on the chesterfield, ignoring the blotches, Ellis said, "They were looking for a drink, eh?"

"Yes, they did seem to be doing that."

"I'm not disturbing your work, sir, I hope."

"Yes, you are, Officer, as a matter of fact. So did they."

"If you wouldn't mind, sir, don't call me 'Officer.' I am one technically. But as a mode of address it's pointless."

"Sorry."

"I'll have to disturb your work a little bit more still, sir, I'm afraid. Now, if I may ask, did this...this *pair* say anything to you about their plans?"

"Did they say anything to anyone else?"

"Yes, Mr. Bradley, to about half the population of South Devon."

"Well, I can tell you what they said to me. They said they were going to get a boat from Torquay to Jersey, and then a plane from Jersey to Guernsey, and then a Hovercraft from Guernsey to France. They were going to go over to France on day passes, but they were going to carry their passports with them, and cash sewn into the linings of their clothes. Then they were going on from France to some other country, where they could get jobs without a *permis de séjour*."

"Some countries, there's loopholes as big as camels' gates," said Ellis, biblically.

I said, "They'll make a mess of it, you know."

"Hash-slinging for her," said Ellis despondently, "and driving a taxi for him. What was the last you saw of them?"

"They drove off."

"Yes, but when?"

"Oh, after dark. Perhaps seven. What happened to them after that?"

"The Falls."

"Sorry?"

"The *Falls*. Their car was found abandoned there."

"Oh."

"No luggage in it."

"Oh."

"So presumably they got on the Torquay bus."

"You can't find out?"

Ellis wriggled on the cushions. "Driver's an idiot. Doesn't see or hear *anything*."

"I was out at the Falls myself."

"Pardon?"

"I say, I was out at the Falls myself. I followed them on foot—though of course, I didn't *know* I was doing that."

"Did you see their car there?" Ellis asked.

"I saw several cars, but they all look alike nowadays. And they all had their lights off. You don't go around peering into cars at the Falls which have their lights off."

"And then, sir?"

"I just walked back. It's a fairly normal walk for me in the evenings, after I've eaten. I mean, it's a walk I quite often take."

(And I had, in fact, walked back by the lanes as usual, resisting the temptation to skulk across the fields. Good for me to have dumped the car unnoticed near the bus-stop, and good for me to have remembered about the luggage before I set out.)

"Good for me," I said.

"Pardon?"

"Good for me to be able to do that walk, still."

Ellis unfolded himself, getting up from the chesterfield. Good for me that he hadn't got a kit with him to test the blotches.

"It's just a routine inquiry, Mr. Bradley," he said faintly, his vitality seemingly at a low ebb. "Mrs. Fiddler's husband, Mr. Oates's ex-wife, they felt they should inquire. Missing Persons, you see. But just between ourselves," he added, his voice livening momentarily, "they neither of 'em care a button. It's obvious what's happened, and they neither of 'em care a button. Least said, Mr. Bradley, soonest mended."

He went.

I should feel guilty; but in fact, I feel purged.

Catharsis.

Am I purged of pity? I hope not. I feel pity for Daphne and Stanislas, at the same time as irritation at their unconscionable folly.

Purged of fear?

Well, in an odd sort of way, yes.

Things have got worse for me. The strain of reducing my overdraft by £250 has left me with Mrs. Prance only two days a week, and, rather more importantly, I now have to count the tins of baked beans and the loaves I shall use for toasting.

But I feel better.

The interruptions are no less than before. Wimpole, Chris, my tax accountant all help to fill my working hours, in the same old way.

But now I feel almost indulgent toward them. Toward everyone, even Mrs. Prance.

For one thing, I garden a lot.

I get a fair number of flowers, but this is more luck than judgment. Vegetables are my chief thing.

And this autumn, the cabbages have done particularly well. Harvest cabbages, they stand up straight and conical, their dark green outer leaves folded close, moisture-globed, protecting firm, crisp hearts.

For harvest cabbages, you can't beat nicely rotted organic fertilizers.

Can I ever bring myself to cut my harvest cabbages, and eat them?

At the *moment* I don't want to eat my harvest cabbages. But I dare say in the end I shall.

After all, it's only them.

Chapter and Verse

Ngaio Marsh

Edith Ngaio Marsh was born in 1895 in Christchurch, New Zealand. She travelled to England in 1928 and said in an essay that her series detective Roderick Alleyn "was born with the rank of Detective-Inspector, C.I.D., on a very wet Saturday afternoon in a basement flat, off Sloane Square, in London. The year was 1931." She explained that, at the time, most of the leading fictional detectives were eccentrics, but she resolved to create a character who was more like the English people she'd actually met. Her father was an old boy of Dulwich College, an "old Alleynian," hence the name she bestowed upon her sleuth.

A Man Lay Dead, Ngaio Marsh's first novel featuring this new detective, did not appear until 1934, but he continued to appear in her books until 1982, the year of her death. He is also to be found in a posthumous "completion novel" by Stella Duffy, *Money in the Morgue* (2018), which Marsh began to write during the Second World War but abandoned. On British television, he has been portrayed by such different actors as Geoffrey Keen, Michael Allinson, Simon Williams, and Patrick Malahide. Marsh's short stories were relatively infrequent. "Chapter and Verse" was published in *Ellery Queen's Mystery Magazine* in March 1973, but is very much in the traditional vein.

———

WHEN THE TELEPHONE RANG, TROY CAME IN, SUN-dazzled, from the cottage garden to answer it, hoping it would be a call from London.

"Oh," said a strange voice uncertainly. "May I speak to Superintendent Alleyn, if you please?"

"I'm sorry. He's away."

"Oh, dear!" said the voice, crestfallen. "Er—would that be—am I speaking to Mrs. Alleyn?"

"Yes."

"Oh. Yes. Well, it's Timothy Bates here, Mrs. Alleyn. You don't know me," the voice confessed wistfully, "but I had the pleasure several years ago of meeting your husband. In New Zealand. And he did say that if I ever came home I was to get in touch, and when I heard quite by accident that you were here—well, I *was* excited. But, alas, no good after all."

"I *am* sorry," Troy said. "He'll be back, I hope, on Sunday night. Perhaps—"

"Will he! Come, *that's* something! Because here I am at the Star and Garter, you see, and so—" The voice trailed away again.

"Yes, indeed. He'll be delighted," Troy said, hoping that he would.

"I'm a bookman," the voice confided. "Old books, you know. He used to come into my shop. It was always such a pleasure."

"But, of course!" Troy exclaimed. "I remember perfectly now. He's often talked about it."

"*Has* he? Has he, really! Well, you see, Mrs. Alleyn, I'm here on business. Not to *sell* anything, please don't think that, but on a voyage of discovery; almost, one might say, of detection, and I think it might amuse him. He has such an eye for the curious. Not," the voice hurriedly amended, "in the trade sense. I mean curious in the sense of mysterious and unusual. But I mustn't bore you."

Troy assured him that he was not boring her and indeed it was true. The voice was so much coloured by odd little overtones that she found herself quite drawn to its owner. "I know where you are," he was saying. "Your house was pointed out to me."

After that there was nothing to do but ask him to visit. He seemed to cheer up prodigiously. "May I? May I, really? Now?"

"Why not?" Troy said. "You'll be here in five minutes."

She heard a little crow of delight before he hung up the receiver.

He turned out to be exactly like his voice—a short, middle-aged, bespectacled man, rather untidily dressed. As he came up the path she saw that with both arms he clutched to his stomach an enormous Bible. He was thrown into a fever over the difficulty of removing his cap.

"How ridiculous!" he exclaimed. "Forgive me! One moment."

He laid his burden tenderly on a garden seat. "There!" he cried. "Now! How do you do!"

Troy took him indoors and gave him a drink. He chose sherry and sat in the window seat with his Bible beside him. "You'll wonder," he said, "why I've appeared with this unusual piece of baggage. I *do* trust it arouses your curiosity."

He went into a long excitable explanation. It appeared that the Bible was an old and rare one that he had picked up in a job lot of books in New Zealand. All this time he kept it under his square little hands as if it might open of its own accord and spoil his story.

"Because," he said, "the *really* exciting thing to me is *not* its undoubted authenticity but—" He made a conspiratorial face at Troy and suddenly opened the Bible. "Look!" he invited.

He displayed the flyleaf. Troy saw that it was almost filled with entries in a minute, faded copperplate handwriting.

"The top," Mr. Bates cried. "Top left-hand. Look at *that*."

Troy read: "*Crabtree Farm at Little Copplestone in the County of Kent.* Why, it comes from our village!"

"Ah, ha! So it does. Now, the entries, my dear Mrs. Alleyn. The entries."

They were the recorded births and deaths of a family named Wagstaff, beginning in 1705 and ending in 1870 with the birth of William James Wagstaff. Here they broke off but were followed by three further entries, close together.

Stewart Shakespeare Hadet. Died: Tuesday, 5th April, 1779. 2nd Samuel 1.10.

Naomi Balbus Hadet. Died: Saturday, 13th August, 1779. Jeremiah 50.24.

Peter Rook Hadet. Died: Monday, 12th September, 1779. Ezekiel 7.6.

Troy looked up to find Mr. Bates's gaze fixed on her. "And what," Mr. Bates asked, "my dear Mrs. Alleyn, do you make of *that*?"

"Well," she said cautiously, "I know about Crabtree Farm. There's the farm itself, owned by Mr. De'ath, and there's Crabtree House, belonging to Miss Hart, and—yes, I fancy I've heard they both belonged originally to a family named Wagstaff."

"You are perfectly right. Now! What about the Hadets? What about *them*?"

"I've never heard of a family named Hadet in Little Copplestone. But—"

"Of course you haven't. For the very good reason that there never have been any Hadets in Little Copplestone."

"Perhaps in New Zealand, then?"

"The dates, my dear Mrs. Alleyn, the dates! New Zealand was not colonized in 1779. Look closer. Do you see the sequence of double dots—ditto marks—under the address? Meaning, of course, 'also of Crabtree Farm at Little Copplestone in the County of Kent.'"

"I suppose so."

"Of course you do. And how right you are. Now! You have noticed that throughout there are biblical references. For the Wagstaffs they are the usual pious offerings. You need not trouble yourself with them. But consult the text awarded to the three Hadets. Just you look *them* up! I've put markers."

He threw himself back with an air of triumph and sipped his sherry. Troy turned over the heavy bulk of pages to the first marker. "Second of Samuel, one, ten," Mr. Bates prompted, closing his eyes.

The verse had been faintly underlined.

"*So I stood upon him,*" Troy read, "*and slew him.*"

"That's Stewart Shakespeare Hadet's valedictory," said Mr. Bates. "Next!"

The next was at the 50th chapter of Jeremiah, verse 24: "*I have laid a snare for thee and thou are taken.*"

Troy looked at Mr. Bates. His eyes were still closed and he was smiling faintly.

"That was Naomi Balbus Hadet," he said. "Now for Peter Rook Hadet. Ezekiel, seven, six."

The pages flopped back to the last marker.

"*An end is come, the end is come: it watcheth for thee; behold it is come.*"

Troy shut the Bible.

"How very unpleasant," she said.

"And how very intriguing, don't you think?" And when she didn't answer, "Quite up your husband's street, it seemed to me."

"I'm afraid," Troy said, "that even Rory's investigations don't go back to 1779."

"What a pity!" Mr. Bates cried gaily.

"Do I gather that you conclude from all this that there was dirty work among the Hadets in 1779?"

"I don't know, but I'm dying to find out. *Dying* to. Thank you, I should enjoy another glass. Delicious!"

He had settled down so cosily and seemed to be enjoying

himself so much that Troy was constrained to ask him to stay to lunch.

"Miss Hart's coming," she said. "She's the one who bought Crabtree House from the Wagstaffs. If there's any gossip to be picked up in Copplestone, Miss Hart's the one for it. She's coming about a painting she wants me to donate to the Harvest Festival raffle."

Mr. Bates was greatly excited. "Who knows!" he cried. "A Wagstaff in the hand may be worth two Hadets in the bush. I am your slave forever, my dear Mrs. Alleyn!"

Miss Hart was a lady of perhaps sixty-seven years. On meeting Mr. Bates she seemed to imply that some explanation should be advanced for Troy receiving a gentleman caller in her husband's absence. When the Bible was produced, she immediately accepted it in this light, glanced with professional expertise at the inscriptions and fastened on the Wagstaffs.

"No doubt," said Miss Hart, "it was their family Bible and much good it did them. A most eccentric lot they were. Very unsound. Very unsound, indeed. Especially Old Jimmy."

"Who," Mr. Bates asked greedily, "was Old Jimmy?"

Miss Hart jabbed her forefinger at the last of the Wagstaff entries. "William James Wagstaff. Born 1870. And died, although it doesn't say so, in April, 1921. Nobody was left to complete the entry, of course. Unless you count the niece, which I don't. Baggage, if ever I saw one."

"The niece?"

"Fanny Wagstaff. Orphan. Old Jimmy brought her up. Dragged would be the better word. Drunken old reprobate he was and he came to a drunkard's end. They said he beat her *and* I daresay she needed it." Miss Hart lowered her voice to a whisper and confided in Troy. "Not a *nice* girl. You know what I mean."

Troy, feeling it was expected of her, nodded portentously.

"A drunken end, did you say?" prompted Mr. Bates.

"Certainly. On a Saturday night after Market. Fell through the top landing stair rail in his nightshirt and split his skull on the flagstoned hall."

"And your father bought it, then, after Old Jimmy died?" Troy ventured.

"Bought the house and garden. Richard De'ath took the farm. He'd been after it for years—wanted it to round off his own place. He and Old Jimmy were at daggers drawn over *that* business. And, of course, Richard being an atheist, over the Seven Seals."

"I beg your pardon?" Mr. Bates asked.

"Blasphemous!" Miss Hart shouted. "That's what it was, rank blasphemy. It was a sect that Wagstaff founded. If the rector had known his business he'd have had him excommunicated for it."

Miss Hart was prevented from elaborating this theory by the appearance at the window of an enormous woman, stuffily encased in black, with a face like a full moon.

"Anybody at home?" the newcomer playfully chanted. "Telegram for a lucky girl! Come and get it!"

It was Mrs. Simpson, the village postmistress. Miss Hart said, "Well, *really*!" and gave an acid laugh.

"Sorry, I'm sure," said Mrs. Simpson, staring at the Bible which lay under her nose on the window seat. "I didn't realise there was company. Thought I'd pop it in as I was passing."

Troy read the telegram while Mrs. Simpson, panting, sank heavily on the window ledge and eyed Mr. Bates, who had drawn back in confusion. "I'm no good in the heat," she told him. "Slays me."

"Thank you so much, Mrs. Simpson," Troy said. "No answer."

"Righty-ho. Cheerie-bye," said Mrs. Simpson and with another stare at Mr. Bates and the Bible, and a derisive grin at Miss Hart, she waddled away.

"It's from Rory," Troy said. "He'll be home on Sunday evening."

"As that woman will no doubt inform the village," Miss Hart pronounced. "A busybody of the first water and ought to be taught her place. Did you ever!"

She fulminated throughout luncheon and it was with difficulty that Troy and Mr. Bates persuaded her to finish her story of the last of the Wagstaffs. It appeared that Old Jimmy had died intestate, his niece succeeding. She had at once announced her intention of selling everything and had left the district to pursue, Miss Hart suggested, a life of freedom, no doubt in London or even in Paris. Miss Hart wouldn't, and didn't want to, know. On the subject of the Hadets, however, she was uninformed and showed no inclination to look up the marked Bible references attached to them.

After luncheon Troy showed Miss Hart three of her paintings, any one of which would have commanded a high price at an exhibition of contemporary art, and Miss Hart chose the one that, in her own phrase, really did look like something. She insisted that Troy and Mr. Bates accompany her to the parish hall where Mr. Bates would meet the rector, an authority on village folklore. Troy in person must hand over her painting to be raffled.

Troy would have declined this honour if Mr. Bates had not retired behind Miss Hart and made a series of beseeching gestures and grimaces. They set out therefore in Miss Hart's car which was crammed with vegetables for the Harvest Festival decorations.

"And if the woman Simpson thinks she's going to hog the lectern with *her* pumpkins," said Miss Hart, "she's in for a shock. Hah!"

St. Cuthbert's was an ancient parish church round whose flanks the tiny village nestled. Its tower, an immensely high one, was said to be unique. Nearby was the parish hall where Miss Hart pulled up with a masterful jerk.

Troy and Mr. Bates helped her unload some of her lesser marrows to be offered for sale within. They were observed by a truculent-looking man in tweeds who grinned at Miss Hart. "Burnt offerings," he jeered, "for the tribal gods, I perceive." It was Mr. Richard De'ath, the atheist. Miss Hart cut him dead and led the way into the hall.

Here they found the rector, with a crimson-faced elderly man and a clutch of ladies engaged in preparing for the morrow's sale.

The rector was a thin gentle person, obviously frightened of Miss Hart and timidly delighted by Troy. On being shown the Bible he became excited and dived at once into the story of Old Jimmy Wagstaff.

"Intemperate, I'm afraid, in everything," sighed the rector. "Indeed, it would not be too much to say that he both preached and drank hellfire. He *did* preach, on Saturday nights at the crossroads outside the Star and Garter. Drunken, blasphemous nonsense it was and although he used to talk about his followers, the only one he could claim was his niece, Fanny, who was probably too much under his thumb to refuse him."

"Edward Pilbrow," Miss Hart announced, jerking her head at the elderly man who had come quite close to them. "Drowned him with his bell. They had a fight over it. Deaf as a post," she added, catching sight of Mr. Bates's startled expression. "He's the verger now. *And* the town crier."

"What!" Mr. Bates exclaimed.

"Oh, yes," the rector explained. "The village is endowed with a town crier." He went over to Mr. Pilbrow, who at once cupped his hand round his ear. The rector yelled into it.

"When did you start crying, Edward?"

"Twenty-ninth September, 'twenty-one," Mr. Pilbrow roared back.

"I thought so."

There was something in their manner that made it difficult to remember, Troy thought, that they were talking about events that were almost fifty years back in the past. Even the year 1779 evidently seemed to them to be not so long ago, but, alas, none of them knew of any Hadets.

"By all means," the rector invited Mr. Bates, "consult the church records, but I can assure you—no Hadets. Never any Hadets."

Troy saw an expression of extreme obstinacy settle round Mr. Bates's mouth.

The rector invited him to look at the church and as they both seemed to expect Troy to tag along, she did so. In the lane they once more encountered Mr. Richard De'ath out of whose pocket protruded a paper-wrapped bottle. He touched his cap to Troy and glared at the rector, who turned pink and said, "Afternoon, De'ath," and hurried on.

Mr. Bates whispered imploringly to Troy, "*Would* you mind? I *do* so want to have a word—" and she was obliged to introduce him. It was not a successful encounter. Mr. Bates no sooner broached the topic of his Bible, which he still carried, than Mr. De'ath burst into an alcoholic diatribe against superstition, and on the mention of Old Jimmy Wagstaff, worked himself up into such a state of reminiscent fury that Mr. Bates was glad to hurry away with Troy.

They overtook the rector in the churchyard, now bathed in the golden opulence of an already westering sun.

"There they all lie," the rector said, waving a fatherly hand at the company of headstones. "All your Wagstaffs, right back to the sixteenth century. But no Hadets, Mr. Bates, I assure you."

They stood looking up at the spire. Pigeons flew in and out of a balcony far above their heads. At their feet was a little flagged area edged by a low coping. Mr. Bates stepped forward and the rector laid a hand on his arm.

"Not there," he said. "Do you mind?"

"Don't!" bellowed Mr. Pilbrow from the rear. "Don't you set foot on them bloody stones, Mister."

Mr. Bates backed away.

"Edward's not swearing," the rector mildly explained. "He is to be taken, alas, literally. A sad and dreadful story, Mr. Bates."

"Indeed?" Mr. Bates asked eagerly.

"Indeed, yes. Some time ago, in the very year we have been discussing—1921, you know—one of our girls, a very beautiful girl she was, named Ruth Wall, fell from the balcony of the tower and was, of course, killed. She used to go up there to feed the pigeons and it was thought that in leaning over the low balustrade she overbalanced."

"Ah!" Mr. Pilbrow roared with considerable relish, evidently guessing the purport of the rector's speech. "Terrible, terrible! And 'er sweetheart after 'er, too. Terrible!"

"Oh, no!" Troy protested.

The rector made a dabbing gesture to subdue Mr. Pilbrow. "I wish he wouldn't," he said. "Yes. It was a few days later. A lad called Simon Castle. They were to be married. People said it must be suicide but—it may have been wrong of me—I couldn't bring myself—in short, he lies beside her over there. If you would care to look."

For a minute or two they stood before the headstones.

"Ruth Wall. Spinster of this Parish. 1903–1921. *I will extend peace to her like a river.*"

"Simon Castle. Bachelor of this Parish. 1900–1921. *And God shall wipe away all tears from their eyes.*"

The afternoon having by now worn on, and the others having excused themselves, Mr. Bates remained alone in the churchyard, clutching his Bible and staring at the headstones. The light of the hunter's zeal still gleamed in his eyes.

Troy didn't see Mr. Bates again until Sunday night service when, on her way up the aisle, she passed him, sitting in the rearmost pew. She was amused to observe that his gigantic Bible was under the seat.

"*We plough the fields,*" sang the choir, "*and scatter—*" Mrs. Simpson roared away on the organ, the smell of assorted greengrocery rising like some humble incense. Everybody in Little Copplestone except Mr. Richard De'ath was there for the Harvest Festival. At last the rector stepped over Miss Hart's biggest pumpkin and ascended the pulpit, Edward Pilbrow switched off all the lights except one and they settled down for the sermon.

"A sower went forth to sow," announced the rector. He spoke simply and well but somehow Troy's attention wandered. She found herself wondering where, through the centuries, the succeeding generations of Wagstaffs had sat until Old Jimmy took to his freakish practices; and whether Ruth Wall and Simon Castle, poor things, had shared the same hymn book and held hands during the sermon; and whether, after all, Stewart Shakespeare Hadet and Peter Rook Hadet had not, in 1779, occupied some dark corner of the church and been unaccountably forgotten.

Here we are, Troy thought drowsily, and there, outside in the churchyard, are all the others going back and back—

She saw a girl, bright in the evening sunlight, reach from a balcony toward a multitude of wings. She was falling—dreadfully—into nothingness. Troy woke with a sickening jerk.

"—on stony ground," the rector was saying. Troy listened guiltily to the rest of the sermon.

Mr. Bates emerged on the balcony. He laid his Bible on the coping and looked at the moonlit tree tops and the churchyard so dreadfully far below. He heard someone coming up the stairway. Torchlight danced on the door jamb.

"You were quick," said the visitor.

"I am all eagerness and, I confess, puzzlement."

"It had to be here, on the spot. If you *really* want to find out—"

"But I do, I do!"

"We haven't much time. You've brought the Bible?"

"You particularly asked—"

"If you open it at Ezekiel, chapter twelve. I'll shine my torch."

Mr. Bates opened the Bible.

"The thirteenth verse. There!"

Mr. Bates leaned forward. The Bible tipped and moved.

"Look out!" the voice urged.

Mr. Bates was scarcely aware of the thrust. He felt the page tear as the book sank under his hands. The last thing he heard was the beating of a multitude of wings.

"—and forevermore," said the rector in a changed voice, facing east. The congregation got to its feet. He announced the last hymn. Mrs. Simpson made a preliminary rumble and Troy groped in her pocket for the collection plate. Presently they all filed out into the autumnal moonlight.

It was coldish in the churchyard. People stood about in groups. One or two had already moved through the lychgate. Troy heard a voice, which she recognised as that of Mr. De'ath. "I suppose," it jeered, "you all know you've been assisting at a fertility rite."

"Drunk as usual, Dick De'ath," somebody returned without rancour. There was a general laugh.

They had all begun to move away when, from the shadows

at the base of the church tower, there arose a great cry. They stood, transfixed, turned toward the voice.

Out of the shadows came the rector in his cassock. When Troy saw his face she thought he must be ill and went to him.

"No, no!" he said. "Not a woman! Edward! Where's Edward Pilbrow?"

Behind him, at the foot of the tower, was a pool of darkness; but Troy, having come closer, could see within it a figure, broken like a puppet on the flagstones. An eddy of night air stole round the church and fluttered a page of the giant Bible that lay pinned beneath the head.

It was nine o'clock when Troy heard the car pull up outside the cottage. She saw her husband coming up the path and ran to meet him, as if they had been parted for months.

He said, "This is mighty gratifying!" And then, "Hullo, my love. What's the matter?"

As she tumbled out her story, filled with relief at telling him, a large man with uncommonly bright eyes came up behind them.

"Listen to this, Fox," Roderick Alleyn said. "We're in demand, it seems." He put his arm through Troy's and closed his hand round hers. "Let's go indoors, shall we? Here's Fox, darling, come for a nice bucolic rest. Can we give him a bed?"

Troy pulled herself together and greeted Inspector Fox. Presently she was able to give them a coherent account of the evening's tragedy. When she had finished, Alleyn said, "Poor little Bates. He was a nice little bloke." He put his hand on Troy's. "You need a drink," he said, "and so, by the way, do we."

While he was getting the drinks he asked quite casually,

"You've had a shock and a beastly one at that, but there's something else, isn't there?"

"Yes," Troy swallowed hard, "there is. They're all saying it's an accident."

"Yes?"

"And, Rory, I don't think it is."

Mr. Fox cleared his throat. "Fancy," he said.

"Suicide?" Alleyn suggested, bringing her drink to her.

"No. Certainly not."

"A bit of rough stuff, then?"

"You sound as if you're asking about the sort of weather we've been having."

"Well, darling, you don't expect Fox and me to go into hysterics. Why not an accident?"

"He knew all about the other accidents, he *knew* it was dangerous. And then the oddness of it, Rory. To leave the Harvest Festival service and climb the tower in the dark, carrying that enormous Bible!"

"And he was hellbent on tracing these Hadets?"

"Yes. He kept saying you'd be interested. He actually brought a copy of the entries for you."

"Have you got it?"

She found it for him. "The selected texts," he said, "are pretty rum, aren't they, Br'er Fox?" and handed it over.

"Very vindictive," said Mr. Fox.

"Mr. Bates thought it was in your line," Troy said.

"The devil he did! What's been done about this?"

"The village policeman was in the church. They sent for the doctor. And—well, you see, Mr. Bates had talked a lot about you and they hope you'll be able to tell them something about him—whom they should get in touch with and so on."

"Have they moved him?"

"They weren't going to until the doctor had seen him."

Alleyn pulled his wife's ear and looked at Fox. "Do you fancy a stroll through the village, Foxkin?"

"There's a lovely moon," Fox said bitterly and got to his feet.

The moon was high in the heavens when they came to the base of the tower and it shone on a group of four men—the rector, Richard De'ath, Edward Pilbrow, and Sergeant Botting, the village constable. When they saw Alleyn and Fox, they separated and revealed a fifth, who was kneeling by the body of Timothy Bates.

"Kind of you to come," the rector said, shaking hands with Alleyn. "And a great relief to all of us."

Their manner indicated that Alleyn's arrival would remove a sense of personal responsibility. "If you'd like to have a look—?" the doctor said.

The broken body lay huddled on its side. The head rested on the open Bible. The right hand, rigid in cadaveric spasm, clutched a torn page. Alleyn knelt and Fox came closer with the torch. At the top of the page Alleyn saw the word Ezekiel and a little farther down, Chapter 12.

Using the tip of his finger Alleyn straightened the page. "Look," he said, and pointed to the thirteenth verse. "*My net also will I spread upon him and he shall be taken in my snare.*"

The words had been faintly underlined in mauve.

Alleyn stood up and looked round the circle of faces.

"Well," the doctor said, "we'd better see about moving him."

Alleyn said, "I don't think he should be moved just yet."

"Not!" the rector cried out. "But surely—to leave him like this—I mean, after this terrible accident—"

"It has yet to be proved," Alleyn said, "that it was an accident."

There was a sharp sound from Richard De'ath.

"—and I fancy," Alleyn went on, glancing at De'ath, "that it's going to take quite a lot of proving."

After that, events, as Fox observed with resignation, took the course that was to be expected. The local Superintendent said that under the circumstances it would be silly not to ask Alleyn to carry on, the Chief Constable agreed, and appropriate instructions came through from Scotland Yard. The rest of the night was spent in routine procedure. The body having been photographed and the Bible set aside for finger-printing, both were removed and arrangements put in hand for the inquest.

At dawn Alleyn and Fox climbed the tower. The winding stair brought them to an extremely narrow doorway through which they saw the countryside lying vaporous in the faint light. Fox was about to go through to the balcony when Alleyn stopped him and pointed to the door jambs. They were covered with a growth of stonecrop.

About three feet from the floor this had been brushed off over a space of perhaps four inches and fragments of the microscopic plant hung from the scars. From among these, on either side, Alleyn removed morsels of dark coloured thread. "And here," he sighed, "as sure as fate, we go again. O Lord, O Lord!"

They stepped through to the balcony and there was a sudden whirr and beating of wings as a company of pigeons flew out of the tower. The balcony was narrow and the balustrade indeed very low. "If there's any looking over," Alleyn said, "you, my dear Foxkin, may do it."

Nevertheless he leaned over the balustrade and presently knelt beside it. "Look at this. Bates rested the open Bible here—blow me down flat if he didn't! There's a powder of leather where it scraped on the stone and a fragment where it tore. It must have been moved—outward. Now, why, *why*?"

"Shoved it accidentally with his knees, then made a grab and overbalanced?"

"But why put the open Bible there? To read by moonlight? *My net also will I spread upon him and he shall be taken in my snare.* Are you going to tell me he underlined it and then dived overboard?"

"I'm not going to tell you anything," Fox grunted and then: "That old chap Edward Pilbrow's down below swabbing the stones. He looks like a beetle."

"Let him look like a rhinoceros if he wants to, but for the love of Mike don't leer over the edge—you give me the willies. Here, let's pick this stuff up before it blows away."

They salvaged the scraps of leather and put them in an envelope. Since there was nothing more to do, they went down and out through the vestry and so home to breakfast.

"Darling," Alleyn told his wife, "you've landed us with a snorter."

"Then you *do* think—?"

"There's a certain degree of fishiness. Now, see here, wouldn't *somebody* have noticed little Bates get up and go out? I know he sat all alone on the back bench, but wasn't there *someone*?"

"The rector?"

"No. I asked him. Too intent on his sermon, it seems."

"Mrs. Simpson? If she looks through her little red curtain she faces the nave."

"We'd better call on her, Fox. I'll take the opportunity to send a couple of cables to New Zealand. She's fat, jolly, keeps the shop-cum-post-office, and is supposed to read all the postcards. Just your cup of tea. You're dynamite with post-mistresses. Away we go."

Mrs. Simpson sat behind her counter doing a crossword puzzle and refreshing herself with liquorice. She welcomed Alleyn with enthusiasm. He introduced Fox and then he retired to a corner to write out his cables.

"What a catastrophe!" Mrs. Simpson said, plunging straight into the tragedy. "Shocking! As nice a little gentle-man as you'd wish to meet, Mr. Fox. Typical New Zealander. Pick him a mile away and a friend of Mr. Alleyn's, I'm told, and if I've said it once I've said it a hundred times, Mr. Fox, they ought to have put something up to prevent it. Wire netting or a bit of ironwork; but, no, they let it go on from year to year and now see what's happened—history repeating itself and giving the village a bad name. Terrible!"

Fox bought a packet of tobacco from Mrs. Simpson and paid her a number of compliments on the layout of her shop, modulating from there into an appreciation of the village. He said that one always found such pleasant company in small communities. Mrs. Simpson was impressed and offered him a piece of liquorice.

"As for pleasant company," she chuckled, "that's as may be, though by and large I suppose I mustn't grumble. I'm a cockney and a stranger here myself, Mr. Fox. Only twenty-four years and that doesn't go for anything with this lot."

"Ah," Fox said, "then you wouldn't recollect the former tragedies. Though to be sure," he added, "you wouldn't do that in any case, being much too young, if you'll excuse the liberty, Mrs. Simpson."

After this classic opening Alleyn was not surprised to hear Mrs. Simpson embark on a retrospective survey of life in Little Copplestone. She was particularly lively on Miss Hart, who, she hinted, had had her eye on Mr. Richard De'ath for many a long day.

"As far back as when Old Jimmy Wagstaff died, which was why she was so set on getting the next door house; but Mr. De'ath never looked at anybody except Ruth Wall, and her head-over-heels in love with young Castle, which together with her falling to her destruction when feeding pigeons led Mr. De'ath to forsake religion and take to drink, which he has done something cruel ever since.

"They do say he's got a terrible temper, Mr. Fox, and it's well known he give Old Jimmy Wagstaff a thrashing on account of straying cattle and threatened young Castle, saying if he couldn't have Ruth, nobody else would, but fair's fair and personally I've never seen him anything but nice-mannered, drunk or sober. Speak as you find's my motto and always has been, but these old maids, when they take a fancy they get it pitiful hard. You wouldn't know a word of nine letters meaning 'pale-faced lure like a sprat in a fishy story', would you?"

Fox was speechless, but Alleyn, emerging with his cables, suggested "whitebait."

"Correct!" shouted Mrs. Simpson. "Fits like a glove. Although it's not a bit like a sprat and a quarter the size. Cheating, I call it. Still, it fits." She licked her indelible pencil and triumphantly added it to her crossword.

They managed to lead her back to Timothy Bates. Fox, professing a passionate interest in organ music, was able to extract from her that when the rector began his sermon she had in fact dimly observed someone move out of the back bench and through the doors. "He must have walked round the church and in through the vestry and little did I think he was going to his death," Mrs. Simpson said with considerable relish and a sigh like an earthquake.

"You didn't happen to hear him in the vestry?" Fox ventured, but it appeared that the door from the vestry into the organ loft was shut and Mrs. Simpson, having settled herself to enjoy the sermon with, as she shamelessly admitted, a bag of chocolates, was not in a position to notice.

Alleyn gave her his two cables: the first to Timothy Bates's partner in New Zealand and the second to one of his own colleagues in that country asking for any available information about relatives of the late William James Wagstaff of Little Copplestone, Kent, possibly resident in New Zealand after 1921, and of any persons of the name of Peter Rook Hadet or Naomi Balbus Hadet.

Mrs. Simpson agitatedly checked over the cables,

professional etiquette and burning curiosity struggling together in her enormous bosom. She restrained herself, however, merely observing that an event of this sort set you thinking, didn't it?

"And no doubt," Alleyn said as they walked up the lane, "she'll be telling her customers that the next stop's blood-hounds and manacles."

"Quite a tidy armful of lady, isn't she, Mr. Alleyn?" Fox calmly rejoined.

The inquest was at 10:20 in the smoking room of the Star and Garter. With half an hour in hand, Alleyn and Fox visited the churchyard. Alleyn gave particular attention to the headstones of Old Jimmy Wagstaff, Ruth Wall, and Simon Castle. "No mention of the month or day," he said. And after a moment: "I wonder. We must ask the rector."

"No need to ask the rector," said a voice behind them. It was Miss Hart. She must have come soundlessly across the soft turf. Her air was truculent. "Though why," she said, "it should be of interest, I'm sure I don't know. Ruth Wall died on August thirteenth, 1921. It was a Saturday."

"You've a remarkable memory," Alleyn observed.

"Not as good as it sounds. That Saturday afternoon I came to do the flowers in the church. I found her and I'm not likely ever to forget it. Young Castle went the same way almost a month later. September twelfth. In my opinion there was never a more glaring case of suicide. I believe," Miss Hart said harshly, "in facing facts."

"She was a beautiful girl, wasn't she?"

"I'm no judge of beauty. She set the men by the ears. *He*

was a fine-looking young fellow. Fanny Wagstaff did her best to get *him*."

"Had Ruth Wall," Alleyn asked, "other admirers?"

Miss Hart didn't answer and he turned to her. Her face was blotted with an unlovely flush. "She ruined two men's lives, if you want to know. Castle and Richard De'ath," said Miss Hart. She turned on her heel and without another word marched away.

"September twelfth," Alleyn murmured. "That would be a Monday, Br'er Fox."

"So it would," Fox agreed, after a short calculation, "so it would. Quite a coincidence."

"Or not, as the case may be. I'm going to take a gamble on this one. Come on."

They left the churchyard and walked down the lane, overtaking Edward Pilbrow on the way. He was wearing his town crier's coat and hat and carrying his bell by the clapper. He manifested great excitement when he saw them.

"Hey!" he shouted, "what's this I hear? Murder's the game, is it? What a go! Come on, gents, let's have it. Did 'e fall or was 'e pushed? Hor, hor, hor! Come on."

"Not until after the inquest," Alleyn shouted.

"Do we get a look at the body?"

"Shut up," Mr. Fox bellowed suddenly.

"I got to know, haven't I? It'll be the smartest bit of crying I ever done, this will! I reckon I might get on the telly with this. 'Town crier tells old world village death stalks the churchyard.' Hor, hor, hor!"

"Let us," Alleyn whispered, "leave this horrible old man."

They quickened their stride and arrived at the pub, to be met with covert glances and dead silence.

The smoking room was crowded for the inquest. Everybody was there, including Mrs. Simpson who sat in the back row with her candies and her crossword puzzle. It went through very quickly. The rector deposed to finding the body. Richard De'ath, sober and less truculent than usual, was questioned as to his sojourn outside the churchyard and said he'd noticed nothing unusual apart from hearing a disturbance among the pigeons roosting in the balcony. From where he stood, he said, he couldn't see the face of the tower.

An open verdict was recorded.

Alleyn had invited the rector, Miss Hart, Mrs. Simpson, Richard De'ath, and, reluctantly, Edward Pilbrow, to join him in the Bar-Parlour and had arranged with the landlord that nobody else would be admitted. The Public Bar, as a result, drove a roaring trade.

When they had all been served and the hatch closed, Alleyn walked into the middle of the room and raised his hand. It was the slightest of gestures but it secured their attention.

He said, "I think you must all realise that we are not satisfied this was an accident. The evidence against accident has been collected piecemeal from the persons in this room and I am going to put it before you. If I go wrong I want you to correct me. I ask you to do this with absolute frankness, even if you are obliged to implicate someone who you would say was the last person in the world to be capable of a crime of violence."

He waited. Pilbrow, who had come very close, had his ear cupped in his hand. The rector looked vaguely horrified. Richard De'ath suddenly gulped down his double whisky. Miss Hart coughed over her lemonade, and Mrs. Simpson avidly popped a peppermint cream in her mouth and took a swig of her port and raspberry.

Alleyn nodded to Fox, who laid Mr. Bates's Bible, open at the flyleaf, on the table before him.

"The case," Alleyn said, "hinges on this book. You have all seen the entries. I remind you of the recorded deaths in 1779 of the three Hadets—Stewart Shakespeare, Naomi Balbus, and Peter Rook. To each of these is attached a biblical text suggesting that they met their death by violence. There have never been any Hadets in this village and the days of the week are wrong for the given dates. They are right, however, for the year 1921 and *they fit the deaths,* all by falling from a height, of William Wagstaff, Ruth Wall, and Simon Castle.

"By analogy the Christian names agree. William suggests Shakespeare. Naomi—Ruth; Balbus—a wall. Simon—Peter; and a Rook is a Castle in chess. And Hadet," Alleyn said without emphasis, "is an anagram of Death."

"Balderdash!" Miss Hart cried out in an unrecognisable voice.

"No, it's not," said Mrs. Simpson. "It's jolly good crossword stuff."

"Wicked balderdash. Richard!"

De'ath said, "Be quiet. Let him go on."

"We believe," Alleyn said, "that these three people met their deaths by one hand. Motive is a secondary consideration, but it is present in several instances, predominantly in one. Who had cause to wish the death of these three people? Someone whom old Wagstaff had bullied and to whom he had left his money and who killed him for it. Someone who was infatuated with Simon Castle and bitterly jealous of Ruth

Wall. Someone who hoped, as an heiress, to win Castle for herself and who, failing, was determined nobody else should have him. Wagstaff's orphaned niece—Fanny Wagstaff."

There were cries of relief from all but one of his hearers. He went on. "Fanny Wagstaff sold everything, disappeared, and was never heard of again in the village. But twenty-four years later she returned, and has remained here ever since."

A glass crashed to the floor and a chair overturned as the vast bulk of the postmistress rose to confront him.

"Lies! *Lies!*" screamed Mrs. Simpson.

"Did you sell everything again, before leaving New Zealand?" he asked as Fox moved forward. "Including the Bible, Miss Wagstaff?"

"But," Troy said, "how could you be so sure?"

"She was the only one who could leave her place in the church unobserved. She was the only one fat enough to rub her hips against the narrow door jambs. She uses an indelible pencil. We presume she arranged to meet Bates on the balcony, giving a cock-and-bull promise to tell him something nobody else knew about the Hadets. She indicated the text with her pencil, gave the Bible a shove, and, as he leaned out to grab it, tipped him over the edge.

"In talking about 1921 she forgot herself and described the events as if she had been there. She called Bates a typical New Zealander but gave herself out to be a Londoner. She said whitebait are only a quarter of the size of sprats. New Zealand whitebait are—English whitebait are about the same size.

"And as we've now discovered, she didn't send my cables. Of course she thought poor little Bates was hot on her tracks, especially when she learned that he'd come here to see me. She's got the kind of crossword-puzzle mind that would think up the biblical clues, and would get no end of a kick in writing them in. She's overwhelmingly conceited and vindictive."

"Still—"

"I know. Not good enough if we'd played the waiting game. But good enough to try shock tactics. We caught her off her guard and she cracked up."

"Not," Mr. Fox said, "a nice type of woman."

Alleyn strolled to the gate and looked up the lane to the church. The spire shone golden in the evening sun.

"The rector," Alleyn said, "tells me he's going to do something about the balcony."

"Mrs. Simpson, née Wagstaff," Fox remarked, "suggested wire netting."

"And she ought to know," Alleyn said and turned back to the cottage.

If you've enjoyed *Murder by the Book*,
you won't want to miss

TILL DEATH DO US PART
by John Dickson Carr

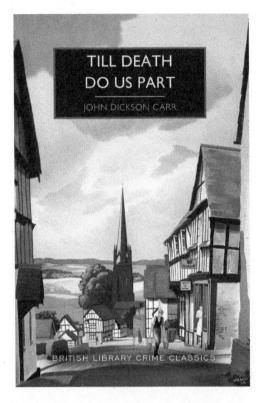

the most recent BRITISH LIBRARY CRIME CLASSIC
published by Poisoned Pen Press,
an imprint of Sourcebooks.

poisonedpenpress.com